"I'M JOHAN. JUST GOT HERE."

He flashed that grin again, and Christina thought she might melt into the ground. Her stomach felt hot, and her heart zipped into her throat. Johan glanced around the yard. "I was looking for the river. My brother and I set up camp nearby."

Christina noticed the wooden yoke and buckets on the ground nearby. "I guess Bruno had other ideas."

"He's a good guard dog." Johan restacked the loose logs atop the woodpile, then reached down to pat Bruno's head. Bruno showed his teeth and let out a warning growl. Johan pulled his hand back and chuckled.

Christina smiled. Johan was friendly and easygoing *as well as* handsome. She wondered if he was witty too. That would be too much. She cleared her throat and hoped that her face had not given her away. She had an unfortunate habit of turning pink whenever she felt a strong emotion. "*Ja*. He's a good sheepdog too. I thought you were a wolf. But you're not. You're . . ." Christina didn't finish the sentence because she wanted to say, *You're exactly what I've been waiting for*. Christina cleared her throat again. "Welcome to New Canaan. I hope you like it here."

Also by Virginia Wise

Where the Heart Takes You

When Love Finds You

Published by Kensington Publishing Corp.

What the Heart Wants

An Amish
New World Romance

Virginia Wise

ZEBRA BOOKS
KENSINGTON PUBLISHING CORP.
www.kensingtonbooks.com

ZEBRA BOOKS are published by

Kensington Publishing Corp.
119 West 40th Street
New York, NY 10018

All Kensington titles, imprints, and distributed lines are available at special quantity discounts for bulk purchases for sales promotion, premiums, fund-raising, educational, or institutional use.

Special book excerpts or customized printings can also be created to fit specific needs. For details, write or phone the office of the Kensington Sales Manager: Attn.: Sales Department. Kensington Publishing Corp., 119 West 40th Street, New York, NY 10018. Phone: 1-800-221-2647.

Zebra and the Z logo Reg. U.S. Pat. & TM Off.
BOUQUET Reg. U.S. Pat. & TM Off.

First Printing: January 2021
ISBN-13: 978-1-4201-4781-0
ISBN-10: 1-4201-4781-1

ISBN-13: 978-1-4201-4784-1 (eBook)
ISBN-10: 1-4201-4784-6 (eBook)

10 9 8 7 6 5 4 3 2 1

Printed in the United States of America

To my sons, who are everything to me.

Chapter One

The cabin felt snug and warm as the sun slipped below the tree line. The sheep were safe in their pen for the night, and a fire flickered in the hearth. Christina and Hilda sat with their sewing as the evening shadows lengthened across the hard-packed dirt floor.

"New Canaan feels so isolated compared to the German countryside," Christina said as she ripped out a misplaced stitch. "Have you adjusted to the quiet?"

"I've always enjoyed the quiet," her sister, Hilda, answered. She smiled, but did not look up from her work.

"That's because you don't like to be interrupted."

Hilda laughed. "You are interrupting me, you know."

Christina grinned. "I know. But we ought to take a break."

"I'll have this bodice resized by the morrow if I maintain my pace."

"I feel as if we've been sitting here for hours." Christina rubbed her eyes and tried to focus on sewing an even stitch.

"We've only just sat down."

"Oh?"

Hilda shook her head as she pushed her needle through the linsey-woolsey fabric.

Christina sighed and set down her needle and thread. "Don't you ever feel like something's missing? It's so . . ." She waved her hand from one side of the room to the other. ". . . quiet."

"Yes. You mentioned that. And I mentioned that I—"

"Like the quiet," Christina interrupted. "I know."

Hilda smiled. "I get more done this way."

Christina sighed again. "You mentioned that too."

Hilda nodded, but kept her eyes on her sewing.

"Don't you ever feel as if you need an adventure?"

"An adventure? Heavens no. We've had adventure enough traipsing through the wilderness and setting up a home here, in the middle of nowhere. New Canaan is a wonderful good settlement, but when I think of the dangers, it sends a shiver down my spine, let me tell you. I really—"

"But there's still one adventure that we've not yet had," Christina said.

"Making a home in the backcountry, protecting our sheep from the wolves and goodness knows what else, making meals from whatever we can get our hands on— that's not adventure enough?" Hilda furrowed her brow as she pulled a length of thread through the fabric. "It keeps me busy enough, anyway."

"Oh, Hilda, you know exactly what adventure I mean."

"I most certainly do not."

Christina raised an eyebrow. Her sister did not look up. "Love, Hilda. Love!"

"Foolishness, Christina. Foolishness."

Christina released a long, heavy breath and turned her gaze to the window. "Just imagine who could be out there, waiting for us."

"The only thing waiting for us out there right now is a fever. The air has quite a chill for late spring."

"Don't you have any dreams left?"

"I never had any to begin with, Christina. There's no need. I have everything I want right here—a good home, an honest living, and the freedom to worship as Amish. What more is there to want?"

Christina laughed. "Sometimes I don't know if you are trying to be funny or if you really mean what you say."

"There is nothing funny about what I say."

"Hilda, you know there is."

"You ought to put aside those girlish dreams and settle for what you have."

"I'm happy for what I have—I just want more!" Christina's eyes flashed as she drew her hands together and clasped them under her chin. "Just imagine a man on his way to this cabin, right now. He'd be tall and handsome and witty. And he would appreciate all of my jokes."

"Any man is taller than you, Christina." Christina was forever standing on her tiptoes to reach things. And she always had to tilt her head back and stare upward during conversations with others.

"Handsome and witty then."

"Yes, yes, I'm sure he would be." Hilda frowned and looked up for the first time in the conversation. "Did you just sew that fabric to your skirt?"

"What?" Christina pulled her eyes from the window and tried to lift the white linen shift she had been hemming. Her skirt lifted with it. "Oh, for goodness' sake!"

Hilda gave a slight smile, then turned back to her sewing. "And that is what dreaming gets you."

Christina laughed. "One day, Hilda, a man will walk

through that door and you will never be the same. Just wait, sister mine. The day will come."

"Ha!" Hilda's laugh sounded more like a dry bark. "We both know those days are past. I'm on the shelf, as they say. A thirty-two-year-old woman simply does not find a husband." Hilda reached over and patted Christina's knee. "You are a dear, but you must stop dreaming. It serves no purpose, save to create disappointment."

Christina opened her mouth to argue. She knew that, once dreamed, a dream never died. It would go on and on, fighting and aching to be realized. But as she worked to form a clever argument, a low growl interrupted the quiet. The growl erupted into a fierce round of barking. Christina leapt to her feet. "The sheep!"

"Wolves, like as not."

"I'll go," Christina said as she hurried for the door.

"Thank you. I want to finish working on this bodice." Hilda glanced up from her stitching. "Do be careful. Although I'm sure Bruno will take care of it. He's certainly bigger than any of the wolves." The enormous sheepdog had proven indispensable in the backcountry. "And stay close to the cabin."

"*Ja.*" Christina made sure to pull the door shut behind her—just in case. She had an unreasonable fear that a wild animal would sneak into the cabin—or at least Hilda claimed it was unreasonable. Christina found it very reasonable, indeed.

Bruno stood at the base of the woodpile with his four legs firmly planted and his sharp, white teeth bared. A man balanced on top of the woodpile.

A man!

And not just any man. A *tall, handsome* man. Christina

stared for a moment. She could not quite believe her eyes. A wet growl sounded in the back of Bruno's throat. The man shifted his weight from one foot to the other to maintain his balance and stay clear of Bruno's jaws. "Call him off, would you?" The man flashed a boyish grin. "It seems we got off on the wrong foot."

Christina realized that she had been staring in a most unladylike fashion. "Oh!" She ran toward her dog. "Bruno! Down, boy! Down!" Bruno fell silent and turned his big, black eyes to Christina. "That's right. Let the poor man go." Bruno looked up at the man, then back to Christina. "It's all right, you big bully." Christina reached down and ruffled Bruno's long, shaggy fur. "Now go on and watch the sheep, won't you?" Bruno whined softly and stayed by Christina's side. "It's all right. He's a stranger, but he's one of us."

Christina looked up at the man. "Aren't you? One of us, I mean." She noticed the youthful spark in his gray eyes and the cheerful expression on his face—and not just any face. A confident, chiseled face. *My goodness!* Was that all she could think about? This poor man was under attack from her dog and all she could think was how handsome he was! But it wasn't every day that a handsome stranger appeared on one's woodpile.

The man leapt from the top of the woodpile and landed with a heavy thud beside Christina. A couple of logs rattled to the ground, and he bent to pick them up. When he straightened up to his full height, Christina nearly gasped. Handsome and the perfect height too? He looked tall, but not too tall for her. She did not have to strain her neck too much to look into his eyes. Who was this man?

"I'm Johan. Just got here." He flashed that grin again,

and Christina thought she might melt into the ground. Her stomach felt hot and her heart zipped into her throat. Johan glanced around the yard. "I was looking for the river. My brother and I set up camp nearby."

Christina noticed the wooden yoke and buckets on the ground nearby. "I guess Bruno had other ideas."

"He's a good guard dog." Johan restacked the loose logs atop the woodpile, then reached down to pat Bruno's head. Bruno showed his teeth and let out a warning growl. Johan pulled his hand back and chuckled.

Christina smiled. Johan was friendly and easygoing *as well as* handsome. She wondered if he was witty too. That would be too much. She cleared her throat and hoped that her face had not given her away. She had an unfortunate habit of turning pink whenever she felt a strong emotion. "*Ja*. He's a good sheepdog too. I thought you were a wolf. But you're not. You're . . ." Christina didn't finish the sentence because she wanted to say, *You're exactly what I've been waiting for*. Christina cleared her throat again. "Welcome to New Canaan. I hope you like it here."

"I'm off to a good start."

"Are you?" Christina smiled and patted Bruno's neck. "You haven't had a friendly welcome."

"No?" Johan gave a dazzling smile that made Christina's face flush. "It feels very friendly to me."

"Oh." Oh! He meant . . . Oh my! Christina knew she had turned pink, now. She felt her cheeks. "It's cold out, isn't it?"

Johan's smile softened into a knowing half grin. "*Ja*. So cold that it's turned your face red."

Christina swallowed hard. "I'm very sensitive."

"I can see that." He looked down, and those twinkling gray eyes locked on hers.

Christina's tongue couldn't form the right words. She tried to calm her heart, but it pounded against her breastbone. She could feel her cheeks grow redder until she knew she resembled a ripe beet. Favoring a root vegetable was no way to win a man. "The river's that way," she managed to say as she pointed to the woods, hoping her face would return to a more natural color.

"Ah. I see." Johan tipped his black beaver felt hat at her and grinned. "Until next time. Which will be soon, *ja*?"

Christina swallowed again. He wanted to see her again soon? "It will?"

"Worship service tomorrow, *ja*?"

A worship service. Of course. He hadn't meant that he would call on her. Could her face flush any redder now? No, it most certainly could not. Christina nodded. She did not trust herself to speak.

"You know, I never caught your name."

"Christina. My name is Christina. Hello." *Hello? Why on earth did I say that?*

"Hello, Christina." His voice sounded so deep and masculine when he spoke her name that Christina had to remind her knees to hold her weight.

Johan nodded, winked, and turned on one heel. He retrieved the bucket and yoke he had dropped and strode into the forest without looking back. Christina stared at the tree line for a long time even though she knew she should go back inside. If he could see her, she would look foolish for staring. And yet, she could not look away. *Oh my*, she thought as she stared into the silent evening shadows. *Oh, my!*

* * *

Johan had not expected to meet a beautiful woman while standing on a woodpile to escape the jaws of a sheepdog. It was not his most dignified meeting. When a man wants to make a good impression, he does not want to be rescued—he wants to swoop in and do the rescuing. But *she* had rescued *him*. The embarrassment stuck to his throat. She must think him quite foolish.

Oh well, it couldn't be helped. Johan shrugged as he tramped through the woods and whistled a happy tune. He couldn't stay discouraged for long. It wasn't in his nature. The important thing was that he had met a lovely young lady—a lovely young *single* lady. New Canaan was already better than he had expected.

When Johan returned to the campsite, his older brother, Wilhelm, was crouched by the fire as a toddler pulled at his sleeve and a young boy clamored up his back. Another little boy ran across the clearing with a branch in his hand. "I'll keep the wolves away!" he shouted.

"Don't run with sticks, Fritz!" Wilhelm said as he plucked the other child from his shoulders and pulled him into his lap. "And don't climb on Papa, Franz. I'm not as young as I used to be, you know." The little boy looked up at him, then settled into his lap and laid his head against his father's chest. The toddler continued to tug on Wilhelm's sleeve. "All right, you too, Felix." Wilhelm pulled the child into his lap and tried to stoke the fire with his free hand.

"Another relaxing night around the campfire, I see." Johan grinned as he strode into the clearing and eased the yoke off his shoulders. Water sloshed over the sides of the wooden buckets as he set them onto the ground.

"*Ja,*" Wilhelm said as Fritz ran back across the clearing. "Very relaxing." This time, Fritz held a frog instead of a stick. "Where did you get that—" Wilhelm cut the sentence short, sighed, and shook his head. "As long as no one gets hurt."

"We're off to a good start," Johan said as he settled onto a log and held his hands to the fire.

"Are we?" Wilhelm pulled a half-eaten leaf from Felix's hand.

Johan broke into a carefree grin. "Yes."

"Put that poor frog down," Wilhelm shouted to Fritz, then turned to Johan. "Why are you smiling like that?"

"Because I met someone."

"I don't guess she's on her way with a hot meal and a bedtime story for these three boys?"

Johan laughed. "If only life were that simple."

Wilhelm pulled an arm away from the children in his lap to rub his eyes with a thumb and forefinger. "If only."

The journey through the wilderness to reach New Canaan would have been difficult enough—but with three young children, it had been nearly impossible. Johan had convinced Wilhelm to make a new start after Wilhelm's wife died. And where better for a new start than the first Amish settlement in America? There, the brothers had reasoned, Wilhelm would have the support of a likeminded community as he navigated single fatherhood. And, they had the promise of land. In the Pennsylvania backcountry, a man could make his own way and build a future for himself. In Germany, the brothers had been poor tenant farmers with little hope of a better life.

"At least we've found a place where we belong as Amish." Johan reached over and tousled his nephew's hair. "It's a start."

"*Ja.*" Wilhelm exhaled and ran his fingers through his own hair. "The question is, now what?"

Johan laughed. "Tomorrow, we go to the worship service. Day after tomorrow, we start clearing the land."

"And after that?" Wilhelm asked.

"We build a cabin and plant our crops."

Wilhelm's oldest son raced by again. The frog was gone, but so were the boy's waistcoat and woolen hose. Wilhelm opened his mouth, then closed it again. He squeezed his eyes shut and pinched the bridge of his nose. "And then what?"

"We'll take it one day at a time after that. Who knows where life will take us?"

"That's what I'm afraid of," Wilhelm said.

Johan laughed. "Look at life as an adventure."

Fritz barreled toward Wilhelm, leapfrogged over his lap—and his two brothers—and kept running.

"I'd settle for something more predictable," Wilhelm said.

Johan grinned. "There's no fun in that!"

"I'll take predictability over fun any day." As Wilhelm spoke, Fritz's feet slid out from under him and he landed flat on his face in a mud puddle. Brown water splashed upward and splattered Wilhelm in the eye. He sighed, took out a handkerchief, wiped his face, and stuffed the handkerchief back in his pocket. "As I was saying . . ."

"Point taken." Johan wanted to tell Wilhelm more about the captivating young woman he had met. But he hesitated. What good would it do to mention it? Wilhelm needed a wife far more than Johan did. In fact, Johan did not think he needed a wife at all. He rather enjoyed the carefree bachelor life—or he had before he'd started helping his widowed brother care for three motherless children. Life had not been carefree since then.

Indeed, Johan had learned a powerful lesson. Family life could be difficult. Children were not always sweet and silent. In fact, they could be quite loud. And boisterous. And downright dangerous. Especially when they ran with sticks and hid frogs in their uncle's bedcovers. No, Johan was quite happy to stay single. One family was enough to handle—he didn't need to start his own!

It was too bad he couldn't get that lovely Christina out of his mind. He hoped it was a passing fancy. Anything else would be quite inconvenient.

Chapter Two

Christina danced into the cabin. Her feet felt as light as a cloud in a springtime sky. Something wonderful had happened. Something momentous and unprecedented. Something she had always dreamed would happen. A man *had* been waiting outside her door! What madness! What glory!

"What in heaven's name has come over you?" Hilda glanced up from her sewing, shook her head, and turned her attention back to her needle and thread.

"You won't believe it."

"Hmmmm. Probably not." Hilda frowned as she pulled the thread taut. "Let me guess. You just met the man of your dreams and we will all live happily ever after now."

Christina clapped her hands. Her face still had a happy pink glow. "How did you guess?"

"Because it's all you ever talk about."

"That is not true, strictly speaking. I also talk about *you* meeting the man of your dreams."

"Hmmmm." Hilda did not look up. "You took care of the sheep?"

"I didn't need to."

Hilda gave a curt nod as she snipped the end of the thread. "So it was nothing."

"Nothing? I told you, it was a man!"

"Ah."

"Don't you want the details? He was—"

"All finished." Hilda held up the bodice she had been stitching. "Good as new, *ja*? You'd never know it's been taken in."

"Don't you want to hear about—"

Hilda picked a loose thread from the bodice. "Oh, Christina." She shook her head. "You have to stop this."

"Hilda, you don't understand."

"Christina, the man of your dreams won't just appear. This is the real world. You have to stop dreaming. Can't you see life is hard enough without adding unrealistic expectations? You'll make yourself sick with all that hope." Hilda stood and hung the bodice on a peg in the wall. "Try and be satisfied with what you have."

"I am satisfied. I just want more."

Hilda laughed, but it sounded small and hollow. "This is all there is."

Christina wanted to say more. She wanted to shout out every detail about Johan. She wanted to take her sister by the hand and dance around the cabin and tell her everything. But Christina said nothing. How could she? Hilda had given up her life to take care of Christina when their parents died. Hilda had sacrificed and struggled and found a way to bring them from their German village to the New World, where they could live free as Amish. Now, at thirty-two years old, Hilda had no hope left for a match. She was far past marriageable age. Hilda would never admit regret, but Christina could sense the loss her sister felt. Hilda would never have a family of her own, and Christina felt responsible.

How could Christina talk about meeting the man of her dreams when Hilda had no one? How could Christina think of leaving Hilda alone? Christina closed her eyes and pushed the temptation away. She would find a man for her sister. She must. Then, and only then, would she dare to dream of a man of her own.

The next day dawned bright and fair. Wildflowers dotted the woodlands and ran along the edges of cleared land, where wild grass fought to overtake freshly plowed fields. Christina's thoughts stayed on Johan as she and Hilda walked to the worship service. Every step along the narrow footpath led her another step closer to the man she had met—she had no doubt he was, indeed, the man of her dreams. How could he be anything else? Men didn't just fall from the sky and land atop one's woodpile—not unless they were meant to find you. Christina shivered with expectation. What did *der Herr* have planned for her?

"Isn't that right, Christina?"

Christina flinched. "What?" She had not meant to daydream.

"The shearing. It should be a good year, *ja*?"

"Oh, *ja*. A very good year." Christina turned her face toward the rising sun. The rays felt warm and soft on her skin. She wanted to melt into the warmth and dream of melting into Johan's arms—but she could not. Christina straightened her spine and cleared her throat. What foolishness. She had already promised herself she would banish Johan from her mind until Hilda found a match.

How Hilda would find a match here in the backcountry, where wolves and cougars outnumbered eligible bachelors, she did not know. But there had to be a way. Christina squeezed her fists together. There *had* to be a way. She could not leave Hilda alone.

"Christina, dear, are you quite well? You look as if you might punch something."

Christina loosened her fists and flashed a smile. "What? I haven't any idea what you mean."

"Hmmmm. Ah, here we are." Hilda turned off the path and picked her way down an embankment toward a stout little cabin. Hemlocks towered over the dirt yard. Sunlight glistened across the dark green needles that shaded the clearing.

Christina's heart leapt into her throat as she scanned the yard. She saw Jacob and Greta, the hosts of this week's service, as well as the Widow Yoder, Eli and his new bride Catrina, the Gruber and Stolzfus families and . . . oh, where could he be? Christina's eyes darted about the clearing. He *had* to come. Surely he wouldn't miss a service.

Surely he wouldn't miss a chance to see her again.

Christina stood on her tiptoes to peer above the cluster of settlers, but she couldn't see anything but the backs of starched, white prayer *kappes*. Christina pursed her lips and jumped up to see better. Hilda gave her a warning glance. Then Jonah Gruber stepped aside to say hello to Bishop Riehl. A gap opened in the crowd and a pair of sparkling gray eyes came into view. There he was!

Johan glanced up and spotted Christina. Their eyes met and his lips curled into a grin. Christina heard herself gasp as her stomach dropped to her toes. He had noticed her. He had even smiled at her! She felt a happy glow spread across her cheeks and knew she was blushing. Of course he had smiled at her. He was the man she had been dreaming of all these years.

"Christina, are you well?"

Hilda's voice sounded far away. Christina's focus stayed on the young man with the glint in his gray eyes and that charming, disarming smile. "Yes," she answered. "I am very well, indeed." Oh, yes. She had never been so well.

The crowd shifted, and Amos Knepp filled in the empty space and blocked Johan from Christina's view. Everyone wanted a chance to say hello to the newcomer. Christina could hear their friendly introductions from across the clearing. She let out a long, dreamy sigh as she stared into the crowd.

"I fear you have taken ill, sister mine." Hilda put a cool hand to Christina's forehead. "You ought to have worn your cloak when you went outside last night. You must have caught a chill." Hilda clucked her tongue. "Or are you just daydreaming again?"

"I am well." Christina's eyes remained on the crowd beside the cabin. "I am very well, indeed."

"You just said that."

"Did I?"

Hilda's eyes narrowed as she studied her younger sister. "You worry me so."

Christina put a hand on her sister's arm. "You worry too much."

"I worry for both of us."

"And I dream for both of us."

Hilda shook her head and patted the hand that Christina had laid on her arm. "Your dreams will only lead to sorrow.

Do try to live in reality. There is nothing more than this for us." Hilda swept her arm across the clearing.

"How right you are, sister dear." Christina smiled her dreamy smile. "I do believe all I need is right here, before us."

Hilda gave a curt nod. "Wonderful good. How pleased I am to hear you speak so practically."

Christina just smiled.

"We have a good life, you and I. We don't need anyone else."

Christina's smile snapped into a frown. She had let her heart overtake her vow. She could not, *would not* leave Hilda alone. Christina knew that she had to act. She had no idea how she would do it. She only knew she would find a man for Hilda. Christina had never backed down from a challenge before. That wasn't to say that her past efforts had not sometimes ended in disaster—they had. But she had always seen those efforts through to the bitter end, no matter what. And this time, Christina told herself, her plan would work out. Failure simply was not an option.

Oh sure, there was that time she accidentally set the outbuilding on fire back in Germany, that time she dropped her best hat down the well, or ended up with fourteen abandoned kittens to feed. And, of course, there was that time she tried to set her sister up with a man who smelled like vinegar and turned out to be forty-five years older than Hilda. To be fair, he had looked a good bit younger, except for that shiny bald head of his. Christina raised her chin and cut off all memories of past schemes gone awry. She would not entertain thoughts of past failures. She would put all her energy into succeeding.

* * *

Johan felt an unexpected lightness when he noticed Christina across the dirt yard. Funny thing, that. Oh, she was pretty enough—but to actually *feel* something for her? Well, that was strange indeed. Johan was used to sweeping young ladies off their feet with his disarming grin, effortless charm, and witty jokes. He didn't mean to do it. It just happened. He couldn't help that he had a personality—and looks—that drew attention. And he couldn't help that he never felt the same way about those charmed ladies as they did about him. If he had a coin for every time he had politely told a hopeful young woman that he had no intention of courting her, then he would be a rich man indeed.

He never led them on, of course. He was always straightforward about his intentions. And his intentions were always to stay happily single. There would be time to marry in the future—the far, distant future. Why not enjoy his youth without the responsibilities of a family?

"You'll start building on the morrow, *ja*?" a male voice asked.

"What's that?" Johan did not move his eyes from Christina. He studied her rosy cheeks, bright blue eyes, and the way her hands danced as she spoke. She looked so animated, so alive. She had a spark of life behind those dreamy eyes of hers.

"Breaking ground on the cabin soon, *ja*?"

Johan noticed that an elderly man was carrying on a conversation with him. Johan tore his eyes from Christina and turned to the man. "Amos Knepp, is it?"

"*Ja*." Amos nodded his head enthusiastically.

"You were asking about our cabin?"

"*Ja*."

"We'll start on that as soon as we can." Johan nodded

toward his nephews. Fritz and Franz ran in circles around Wilhelm. Felix jumped up and down and pulled at his father's waistcoat. "Those boys need a good roof over their heads before they turn as wild as wolves."

Amos raised his eyebrows. "Ah." He watched as Wilhelm's sons pushed for his attention, gave up, and raced away. Fritz glanced back at his younger brothers, flashed a grin, and shouted that he would beat them to the footpath. He kept running with his head turned—until a hand shot out and grabbed his collar. The boy stopped short and flung his head around to see a stern face bending over him.

"That's quite enough," Hilda said in her most no-nonsense voice. "One more step and you would have knocked over Ruth Yoder."

The elderly widow stood directly in the boy's path. She tried to force her face into a serious expression, but Johan could see the mirth in her eyes.

"What would you have done then, with the poor Widow Yoder knocked flat on the ground?" Hilda stared down at the boy. Unlike Ruth's, her eyes held no hint of mirth.

Fritz swallowed hard and glanced at his father. Wilhelm nodded. The boy looked back at Ruth with a contrite expression. "Sorry. But I couldn't help it."

"Why not?"

"I had to get away from Franz." As he said the words, a ball of mud flew through the air. Fritz ducked and the mud landed in the center of Hilda's bodice with a wet splat.

Hilda stared at the stain for a moment, then frowned and dabbed at the mud with the corner of her apron. "I see."

"All's well that ends well, young man," Ruth answered and patted him on the head.

"Tell that to my bodice," Hilda said.

Ruth laughed. "Oh, but what fun. I do love the unexpected."

"Yes." Hilda wiped the spot more vigorously. "What fun." Her voice did not sound as if she were having very much fun.

Catrina Webber hurried over. She looked beautiful in her spotless bodice, ironed skirts, and freshly starched prayer *kappe*. "Oh, you poor darling!" She pulled out a crisp, white linen handkerchief and dabbed at the stain. "What a terrible thing!"

Hilda sighed. "It's all right."

Catrina kept dabbing away.

"Really, it's all right."

"Is there anything worse than mud?" Catrina asked.

"I can think of a few things. . . ."

"Aren't you brave!"

"Really, Catrina."

"Well, that's the best I can do." Her brow creased with sympathy.

"It's fine, really. Thank you." Hilda turned from Catrina to the mud-throwing culprit. The little boy stared at her with big eyes. "Come here, child."

Franz glanced back at his father. Wilhelm nodded, and Franz gave a dramatic sigh, hung his head, and walked to Hilda. He shuffled his feet as he went.

Hilda crouched down to Franz's eye level. She gave him a hard, no-nonsense stare. "Boys ought not to throw mud. It was naughty of you."

He stared back without speaking.

"What do you say when you hit someone like that?"

"It was an accident?"

Hilda's mouth twitched and it looked like she might

smile, but she managed to keep that firm expression on her face. "Accident or no, you owe me an apology."

"I'm sorry."

Hilda nodded. She straightened Franz's black linsey-woolsey jacket and brushed a spot on the sleeve. "Where's your mother? Is she here?"

The boy shook his head. "I don't have a mother. She died a long time ago and I don't remember her."

"Ah." Hilda smiled. "You'll have to come to our cabin for a good meal, *ja*? I'll make something nice just for you. A pudding, perhaps?"

Franz nodded with big, solemn eyes and took off for his father. Then Franz froze, glanced back at Hilda, and slowed to a walk. Hilda nodded her approval, and Franz gave a shy smile.

Johan watched as Franz made his way through the crowd. The boy kept a polite distance as he skirted the adults. "That woman certainly knows how to handle little ones," Johan whispered to his brother.

"Indeed, she does." Wilhelm shook his head. "What I wouldn't give to have a woman like that for my boys."

Johan shrugged. "What's stopping you?"

"Ha! Easy for you to say. You've got women knocking down the door to find you. I'm an old widower with"—he waved his hand in the direction of his unruly children—"three additions to the bargain."

Johan sighed and his voice took on a serious tone. "They're good children, Wilhelm."

"That they are." Wilhelm watched them with tired eyes. "But they've grown wild, as you know. I've worked so hard to provide for them that I've forgotten how to do the simple things. Tucking them in at night, minding their table manners, keeping their hose mended . . ."

Wilhelm ran his fingers through his hair. "It's not something I expected to do on my own. I'm afraid I'm not very good at it."

"Being a father?"

"*Ja.*"

"Nonsense." Johan shook his head. "You're an excellent father. You just need a little help. Everyone needs help sometimes." Johan shrugged. "Too bad I'm not any better at mending stockings or minding table manners than you are."

"That's for certain. I wonder—" Wilhelm stopped midsentence to nod a polite hello to Frena and Georg Witmer. It was difficult to get a private word in when the entire settlement was eager to greet the newcomers. Johan didn't mind. He had always enjoyed meeting new people—especially lovely young ladies. Johan stared in Christina's direction as the settlers drifted by to introduce themselves. He tried to pay attention to the introductions, but he kept wondering what dreams hid behind those wide, blue eyes. He was sure Christina was a dreamer. That much was evident in her soft smile and faraway look as she gazed in his direction.

The only thing that Johan couldn't understand was why he cared. So what if she was a dreamer with wide blue eyes, flushed cheeks, and a faraway look on her face? Bah! He had no interest in settling down, so he had no interest in that face. Even though it was a lovely face. A very lovely face indeed.

Christina had an idea. She did not know if it would work, but the pieces seemed to be before her, just waiting to snap into place. Johan had mentioned that he had a brother. He had not mentioned that his brother was single.

Christina studied the man who stood beside Johan. Kind eyes, a friendly smile, an ordinary but trustworthy face . . . oh *ja*, the man had potential.

Christina took her sister by the hand and pulled her toward Johan and his brother. "We must greet the new family."

"*Ja, ja*. Don't pull so hard." Hilda frowned. "I've already met one of them. And he was an unruly fellow, the poor dear."

"Yes, he was a dear. I'm so glad you agree."

"Humph."

"One day, Hilda, you will look back and wish you had enjoyed life more."

"Humph."

"Don't you like meeting new people?"

"If I did, I would not have moved to the wilderness."

"Hilda! You don't mean that, surely."

"Sometimes I wonder how two sisters can be so different," Hilda muttered as Christina dragged her across the yard.

"You have a way with children, you know. Even if you don't like to admit it."

"Ha! A way with children! I have no patience for children."

"Of course you do. You had patience for me, remember?"

"And now I've none left."

Christina glanced at her sister. Hilda winked.

"I thought you were serious."

"I was. I spent all my patience on you."

Christina laughed. "Now be serious. We ought to be welcoming."

"I'm not the welcoming sort."

"Of course you are!" Christina straightened her sister's prayer *kappe*. "Now, just act natural."

"Act natural? Why in the world wouldn't I act natural? Christina, what in heaven's name has gotten into you?"

"Nothing. Now quiet down before they hear." Christina tried to look calm. She smoothed the front of her apron and adjusted her neck cloth. "You never get a second chance to make a first impression."

"Really, Christina. Why on earth would I care about what impression I make on these men?"

Christina did not answer. She wondered how Hilda could be so blind to the potential before them.

Johan flashed a grin as the sisters drew closer. Christina returned the smile. She waved and picked up her pace.

"Really, Christina. Try not to act so eager! You've not even met the man."

"Oh, I have. I did mention it, if you recall."

Hilda raised an eyebrow.

"Last night."

"I do not recall. But even if you have met him, you ought not to act so eager. The very idea. It isn't decent, running over to him like that!"

Christina forced herself to slow down. She took a deep breath and let it out slowly. *Act natural. Act natural.* Dash it all, she *was* acting natural. Flighty, impulsive, eager— that *was* her natural state. Should she act unnatural?

Christina's concerns disappeared as she drew closer to Johan. Her entire universe narrowed down to that one, gorgeous grin. "Christina." His eyes sparkled as he spoke her name. Christina felt her cheeks redden. So charming, that man. "How good it is to see you again," he said without taking his eyes from hers. Christina felt her knees soften. "Allow me to introduce my brother, Wilhelm." Johan motioned toward the man beside him.

Wilhelm nodded. He looked sheepish as he glanced

down at the three young boys clinging to his black coat and knee breeches. "You've already met one of my sons."

"Ah." Hilda did not smile. "That we have."

"A lovely boy," Christina said.

Wilhelm did not look so certain. "Hmmmm." His eyes met Hilda's, lingered there a moment, then dropped.

Christina watched that momentary interaction and felt encouraged. There was definitely potential there. "The poor child is without a mother, *ja*?"

"*Ja*. I've been widowed since Felix was a newborn baby. Childbed fever. The boys can't remember what it's like to have a mother."

Could everything fall into place this easily? A kind widower materializing the day after a dashing young man appeared on her woodpile . . . oh, this was too good to be true! Hilda always said that if it seems too good to be true than it *isn't* really true. But what did Hilda know? She was far too practical.

Christina smiled to herself. She had a plan. A perfect, foolproof plan. All she had to do was make it happen.

How hard could that be?

Chapter Three

Christina's head swirled with ideas. She had not felt so excited since she had tried to set Hilda up with the bald man who smelled like vinegar. That had been a disaster, but she had learned from her mistakes. Besides, Wilhelm had a good head of hair. He did not look at all like that poor fellow. And he certainly did not smell like him. That was a start, at least.

Christina narrowed her eyes and sized up Wilhelm. She guessed he was in his mid-thirties—a perfect match to Hilda's thirty-two. He looked stouter and more weather-worn than his brother. He wore a gentle expression of exasperation on his face. The man needed a helpmeet—that much was clear.

Oh, this was going to be too easy!

Christina's heart quickened as the plan solidified in her mind. She could imagine Wilhelm's and Hilda's wedding already. Perhaps even a double wedding. That had always been her dream. Christina looked up at Johan and smiled. Oh yes. Definitely a double wedding.

"You look like the cat that ate the canary," Johan said and returned her wry smile.

"Oh. Do I?" Christina giggled.

Hilda pursed her lips. She had no patience for her sister's giggles and dreamy eyes. "We ought to sit down. I'm sure Bishop Riehl would like to start the service."

"Not at all." Abraham Riehl patted Wilhelm on the back. "It's good to have you all. New Canaan is growing from a solitary outpost to a village, *ja*?"

"*Ja*," Christina said before anyone else could answer. "And Hilda has already invited you and your family to dinner, Wilhelm."

"I have?" Hilda looked puzzled.

"You invited little Fritz, dear. Your memory really has been slipping lately."

"Oh, I meant—"

"To invite the whole family? Yes, dear, I know. How lovely of you."

Hilda did not respond. Instead, she shot Christina her sternest look. Then Hilda nodded to Wilhelm and said, "We would be happy to have you." She did not look happy in the least.

Christina clapped her hands. "Wonderful good! Tomorrow night. You all must come over tomorrow night. It's been ages since you had a good meal, *ja*? All those weeks on the trail, with naught but salt pork and corncakes, *ja*?"

Wilhelm nodded his head enthusiastically. "*Ja!*"

Christina beamed. Hilda did not realize how very perfect this was. But she would soon enough.

The cabin became a bustle of activity the next day. Christina flew in every direction, scrubbing this, cleaning that, stoking the fire, sweeping the dirt floor, rolling out the pastry crust for a meat pie. Rabbit would have to do, although she would have preferred beef. The settlement's men always remembered the sisters after a hunt and checked in from time to time to make sure they had food in the larder. Thankfully, Jacob Miller had just given the sisters a good, fat rabbit that needed to be eaten before it spoiled. The sisters would remember to return the favor when they sheared the sheep and had wool to give.

After she skinned and cut the rabbit, Christina salted the meat and wished for nutmeg and black pepper. She had neither. A good meat pie required sugar as well, and she debated whether or not to take from their small reserve. *It is not every day that one works to woo two fine men*, she reminded herself. And so it was decided. Besides, what was sugar for, if not for eating?

Christina spread the salted rabbit meat atop the pastry crust, followed by a layer of sliced apples, a sprinkle of sugar, and a generous slather of sheep's butter. The smooth, rich, and mildly sweet butter would help make up for the lack of spices. She added another layer of salted rabbit meat and sealed everything beneath a pastry crust. She patted the pastry with more sheep's butter and laid the pie in a Dutch oven.

Christina tucked her skirts behind her as she stooped over the fireplace to rake coals onto the hearth. Once she had a good pile of red-hot coals, she set the Dutch oven on top, put the heavy cast-iron lid in place, and added another layer of coals atop the lid. The coals would bake the pie to a lovely golden brown. Christina wiped the perspiration from her forehead and sat back on her heels. She would make a perfect meal for a perfect evening—and a perfect match.

She rested only a moment before jumping up again. So much to do to create a perfect evening. And, she must allow time to change into a clean apron and straighten her hair. Did her prayer *kappe* look clean and crisp? Her hands flew to her head. The fabric felt limp beneath her fingers. If only she had thought to wash it on Saturday. But how could she have known that an eligible man—make that *two* eligible men—would appear out of thin air? So much can change in an instant.

Soon, the scent of roasted meat and wood smoke curled up from the hearth. Christina was too busy to notice. Perfection did not come easily.

"I do wish you would sit down," Hilda said after she came in from tending the sheep. "The flock is safely in for the night. Let's finish our sewing, *ja*? I need to make a new housewife." Because their clothing had no pockets, men and women both carried a pouch called a housewife to hold essentials.

"Oh, Hilda. How could you possibly?"

"Do what I do every evening? Quite easily, thank you."

Christina put her hands on her hips. "You know what I mean. We have guests coming for dinner!"

"Ah, that." Hilda sighed. "I had forgotten." She sank onto the rough wooden bench and picked up her sewing basket. "And I so wanted to get that housewife made." She clucked her tongue. "Well, I suppose it can't be helped."

"Can't be helped!" Christina stared at her sister. "We have guests—two handsome guests, I might add—and that's all you can say?"

"*Ach.* All right. It's the right thing to do to welcome newcomers."

"Come now, *Fraulein* Grumpy. Surely you can find more enthusiasm than that."

Hilda sighed again as she picked through her sewing basket. "Those children are quite unruly, you know. I imagine it will not be a quiet evening. And I do enjoy our quiet evenings."

"They are unruly because they need a mother, the poor dears. Wilhelm is in over his head. He hasn't any notion of effective discipline." Christina paused for emphasis. "Where, I wonder, might he find a good mother for those darling boys?"

"Where, indeed?" Hilda shook her head without looking up. "It was a good thing to bring them here, to be brought up among their own people, but I'm afraid the poor man has condemned himself to remaining a widower." She pulled a scrap of gray wool from the basket. "There simply aren't any candidates here, in the middle of the wilderness."

Christina raised her eyebrows. Hilda did not notice. She was too busy threading her needle. "You know, I do admire him," Hilda said. "To make that sacrifice so that his family can worship freely as Amish. How lonely he will be here, with no hope of a match."

"No hope of a match?" Christina asked. Her eyebrows rose even higher. "No candidates at all?"

Hilda knotted her thread. "I suppose there's the Gruber girl. She's what, sixteen now?" She shook her head. "No, that's too young for Wilhelm. He looks to be in his thirties."

"And you can think of no other candidates? None at all?" Christina's eyebrows rose so high her forehead ached.

"No." Hilda shook her head again. "The poor dear."

"Really, Hilda. None at all?"

Hilda's eyes shot up. "Oh." She studied Christina. "Oh, I see." Hilda looked back down and rummaged through her basket. "It isn't the match I would have predicted, to be sure. Do you really want to take on three little children and a man in his thirties? You're only nineteen. I know most girls your age are already married but . . ."

"Hilda. I am not interested in Wilhelm."

"Hmmmm. Then why so much talk?"

"Never mind."

"I know you are too loyal to leave me, Christina, but leave me you must. You cannot keep scorning suitors out of guilt. If you feel affection for Wilhelm, you must pursue him. You cannot give up your life."

"I feel no affection for Wilhelm."

"Oh, Christina."

"Don't 'oh, Christina' me."

"I know you feel you owe me, but it was my choice to raise you when our parents died. You never asked me to do it. I wanted to stay with you."

"And I want to stay with you," Christina said. "And so I will."

Hilda's face hardened. "If you keep up this nonsense, you will find yourself on the shelf, like me. There is no reason for both of us to end up alone. No reason, save your stubbornness."

"We're not alone. We have each other."

Hilda's firm expression softened into a smile. "That is true. You are a darling girl, Christina." Hilda glanced up at her sister and winked. "And an exasperating one."

Christina smiled at Hilda, but she knew she would get nowhere with her sister. To think that Hilda had called *her*, Christina, the stubborn one! Ha! No matter. She needed to put all her efforts into creating the perfect evening. She had cleaned the house from top to bottom, pulled together a hearty meal for two hungry men and three hungry boys, and tried to talk some sense into Hilda. Now, what was she forgetting?

Hilda's appearance! She could not receive Wilhelm looking like *that*. "Hilda, dear."

"*Ja*?" Hilda's fingers moved over the cloth as her needle went in and out.

"It's time to freshen up."

"No need."

"No need? You've come straight from tending the sheep. You need a fresh apron. And your curls are slipping out of place. Repin your hair, at the least. That frizzy, brown hair of yours. What a sight you are!"

"Calm yourself, dear." Hilda pushed a stray curl under her prayer *kappe*. "There, all better."

"And the apron?"

Hilda dusted a smudge of dirt from the white linen. "Perfectly serviceable."

"I thought you might change into your Sunday best."

"Whatever for? Besides, the sheep might need tending again later. And there's supper to get."

"I've taken care of supper."

"Still, no need to be extravagant."

"A clean apron is hardly extravagant."

"Hmmmm." Hilda held up the half-sewed housewife. "My stitching is not as even as it once was. These eyes are failing already."

"You are much too dramatic." Christina picked up the Betty lamp—a homemade German oil lamp with a tiny flame—and set it down closer to Hilda. "You act as if you are as old as the Widow Yoder."

"I may as well be."

"Hilda, sometimes I think you want to wallow in your own misery. If you would just open your eyes and see the possibilities in front of you!"

Hilda frowned and looked beyond her sister's shoulder.

"The only thing I see in front of me is smoke. Is something burning, dear?"

Christina spun around to see smoke billowing from the hearth. "My supper!" She dashed to the Dutch oven and scrambled to rake the coals off the iron lid. "Oh, my poor perfect supper!" Smoke soared upward and stung her eyes. She covered her mouth and nose with her apron and coughed as she cleared the last coals away. Then she grabbed the iron hook, latched it to the handle on the Dutch oven, and pulled it from the remaining coals. Christina tore open the lid and screeched.

"Not so perfect, I fear," Hilda said from across the cabin.

Christina covered the rest of her face with her apron and sobbed into it. "How could this happen? Everything was going so well. How could I ruin it all?"

"There, there." Hilda set aside her sewing and stood up. "It's only supper."

"It was so much more than supper! Don't you see?" Christina pressed the apron against her eyes. "This will never work."

"Not if you keep up that caterwauling. Now get a hold of yourself and think fast. We've five hungry mouths to feed, not counting us. And I don't know about you, but I intend to eat."

A knock at the door sent a surge of panic down Christina's spine. She couldn't let Johan catch her with red eyes. She leapt up from the hearth even as her stomach plunged to the floor. Oh, how to solve this dilemma? "My eyes!" she whispered to Hilda. "I can't receive company in this state."

"It's all right. They'll think it's the smoke." Hilda coughed and fanned the air. "Heaven knows there's enough of it."

"Thank *der Herr* for small mercies."

"Indeed." Hilda motioned toward the door. "Now get that pie out of this cabin before the bed linens take on the smell of smoke."

Christina hauled the Dutch oven from the hearth by the iron hook, then wrapped a cloth around the hot, metal handles. It took both hands to lift the heavy, cast-iron pot—and the burning pie inside. Smoke trailed upward and engulfed her as she dashed across the cabin. She threw open the door and saw five surprised faces stare at her. No one spoke. They just stared. Christina wanted to melt into the ground and disappear. Could this get any worse?

If her record of previous schemes was any indication, it could. Oh, it could get much, much worse.

Chapter Four

Johan stared as the cabin door was flung open and Christina tore past him. Smoke billowed around her like a halo. Blond hair escaped her prayer *kappe* in messy curls. Her eyes looked wide and red and her lips quivered as if she could not believe the current state of affairs.

In short, she looked adorable.

"What's that?" Franz asked in a loud voice and pointed to the Dutch oven that zipped past them. They turned their heads in unison to watch Christina race across the yard. Smoke trailed behind her as she ran.

"Our supper," Wilhelm said.

"Our supper!" the three boys shouted.

"Shhhh," Johan whispered. "Don't hurt the poor girl's feelings."

"But, Uncle Johan! Our supper!"

"Shhhh."

Johan patted his nephew on the head as he stared at Christina. She made it halfway across the clearing before she dropped the Dutch oven in the dirt. She stretched her back and swallowed hard. The sheepdog licked his chops and trotted over to investigate. He circled the Dutch oven twice, sniffed the smoldering piecrust, and backed away. Christina covered her face with her hands.

"Ran into a bit of trouble?" Johan shouted across the clearing.

Christina nodded without moving her hands from her face.

"That's all right."

Franz tugged at Johan's black woolen jacket. "No, it's not. I'm hungry."

Johan patted the boy's head again and whispered for him to hush. "Could have been worse."

"Really?"

Johan paused and rubbed his chin with a thumb and finger. "Could have burned down the cabin."

Christina's shoulders began to shake.

Now he'd done it. He'd made the poor girl cry. "Now, don't go getting all upset. It's just a pie. We don't mind." Johan shot a firm stare at his nephews. Franz opened his mouth to protest, then closed it again. Christina's shoulders continued to shake. Johan felt downright awkward. He did not know how to comfort a crying woman. He frowned and tried to think of something encouraging to say. But before he could think of the words, Christina dropped her hands from her face. She was not crying. She was laughing!

Johan returned the laughter. He liked the joy and recklessness he saw in Christina's blue eyes. Not many people could laugh at their own mistakes. He admired that. The boys looked at each other in surprise, then up at their father. Their looks of surprise were transformed to grins, and they all broke into laughter too.

"What in heaven's name?" Hilda darted out of the cabin with a corner of her apron pressed over her mouth and nose. She dropped the apron, wiped her eyes, coughed, and shrugged. "Well, at least we got some entertainment out of it." Wilhelm started toward her, but she shooed him away. "No one can go inside. It's filled with smoke."

"Ah." He peered through the open door and frowned. "Best leave the door open to air."

"*Ja.*"

His eyes scanned the cabin's windows. "Still got the oilcloth tacked in place." With no glass to be had in the backcountry, the settlers sealed their windows shut with oiled cloth throughout the winter.

"I'm afraid so. Nights have been chilly of late."

"Hmmm." Wilhelm walked to the threshold and studied the layer of smoke trapped beneath the low roof of the snug little cabin. "Johan and I will take the oilcloth down. Otherwise, that smoke's not going anywhere. The nights should be warm enough from now on."

"I wouldn't hear of it."

Wilhelm looked surprised. "It's the sensible thing to do."

"I mean I wouldn't hear of your doing it. Christina and I can manage."

"Ah." Wilhelm looked amused as he studied Hilda's straight back and firm expression. "*Ja.* I can see that."

Hilda gave a curt nod.

"So we'll do it together."

"That won't be necessary."

"I insist."

Johan smiled as he watched his brother interact with Hilda. Christina's sister was not a pushover. That much was clear. Her determination made her seem formidable, even though she was small of stature. "She insists."

"As do I." Wilhelm nodded.

Hilda shrugged. "Suit yourself."

"I will."

"Three's a crowd," Johan said with a happy sigh as he settled onto a stump. If Hilda wanted to untack the oilcloth herself, who was he to stand in her way?

"What a dear you are, Wilhelm!" Christina shouted from across the clearing. She picked up her skirts, hurried to the cabin, and clapped her hands when she reached the doorway. "Isn't he thoughtful, Hilda? Isn't he, Hilda?" Wilhelm shrugged one shoulder and looked sheepish before escaping into the cabin. Hilda shook her head and followed him inside.

Oh. *Oh.* Johan's happy mood evaporated as he watched Christina's eyes light up at the sight of Wilhelm. Those same blue eyes that had met his across the clearing just a moment ago. He frowned. Now those blue eyes were on his brother, not him. He stared at Christina and tried to understand the strange feeling he had. He had never had such a feeling before. Could it be jealousy? No, that would be preposterous. Absolutely preposterous. Johan had never felt jealous of anyone before. Women always flocked to him, not to other men—and especially not to his poor, overburdened brother. Christina couldn't have eyes for Wilhelm.

Could she?

Not that it mattered. Johan frowned and shifted his weight. It didn't matter one bit. After all, he wasn't inter-ested. He was far too busy being happy and carefree to be concerned.

Franz skipped over to Johan and tugged at his sleeve. "When will we eat?" he asked.

"*What* will we eat?" Fritz added.

Johan's stomach rumbled. "There's always the salt pork."

"Uncle Johan, that's all we've had for ages!" Fritz kicked a pine cone and sent it skipping across the dirt yard.

"So another meal of it won't kill you."

Fritz kicked another pine cone.

Johan sneaked a glance at Christina. She sat in a heap with her knees to her chin, her skirts flowing over her legs and puddled across the ground. The poor girl must feel quite sheepish about burning dinner and causing so much trouble. Johan tried to think of something to say to cheer her up, but decided to stay silent. After all, she clearly did not want to hear from him. The minutes passed slowly. The boys found an anthill to investigate, but Johan and Christina had nothing to do but stare at the dirt and pretend not to notice each other. Of course, Johan had no reason to care. Why should it bother him that Christina's eyes kept sliding back to the cabin door, as if she wanted to catch a glimpse of Wilhelm? Why should it bother him that Christina looked alone and embarrassed?

Dash it all, nothing was the way it should be.

Johan continued not to care when Christina crept to the entrance of the cabin and peered inside. Except that his stomach sank to his feet. Was that what it felt like to care? Surely not. Johan Lantz did not care about such things. He frowned and kept his eyes on Christina as she shouted Wilhelm's name. "You did it!" she said in an adoring tone.

Johan's frown deepened.

"*Ja*," came Wilhelm's voice from inside the cabin. "It was nothing."

"Oh, it was something!" Christina said and clasped her hands together. Johan recognized a strange hope in her eyes. His stomach sank even further, and he looked away.

Hilda and Wilhelm hurried out of the cabin and nearly

bumped into Christina. She took a quick step backward and grinned. "The air will be clear soon, *ja*?"

"Soon enough," Wilhelm said. "Until then, Hilda found us something to eat." He looked down at Hilda with an eager smile as she raised a basket covered with a white linen cloth. Johan jumped up from the stump. "Wonderful good!" Out of the corner of his eye, he saw Christina's shoulders straighten. She looked hopeful and satisfied—not what one would expect after instigating a minor disaster.

Johan could not understand Christina, and he told himself he did not want to. Instead, he scowled and strode over to Hilda. She whipped the cloth from the basket to reveal a two-day-old loaf of bread. "It isn't much, but it will do." She motioned to a hill in the woods perfect for cool, underground storage. "Fritz and Franz, run down to the root cellar and fetch us a block of sheep's cheese."

"This will do very well, indeed," Wilhelm said and rubbed his hands together. "We haven't had bread in ages. No bake ovens on the trail, as you know."

"And even if there were, who would have baked in them?" Christina said. "You two are quite alone. No one to bake for you, *ja*?"

Wilhelm cleared his throat. He looked as if he did not know how to respond. After a moment, he cleared his throat again and turned back to Hilda, as though Christina had not pointed out the obvious and awkward fact that he was single and in need of a wife. Christina did not seem to notice the uncomfortable tension. She just stared at Wilhelm with a glimmer of expectation in her eyes.

"You know how to work wonders, Hilda." Wilhelm's eyes stayed firmly on Hilda.

"Nonsense," Hilda said. "Now, let's eat before it begins to rain."

"Too late," Johan said. He lifted his face to the cold, gray sky as a soft mist settled on his skin. Just when he thought the evening couldn't get any worse. He wondered why everyone else was smiling. Wilhelm and Hilda settled onto a log side by side and chatted about the price of wool or something equally dull, while Christina stared and grinned like she'd been struck by a spell. None of them seemed to notice the rain. The boys fetched the sheep's cheese, then shouted and laughed and ran around the yard with slices of bread grasped in their fat little fists.

Only Johan sat with a glum look on his face. And, for the life of him, he could not understand why he felt so low.

Christina felt very pleased with the state of affairs. True, the meat pie had been a disaster. But the disaster had worked for good in a most miraculous way. Why, Christina would have *planned* to burn dinner if she had known that it would force Hilda and Wilhelm to work together. She almost felt disappointed in herself for *not* planning it that way.

Christina pulled the quilt to her chin and stared through the cracks in the wooden shutters. With the oilcloth gone, she could make out the faint light of stars above the distant shadow of the tree line. She thought she ought to feel alone in the wilderness, with just her sister in the cabin and only a dozen or so families in the settlement, but she did not. She felt a strange sense of belonging in the darkness that surrounded the cabin. Christina knew the darkness was not empty, but alive with *der Herr's* creation. Owls swooped from towering hemlocks. Pine needles rustled in the soft night air. Fat possums waddled through the underbrush while foxes padded across meadows on silent feet. Wolves whispered through the forest in swift and secretive packs, racing with the quiet.

Bruno stood watch between her and the predators that wandered outside her door, and Christina was not afraid. Instead, she felt warm and alive, knowing that an entire world unfolded outside her window that only the night creatures could see. She listened to the distant howl of a wolf and smiled. She was glad she had come to New Canaan—especially now that she had found a man for Hilda. Christina felt sure they were on the right track.

She rolled over and grinned into the darkness. The hard-packed dirt floor pressed into her shoulder, but she did not care. Her heart was too filled with anticipation to be bothered by the fact that she slept on a pallet against bare earth. She had found a way. Hilda and Wilhelm had connected today. She was sure of it. Christina replayed each moment in her mind. She remembered how Hilda and Wilhelm had worked side by side to tear down the oilcloth. She remembered the look that Wilhelm had given Hilda when she emerged from the cabin with the bread and cheese. It had been a look of appreciation, or admiration, even. He had recognized Hilda's resourcefulness. Christina would gladly suffer the humiliation of burning supper to give Hilda credit in Wilhelm's eyes.

No, she could not have planned it better.

A concern tickled the back of her mind, but she could not understand what could have possibly gone wrong in the midst of so much success. Toward the end of the evening she had noticed that poor Johan sat alone with a grimace on that handsome face of his. He was not a man given to grimaces, she could tell, for it had looked quite out of character. The memory of that dour expression nibbled at her victorious mood.

Christina rolled over again to try to find a comfortable position on the dirt floor. As her mood deflated, so did her positive attitude about her sleeping arrangement. She could use a thicker pallet. Tomorrow, she would take the time to gather the wild grass that sprouted in the cleared fields, leave it to dry in the sun, then add it to her thin mattress.

Perhaps it had been the rain that had put that grimace on Johan's face. He had looked rather disconcerted as he sat in a steady drizzle with his arms crossed and his jaw set. The water had beaded on his black beaver felt hat, and dripped off the brim and onto his woolen knee breeches. *Perhaps he is a man who does not enjoy sitting outside in a cold, wet drizzle, eating damp, day-old bread. Yes, that must be it.* It was the only logical answer. The next time they met, she would make sure it was on a fine day with fair weather. Johan would be back to his cheerful self then.

"Hilda?" Christina raised her head and whispered across the small cabin. "Are you awake?"

A quilt rustled in the darkness. "No."

Christina laughed and propped herself on one elbow. "Didn't you have a wonderful good time today?"

Hilda sighed. "I can't talk. I'm asleep."

"Do be serious. I haven't any patience for your nonsense at the moment."

"*My* nonsense?"

"*Ja*. This is a very serious question."

"If I had a wonderful good time?"

"*Ja*."

"That is not a serious question."

"Oh, Hilda. You know that it is."

"I most certainly do not."

"All right. Stop arguing over details and answer the

question. The conversation would be over by now and you could be asleep again if you would just answer the question."

"I am asleep."

"You are not."

"All right. All right." The quilt rustled again, and Christina heard Hilda turn over on her pallet. Dry grass crunched beneath her body weight. "It was fine."

"That's all?"

"It was . . . memorable. It's not every day that one's sister makes such a scene."

"That's the only reason it was memorable?"

"*Ja.*" There was a moment of silence and Christina could hear Hilda's deep, even breathing. She thought her sister had fallen asleep when Hilda added, "Ah, I see. You fear that you have made a fool of yourself. Do not fear, sister mine. There was no harm in the end, and I'm sure the entire evening will soon be forgotten."

"Forgotten?"

"*Ja.*"

"Entirely forgotten?"

"*Ja.*"

"Was there no part worth remembering?" Christina's heart sank. Would Hilda really insist on being so very thick headed?

"Wilhelm made a good neighbor today. He was quick to lend a hand."

"Ah!" Christina smiled into the darkness. "So you will remember him?"

"*Ja.* When the shearing comes, I will remember him with a small gift of wool, perhaps. Particularly since he offered to return to do more of the heavy chores for us."

"That's the only reason you will remember him?"

"Why else would I?"

Humph. Why, indeed? Christina punched her pallet to fluff the dry grass inside, then collapsed onto it in a dramatic heap. Matchmaking was going to prove a greater challenge than she had thought.

Chapter Five

After some deliberation, Wilhelm and Johan agreed that the spring planting should come first. The cabin would have to wait. What good was shelter if they had nothing to eat or trade come fall? When the brothers had sailed into Philadelphia a few months ago, they'd sold their valuables and bought seeds, which they considered more precious than gold. Gold did not fill empty bellies in the back-country. Seeds, an iron spider for cooking, and a few tools were all a man needed to live free here.

The Pennsylvania backcountry was a place for practi-cality and steadfast determination—not for luxuries or fanciful living. Circumstances pushed Plain living upon all who dared to make their way here, and that was just fine with Johan. He was up to the adventure and pleased to live far from the fancy, worldly lifestyles his people had faced in Germany. Besides, he and Johan could not afford their own land in Germany. But here, in the American Colonies, a new world opened to them. They could make their own way, claim their own land, and live for them-selves, safe from German laws that forced Amish pacifists into the military or oppressed free thinkers.

Johan surveyed the thick, silent woods that surrounded their campsite. This was home. He grinned and leaned against the solid trunk of a massive hemlock. Soon, he would transform these woods into rolling green fields that would ripen into a fine crop of barley, wheat, and oats. Johan nodded with satisfaction. This was good land—the breadbasket of the Colonies. The soil was rich, the rains good. Everything was going according to plan.

Except for one thing. It was a very small thing, Johan told himself. An almost imperceptible thing—even if it did cling to his thoughts like mice clung to a good kernel of corn. That reminded him. . . . "Franz, Fritz, and Felix!" The three boys came running from three different directions, each set of legs muddier than the last. "You see these sacks, *ja*?"

"With the seeds?"

"*Ja*." Fritz elbowed Felix in the ribs and Felix howled. "He doesn't know. He's too little."

"He's big enough to do a job for me." Johan put on his most serious expression. "And, just because you said that, I'm putting Felix in charge."

"In charge!" Fritz shouted. "He can barely talk! That's not fair."

"Then next time, remember to be nicer to your brother."

Fritz scowled but said no more. The threat of permanently losing his place as leader was too great a risk.

"Felix, you are in charge of the seed in these bags." Johan stooped down to look his little nephew in the eye. "You have a very important job, *ja*?"

Felix stared back with big, blue eyes and nodded.

"You make sure nothing eats the seeds, *ja*? Chase away the field mice and anything else that tries to steal a bite.

And make sure they stay dry and snug beneath the oilcloth tarp, *ja*?"

Felix nodded again. "No."

Johan paused, then smiled when he remembered that *no* was Felix's favorite word. "And by no, do you mean yes?"

Felix gave a solemn nod.

"Ah. I'm glad that's settled. You are officially Keeper of the Seed. A very important job."

Felix beamed and climbed atop the biggest burlap sack. His legs dangled as he sat guard. Johan tried to keep a serious expression on his face. "Well done, young man. The mice would not dare."

"No."

"No." Johan smiled and tousled his nephew's blond hair.

"What about us?" Fritz asked as he tugged Johan's linen waistcoat.

"Ah. A good question. Big boys need a big job, *ja*?"

"*Ja*," the boys shouted in unison.

"You two will help your father and me clear the forest."

"All of it?" Franz's jaw dropped as he scanned the immense wilderness that seemed to stretch on and on, forever.

Johan laughed. "Just enough for the spring planting."

"And when you're not minding the brush fires, you'll keep an eye on those seeds alongside Felix, *ja*?"

"*Ja!*"

"If you can handle it, that is." Johan shook his head. "It's a mighty important job."

"We can handle it!" Franz shouted as he jumped up and down.

"We can!" Fritz echoed.

"Well, then. It's settled. I'll be out of a job soon."

The boys grinned and Johan gave a satisfied smile. It was almost too easy. He had the boys right where he wanted them. They'd have the fields cleared and planted in no time. And come fall, they'd all eat like kings.

Now, what was it that had been bothering him? The thought returned to tickle his brain. Ah, yes. That was it. His smile sank into a frown as an image of Christina floated across his mind. Those lively blue eyes, rosy cheeks, that dreamy expression . . . Dash it all, why was he thinking of her? Especially after she had kept her eyes on Wilhelm during last night's meal. What a strange predicament.

Johan shook his head. No matter. Thinking of a woman led to settling down with a woman and starting a family— and that was the last thing he wanted. He felt sure he could shake the foolishness from his head if he got to work. And so he did.

Johan's ax rang out across the woodlands. Wilhelm's ax fell in time with his brother's. A deer bounded out of the underbrush and swept past Johan, so close he could have reached out and touched the smooth velvet of spring antlers. "Grab the gun!" Johan said and twisted for the German Jaeger rifle propped against a tree trunk.

Wilhelm did not move. Instead, his eyes followed the deer's swift, graceful escape as it bounded past and disappeared into the shadows of the deep forest. "No," he said. "Let that one go."

"You've always been too soft, brother," Johan said. But his eyes had lingered wistfully on the deer as well. He felt himself smile. The forest seemed wild and alive. There was something mysterious and almost magical in the still, damp air and restless shadows. "It was a beautiful animal."

Wilhelm nodded and raised his ax. "There'll always be another."

"*Ja.*" Johan was glad the deer had escaped, although he could not quite understand why. His mind had been full of foolishness since he had met Christina. He had gone as soft as his brother.

"What troubles you?" Wilhelm asked as his ax thudded into the trunk of a sturdy oak.

"Nothing."

Wilhelm gave his brother a look. "Then what distracts you?"

"Nothing."

"No? I've nearly doubled your efforts." Wilhelm grinned. "I suppose I'm the better woodcutter. Unless you have an explanation, that is."

Johan rolled his eyes. "Always competitive. I'd call you prideful, if I didn't know better."

"No explanation, then?"

"Well, I didn't say that."

Wilhelm glanced over with an expectant look.

Johan frowned and struck the oak with a tremendous thwack. He didn't want to admit he felt distracted. "What did you think of supper last night?"

Wilhelm grinned. "The boys were entertained by the spectacle."

"That's all you noticed? The spectacle?"

"That look on Christina's face when she ran outside with the Dutch oven." He raised the ax again, laughed, and lowered it again. "Now *you're* distracting *me*."

"Christina's antics were all you noticed, then?"

Wilhelm paused, then shrugged. "That Hilda has a head on her shoulders, *ja*?"

"She does. But I wonder if Christina . . ." Johan frowned and cut himself short. What had he been wondering? Whether or not Wilhelm had eyes for Christina? Christina certainly seemed to have eyes for Wilhelm. Had his brother not noticed? Johan clamped his mouth shut and raised his ax over his head. If he said anything, his brother would never let him hear the end of it. He swung the ax with all his strength. The metal blade slammed the wood so hard it made his joints ache. But when Johan raised the ax again he saw that it had barely made a dent. These trees would not be taken down easily. Neither would those confounded thoughts of Christina Dresser.

A dog barked in the distance and a woman shouted. Her clear, high voice drifted through the forest and into the clearing. Johan sighed and lowered his ax. He recognized that voice.

Christina was on a mission. Last night had gone so well that she knew she could finish the job today. By tomorrow, she would have made a match for Hilda.

"Do slow down," Hilda said and stopped to lean against the broad trunk of an ancient oak. "The grass is not going anywhere." Hilda lifted a foot, pulled off her leather shoe, and shook it until a pebble tumbled out. "You've led us on a merry chase this morning." Hilda slipped her shoe back on her foot and readjusted her woolen hose.

"Yes, but the sheep are hungry." The forest rang with the sound of bells as the flock searched for a good patch of weeds. Christina stooped to pat the soft, warm back of a ewe. The animal stared at her with trusting eyes before wandering away. Bruno swept around the sheep with sharp, watchful eyes. He sniffed the air, then ran to cut off a stray lamb.

"We ought to turn around," Hilda said. "I'm sure there's

enough grass growing in the village green, beside the bake-oven and the smokehouse."

"Oh no, they've eaten it all." Christina frowned. She had to be careful not to tell a lie while shuttling her sister in the right direction. "Or most of it at least." She cleared her throat and lowered her voice. "Or a lot of it, anyway."

Hilda glanced at the position of the sun in the sky. "It would be more efficient if I were home getting a head start on the laundry. I ought to go back and leave you to watch the flock."

"No, you mustn't." Christina searched for an excuse. "What of the wolves? Would you have me meet a hungry pack alone?"

"You're not alone. You have Bruno. And besides, when have you ever been afraid of wolves?"

"A bear then. Or a cougar."

"You are acting out of character today, Christina. Shuttling me about, raving about wolves."

Christina could not think of a reply. Fortunately, she heard the cheerful thud of an ax and smelled smoke on the wind. "Who could that be?" she asked in her most innocent voice. "Someone must be clearing land."

"Wilhelm and Johan, no doubt. They've much work to do before the planting."

"What a pleasant surprise," Christina said and tugged her sister's sleeve. "We really must say hello."

"I'm sure they're busy, dear."

"Then they will welcome the respite."

Bruno growled and took off in the direction of the wood smoke.

"Those stays and shifts aren't going to wash themselves, you know."

"Nor will they be going anywhere," Christina said. "Why don't you relax and enjoy the visit?"

"I am relaxed. I am always relaxed."

"Mmmm. Of course you are." Christina was too busy staring at Johan to pay attention to Hilda's protestations. She could make him out through the trees that edged the clearing. Oh, he did look dashing with his sleeves rolled to the elbow, ax in hand, and those blond curls in adorable disarray. She let out a long, wistful sigh.

Then she remembered Bruno. "Come back, boy! He's a friend, I tell you. A friend!"

Bruno bounded out of the forest and hurtled toward Johan with a fierce growl and a flash of teeth. Johan lowered the ax slowly and dropped it on the damp earth. He showed the dog his empty palms and spoke in a low, soothing voice. "It's all right, fellow. We're all friends here, *ja*?"

"He'll take your hand off," Wilhelm said as he jogged to catch up. "Mind yourself."

"It's all right. He knows me. He'll remember."

Wilhelm shook his head.

Bruno stared at Johan with threatening eyes. Johan eased closer. The dog sniffed the man's palm until the growl died in the back of his throat. He whined softly, then pushed his nose into Johan's hand and licked the skin before dashing away.

"You were saying . . ." Johan gave his brother a sly grin.

"A lucky escape."

"Dogs like me. They always have."

"Not always." A female voice rang out from the edge of the clearing. "I believe Bruno was rather slow to warm up to you when first you met." Christina whistled for Bruno as she emerged from the woods and he ran to her side.

"Ah," Johan said with a mischievous glint in his eye. "My defender."

"Don't tease," Christina said. "Bruno would have eaten you alive had I not rescued you that night."

"We were just getting to know each other, that's all."

"From atop a woodpile." Christina raised an eyebrow. "Indeed."

"I'm glad you see it my way."

Christina laughed. "I most certainly do not."

Johan returned her smile, and Christina sensed a sincere connection between them. She could fall into those sly gray eyes and never find her way out again. She cleared her throat and looked away. "We were leading the sheep to pasture and"—Christina's gaze turned to Wilhelm—"we happened upon you. What a pleasant surprise."

Johan's expression hardened when he saw Christina's attention turn to Wilhelm, but Christina did not notice. She was too busy measuring Wilhelm's reaction to the surprise visit.

"*Ja.*" The life had gone out of Johan's voice. "What a pleasant surprise." He watched Christina watching Wilhelm, then bent to pick up his ax.

"Take a rest, brother," Wilhelm said and set his own ax down with a happy thump. "We've company." He settled onto a stump and nodded to Hilda. "Have a seat, won't you? I've no chairs to offer, but there're plenty of stumps."

Hilda stood at the edge of the clearing with a look of frustration on her face. "Thank you, Wilhelm. But I really shouldn't stay. I've the laundry to do."

"*Ach.*" Wilhelm waved his hand. "It will still be there when you get home. It isn't going anywhere."

"Exactly."

"That's just what I was saying!" Christina beamed. "You must have read my mind. How providential."

Johan did not look as if he thought it were providential in the least.

Christina did not notice Johan's expression. Her eyes lingered on Wilhelm for a moment before she turned her attention to Hilda. "Hilda, it's a lovely day for a visit." Christina stalked to her sister and pulled her by the elbow. "And we really should welcome our new neighbors, *ja*?"

Hilda shook her arm free and shot Christina a look. "I never said I didn't want to welcome our neighbors," she whispered.

Christina flashed a smile. "I'm so glad we are in agreement."

"No, what I meant was . . ." Hilda did not finish her sentence, and Christina knew she had won. She patted her sister's arm. Poor Hilda, always distracted by the next chore. A forced visit was just what she needed. Christina steered her sister to a stump near Wilhelm. The stump looked wide enough to fit both sisters, and Christina plopped down beside Hilda. She didn't quite have enough room, and she pushed into Hilda's side. "Move over, *ja*?"

Hilda responded with a longsuffering sigh, but moved over. Christina smiled. Everything was going according to plan. She felt cozy and safe inside the small clearing. The forest rose in a wall around them, a mighty fortress against the mysteries beyond the clearing. Birds twittered and swooped among sharp-smelling pine needles and long, leafy branches. Sunlight filtered through the canopy and dappled the damp earth with light. "I'd rather do laundry than take down that forest, *ja*?"

Hilda rubbed her eyes. "*Ja*. I would too. That's what I was trying to do, in fact."

Christina ignored her sister's response. "Such hard work!" She patted the stump beneath her. "This tree must have been wider than three men standing abreast."

"*Ja.* It was."

"You have to be strong to handle a job such as that!" Christina spoke in her most feminine voice. She felt a little embarrassed, but could not let pride keep her from shoving Wilhelm and Hilda together. If she had to get the conversation going in the right direction, so be it. "Isn't that right, Hilda?" Christina added a giggle for good measure. She felt Hilda stiffen.

"If you say so."

Wilhelm cleared his throat. "Oh, I don't know about that. . . ." He looked away.

"Oh, I do! Look at those arms, Hilda. Strong enough to take down the wilderness, *ja*?" She giggled again and nudged Hilda in the ribs until Hilda elbowed her back to make her stop.

Wilhelm's face turned an interesting shade of red. Johan stared at Christina with a strange expression, then turned away. He clenched his jaw, tightened his grip on his ax, and marched to the nearest tree.

"We really should be going," Hilda said in a flat tone.

"You can't leave now," a boy shouted. "You've just arrived." Fritz, Franz, and Felix ran across the clearing and surrounded Hilda. They jumped and yelled and tugged at her sleeves. "We've been helping," Franz said.

"Ah. I can see that." Hilda patted the boy on the head and adjusted his waistcoat. "Well done."

"No more boring grown-up conversations," Fritz said. "Tell us a story."

"All right." Hilda smiled. "Once upon a time, there were three good boys who lived in a big forest in the backcountry. They helped their father and uncle burn brush and clear the trees so they could plant a good crop that spring and have full bellies the next winter."

Franz frowned. "That's not a very good story."

"That's because I didn't tell you the ending."

Fritz jumped up and down. "Tell it!"

Hilda nodded. "And the three good boys went back to watch the fire as good boys should. The end."

Wilhelm laughed. "I like that ending."

"I don't," Franz said.

"I've a better ending!" Fritz said. He grabbed a stick from the ground and thrust it into the air. "The three boys fought a pack of wolves and saved their father and uncle."

"A practical ending is a better ending," Hilda said with a firm nod. "Now, back to your posts."

The boys shuffled their feet and stuck out their bottom lips, but they did as they were told.

Wilhelm grinned. "Well done, Hilda." Christina could see the appreciation in his eyes as he gazed at her sister.

"Oh, it's nothing." Hilda shrugged and stood up. "They are good boys. They just need to be reminded of that sometimes." She brushed off her skirts and motioned to Christina. "We must be on our way."

"But we just arrived." Christina stayed firmly planted on the stump. "And we are currently engaged in lively conversation with Wilhelm." Christina hoped that no other members of the party would notice her exaggeration. Wilhelm had barely spoken to the sisters during their visit. He had been too busy listening to her talk.

The heavy thud of an ax rang across the clearing. Christina glanced up to see Johan hack into an oak tree with an expression of frustration. She frowned. What could be the matter with him? He really did seem to frustrate easily. Was he not pleased to receive visitors? Ah well, she would address that later. For now, she had more important matters to deal with. Christina turned back to Wilhelm. "You were telling us how strong you are."

"Oh." Wilhelm cleared his throat and shifted his weight. "I don't quite remember it that way."

Christina giggled. "Wilhelm! You are a delight! Isn't he, Hilda?"

Hilda sighed. "Yes. I'm sure he is." Her voice did not sound at all sure.

Johan's ax hit the tree trunk even harder than before. Christina flinched. This didn't seem to be going as well as she had hoped. Hadn't she given her best, most over-the-top giggle? There was only one thing to do: double her efforts. Christina raised her chin and narrowed her eyes. She *would* succeed.

Chapter Six

Johan was not amused. He stole a glance at Christina. She was staring at Wilhelm with big, dreamy eyes. Johan turned back to the stout oak in front of him, sized it up, and tossed the ax onto the ground. He needed to take a break. From everything. Franz shouted from the other side of the handcart. Or was that Fritz? Another boy screeched. Ah, *that* was Fritz. Johan wiped his brow. A cool drink of water should do the trick. Maybe Christina would be gone by the time he returned from the stream.

Not that she was any of his concern. If she had set her sights on his brother, that was fine with him. He was happy to be footloose and fancy-free. Wilhelm needed a wife, not him. Johan scowled as he stomped to the edge of the clearing and plunged into the forest.

"Going somewhere?" Wilhelm shouted after him.

"*Ja.*" Johan did not stop to explain. He felt too frustrated and confused for conversation. Hadn't someone mentioned at the worship service that Georg and Frena Witmer had the fever and ague? That could explain it. Hadn't he been out in the night air for the past fortnight? Why shouldn't he have the fever and ague too? Everyone knew bad air was the fastest way to illness. And an ill head might explain his ridiculous preoccupation with a certain young woman. It couldn't be those sparkling blue eyes, blushing cheeks, or lively wit.

That would be preposterous.

Johan made it halfway to the creek before he realized that he had left the wooden buckets and yoke back at the campsite. Well, if that didn't beat everything. He shook his head and turned on his heels. At least he'd gotten away from that giggle for a few minutes. He could still hear it ringing in his mind like a bell. It was not a bad giggle—a bit excessive, perhaps. The real problem was that the giggle had been directed at the wrong person. Women didn't giggle at Wilhelm. It simply wasn't done.

A twig snapped beneath Johan's boot, and a startled rabbit burst out of the underbrush. "You're all right, little fellow. Haven't got my gun." The rabbit bounded into a carpet of ferns and disappeared. A crow scolded them both from high above the forest floor. The solitary cry echoed through the trees. As the woods sank back into silence, Johan felt as if he were the only man on the earth. How long could a man walk westward? How long did this forest stretch? No one knew. He might walk forever and never reach the end. As far as he could imagine, a vast emptiness surrounded him.

Johan had never felt alone before that moment.

He exhaled slowly. The sound filled the still air. He heard the ruffle of wings as the crow adjusted its feathers, then silence again. Johan had always enjoyed his own company. So why did he feel so lonely all of a sudden? It must be this remarkable countryside. Who could have imagined such isolation? In Germany's Rhine River Valley, there was always the clack of hoof beats on cobblestone, the shout of a traveling peddler, the laughter of children running through the fields. He had never known stillness like this before. The emptiness could drive a man to strange thoughts. Such as the desire to have a woman giggle at him instead of his brother.

Johan nodded his head. That was it. The wilderness had driven him to a strange sort of madness. It wasn't like him to pine after a woman. He just needed to adjust to the backcountry. All would be back to normal soon.

The smell of smoke drifted through the hemlocks and tickled his nose. Ah, the boys must be doing a fine job of burning brush. He had done well to put them to work. Maybe if Wilhelm listened to him a little more, he could keep those wild little ones in line. Johan felt rather smug until he heard a shout.

Was that Hilda? Johan's body tensed. She was not a woman given to shouting. That much was obvious. Another shout tore through the forest, higher pitched and more urgent than the last. Christina. Johan did not wait for a third shout. He took off for the clearing with his heart pounding in his throat. The acrid scent of smoke strengthened as he plunged through tangled thickets and scrambled over boulders. He pushed his legs to go faster, and the leaves faded into a blur. A branch whipped his forehead, and he flinched but did not slow his pace until he skidded into the clearing.

A plume of black smoke billowed upward, filling the sky. He felt the searing heat and heard the sharp crackle of flames, but could see nothing beyond the swirling smoke. Something had gone terribly wrong. There was too much smoke. The brush fire must have spread. Johan coughed and yanked his shirt over his mouth as he scanned the site for his nephews. He could only see smoke and the orange glow of fire deep within.

Johan charged forward, into the smoke and confusion. His eyes and throat burned. "Is anybody there?" A movement caught his eye as he pushed forward. There! Fritz and Franz stood rooted in place as they stared at the smoke with open mouths and wide, shocked eyes. They had not left their posts. "What happened?" Johan shouted as he scooped up the two boys and dragged them across the clearing.

"We only looked away for a moment."

"A moment is all it takes!" Johan dropped them on the ground without stopping. "Where's Felix?"

The boys coughed and shook their heads.

Panic surged up Johan's spine. "Stay away from the smoke. Go get help." Johan did not take the time to watch them go. He whispered a prayer to *der Herr* and plunged into the smoke. He had to find Felix. And Christina. Where were they? Smoke billowed in waves and blackened the sky. His eyes stung and watered. He gasped for a clean breath and stumbled deeper into the heated air.

"Christina!" No answer. "Felix! Wilhelm!" He forced his way through the smoke until the air cleared and he found himself on the far side of the campsite. He could feel the heat behind him and hear the roar of fire in his ears. Wood popped and sparks exploded upward. He turned and forced himself back into the smoke and heat. Tears sprang to his eyes as he blinked and pressed his shirt against his nose and mouth. Where were they?

A hand reached through the smoke and grabbed his waistcoat. He spun around and clasped a pale, slender arm. He knew that arm. Christina. Johan pulled her close and wrapped his arm around her. She felt small and fragile.

He held her so tightly that he had to tell himself to ease his grip. "Are you all right?" he shouted. His voice sounded so ragged and hoarse that he didn't recognize it.

"*Ja*. But the boys. Where are the boys?"

"I've got Franz and Fritz. They've gone for help."

Christina's body relaxed beneath his arms. "And we've got Felix." She pressed her face into Johan's chest. "I couldn't find them."

"It's all right now."

She nodded, then coughed.

"Come." Johan picked her up so that her feet dangled above the ground as he held her against his chest. "I've got you."

"What's happened?" she asked. "I can't see anything for the smoke."

Johan did not know. "You don't worry about that. You just get yourself somewhere safe." He kept his arms wrapped firmly around her as he carried her away from the smoke. "I'll take care of it." He had a job to do, and he would do it. He couldn't let the fire burn out of control. What if it spread to neighboring cabins and crops?

But, for that one precious moment, the fire and the smoke and the fear disappeared. All Johan knew was the feel of Christina against his chest and shoulder. Her breath rose and fell and warmed his bare neck. Her prayer *kappe* had fallen loose and a mass of golden curls tickled his face. Her hands tightened around his shoulders. Nothing had ever felt so right as having this woman in his arms, knowing that she was safe—that *he* had made sure she was safe.

They emerged from the smoke, and Johan looked down to see Christina staring up at him with wide, adoring eyes. Women had looked at him like that before. But he had never felt anything in return. This time, he felt something. Something strange and indescribable.

Something that struck him with a greater fear than the fire had.

Johan inhaled the soft clean scent of Christina's hair one last time and set her on her feet. He swallowed and backed away. He had to regain his senses.

"Are you all right?" Christina blinked, but kept staring up at him in that disarming, adoring way. Soot blackened her chin, and he resisted the urge to pull her close and wipe her face with his handkerchief.

"You don't worry about me. Are you all right?"

She nodded. He turned to look for Wilhelm and Hilda, or to try to put out the flames. But, first, he had to find the flames. He couldn't see the fire through all that confounded smoke. He didn't have a plan. He just knew he had to act. But when he tried to leave, Christina's hands held fast to his waistcoat. He smiled. "You can let go now."

She gasped and looked down at her hands. "Oh." Her fingers opened. "I didn't realize. . . ." Her face reddened from something more than the heat of the fire. She pulled her hands back, but kept staring up at him.

It was quite unnerving. So unnerving that Johan almost forgot his duty. He cleared his throat. "I've got to help the others."

Christina nodded but didn't speak. Her face looked as flushed and innocent as a fawn caught by surprise. Johan felt her eyes on his back long after he hurried away.

A fire was not the time for a celebration. Christina was not that foolish. And yet . . . even as the smoke swirled higher and forced her back, Christina felt a thrill of joy shoot through her heart. He had found her! He had saved her! Oh, what a hero he was! True, she had already been on her way out of the smoke. And she had seen him first and grabbed his waistcoat. An impartial observer might even say that *she* had saved *him*, rather than the other way around.

But he had scooped her up and carried her to safety. True, she did not need to be carried. She had made it on her own up to then. But what joy to be saved! It was like the old German fairy tales, when the handsome prince rushes in to rescue the distraught princess. So what if she didn't actually *need* saving? He had saved her nonetheless!

Now, she needed to see what she could do to help. He had saved her once. If need be, he could save her again. She remembered the strength of his arms, the solid warmth of his chest as he held her close, the rasp of his breath above her ear, the heat of his neck against her cheek. Christina released a dreamy sigh.

Oh, yes, he could save her again.

Christina circled the smoke until she reached Johan and Wilhelm's handcart. She scanned the belongings spread across the small campsite: an iron spider, a stack of quilts, a handsaw, hammers, axes, a bag of nails, and two burlap sacks. The seed crop! Christina gasped and grabbed the burlap sacks. Everything else could burn if it must. She would save the most important thing first.

Christina took off with her heart pounding in her throat. Every step jolted her body as her leather shoes slammed the earth. She ran until her lungs burned with effort, until the air was clear, and she could no longer feel the smoke sting her eyes. She skidded to a stop, threw down the burlap sacks, and raced back toward the campsite.

She would save as much as she could. Christina knew

how precious every item was in the backcountry. A settler couldn't replace something as simple as a needle or a nail. How she had taken those things for granted back in Germany! She longed to wander down a bustling cobblestone street to fetch a lamb shank from the butcher or a pair of shoes from the cobbler.

Smoke rose to meet her as she stumbled out of the forest and back into the campsite. Her eyes flew to a patch of weeds beside the handcart that had caught fire. The flames crackled and danced with orange delight. A spark must have blown from the main fire and landed in the dry grass. If she didn't act fast, those flames would devour the handcart and all the brothers owned.

Christina pulled her white linen neck cloth over her mouth and nose and raced toward the burning weeds. She had returned in the nick of time, for the fire was still small enough to smother. She raised her skirts above her knees to protect the linsey-woolsey fabric from the flames, then stomped with all her strength. She thanked *der Herr* that the screen of smoke protected her from prying eyes, for she must look like a wild creature of the forest with her legs bared and her feet flying in a most undignified dance.

Christina slammed her feet into the earth until she was sure the flames had died completely. Then she kicked a mound of dirt over the blackened weeds for good measure. She stepped back and wiped her forehead. That was a good day's work if she did say so herself. Her knees felt quite weak, which was odd, for she had not noticed feeling the least bit of fear in the moment. She had not even considered the danger of her skirts going up in flames and could not remember hiking them above her knees.

Above her knees! Oh! She realized her legs were exposed in a most scandalous fashion and she dropped her skirts. She glanced around to confirm that no one had seen her legs. She would leave that detail out in the retelling of the tale. Sure, she wore woolen hosen so no skin showed—but still. She smoothed down her skirts and apron. It would not do for Johan to think she took liberties with her reputation. Why, just last year she had heard tell of a shipwreck in which the women chose to drown rather than discard the layers of wet fabric that weighed them down in the water. She had thought it an excessive exercise in modesty—God rest their souls—but she could not fault their devotion to reputation.

A hot, dry wind whipped past Christina's face and blew her golden hair into a tangled halo. She looked into the sky and saw a dim yellow ball behind the haze of smoke. The sun looked so fragile and far away. How could this have happened? How had the smoke overpowered the clearing so fast?

Christina remembered Franz's and Fritz's happy laughter, peppered by the occasional shout from Felix. She remembered when Johan dropped his ax and disappeared into the forest. Then Wilhelm had said something to Hilda that made her smile. Everything had seemed normal. Christina had been so busy listening to Hilda's and Wilhelm's conversation that she hadn't noticed anything untoward.

Christina had leaned back into her hands and tilted her chin upward to watch a fat white cloud drift across the sky. It had reminded her of a rabbit. She had been thinking of rabbits and basking in the glow of spring sunshine when everything had gone suddenly wrong. The boys had shouted in voices tinged with panic as smoke billowed into her face, and she had jumped up with wide, surprised eyes. Hilda had already been on her feet, yelling at the boys to run from the fire.

Christina now heard a cheer from across the hazy clearing. The smoke shifted, and the sky brightened. She could sense a change. The fire was out. It was over. Now, she just needed to find Johan and fall into his arms again. That would be a most satisfactory end to a difficult afternoon.

Chapter Seven

Christina smelled wet ash on the wind and pressed her neck cloth tighter against her nose and mouth. "Is everyone all right?"

"Christina?" Multiple voices called her name.

"Christina?" Johan's voice rang out above the rest, more urgent this time.

"It's all right," she heard Hilda say. "She's run off somewhere safe. Down to the creek, most likely. That's the best place for her."

"I'm here!" Christina shouted. The smoke had thinned but still hung in the clearing like a heavy fog. She ran until she could make out the hazy outlines of figures. The outlines sharpened into bodies and faces as she cleared the last of the smoke. She collapsed into a heap and began to cough as she gazed upward from the trampled earth, searching for Johan. He lunged forward and dropped to his knees beside her.

"Where in heaven's name have you been?" Johan asked in a panic-tinged voice. He picked up her arms, dropped them, then gripped her shoulders, pulled her forward, ran his eyes down her back, and gently pushed her away to study her face.

"What in heaven's name are you doing?" Christina asked in return.

"Checking to see that you're all right. You're not hurt? Not burned?" His eyes scanned her body in frantic, jerky movements.

"No."

"You sure?" He picked up a tangle of golden curls and peered beneath, at the white skin of her neck.

"I'd know if I were."

"Right." Johan's expression morphed from concern to sheepishness. He cleared his throat and dropped her hair. He cleared his throat again as he tried to smooth the curls back into place. "Right." He stood and took a quick step back.

A different male voice murmured above her, and someone else whispered. Christina realized that a small group hovered over her, staring. She flung her hands over her bare head and realized she had lost her prayer *kappe*. How could she be so exposed! Why, she must look like a wanton woman with her hair unbound and flying all over the place! She could cover her head with her neck cloth . . . but that would leave her neckline exposed and an Amish woman would never show the skin beneath her collarbone the way the fashionable women of the world did.

Collapsing onto the ground in a dramatic faint had seemed like a good idea at the time. And it had caught Johan's attention. But she had not meant to get *everyone's* attention. . . .

"What on earth happened to you?" Hilda asked. She stood with her hands on her hips and a serious expression on her face.

"You went somewhere safe like I told you, *ja*?" Johan asked.

"Looks like she's been dragged through the mud by wild horses," a deep voice murmured. Christina's attention shot upward, and she recognized Jacob Miller standing over her. His wife, Greta, stood beside him with a concerned expression on her face. Jacob's expression looked more amused than concerned.

"Mud! The poor dear!" A high-pitched female voice rose above the rest as a stunning, blue-eyed woman with porcelain skin and raven black hair stepped forward and crouched down. "It's all right now," Catrina Webber said. "We'll have you clean again in no time. You poor darling!" She pulled out a crisp white handkerchief and began to dab at Christina's face. "You're as dirty as a chimney sweep." She rubbed harder, and Christina winced. "All that horrible soot!" Catrina leaned back a fraction to study Christina, then clucked her tongue and scrubbed even harder.

"I'm all right." Christina tried to wave her friend away. "Really."

"You brave little thing!" Catrina clucked her tongue again. "Such lovely hair," she whispered. "But we've got to get it covered, *ja*?" She placed the handkerchief squarely atop Christina's head. Catrina shook her head and gave a sympathetic look. "It isn't very dignified, I'm afraid. But we must make do, *ja*?" She adjusted the cloth. "Perhaps we can tie the ends beneath your chin?"

Christina squeezed her eyes shut. "Oh. No. Let's not. Thank you. You're very kind. But really, that's quite enough. Thank you." Christina did not open her eyes. She did not want to see the small crowd staring down at her. What must Johan think of her sooty face and handkerchief-covered head? Had anyone ever looked so undignified?

Was humiliation her reward for saving the seed crop? Just moments ago, Johan had rescued her in a most dramatic and heroic fashion—and she had played the damsel in distress to perfection. Now, she just looked ridiculous. How had she fallen from lovely, ready-to-be-rescued damsel to unkempt gutter rat? Her plan had been going so well.

Well, the seed crop had to be saved, and that was that. But if only she could have managed to save it while still looking lovely and delicate. It was a waste of a good natural disaster was what it was. She could have been saved twice, but instead, she had collapsed (in a most dramatic, ready-to-be-rescued fashion) and Johan had not taken her into his arms as she had expected. And why had Catrina insisted on wiping her clean and dropping a handkerchief atop her head? It had only added to the indignity.

"Catrina," a tall, redheaded man said. "Let the poor girl get some air. She looks about to faint."

"Eli, she'll feel much better now that she's cleaned up . . . a bit." Catrina stood up, patted her husband's hand, and frowned while she stared at Christina. "Or at least I tried to clean her up." Catrina smoothed her own skirts and brushed a blade of grass from the fabric. "The poor dear."

"Ever thoughtful," Eli said. He pulled Catrina to his side and draped his long, lanky arm over her shoulders. "You are a wonder, you know."

"Mmmm." Catrina smiled and rested her head against his arm.

"Catrina, really. I am quite all right," Christina said as she readjusted the handkerchief atop her head. They all kept staring at her. It was just too awkward. "I did not expect to see you here."

"Franz and Fritz raised the alarm, and we came to see

what we could do." Eli reached down and tousled Franz's hair. "Well done."

"Jacob and Greta too? Has the entire settlement come to see me in this state?"

A round of laughter passed through the circle.

"Ah, well." Johan's eyes twinkled. "You know what they say: smoke follows beauty. It's quite uncanny, really. First the incident with the meat pie, and now this. It seems the saying is true."

"Oh." *Oh!* Had Johan Lantz just called her beautiful in front of half the settlement? If so, her humiliation felt very much worth the compliment.

"Smoke follows the foolhardy, I should say," Hilda noted as she stood with her hands on her hips. She looked tired and entirely unamused. "For disaster follows my sister as surely as night follows day."

Johan leaned down and offered a large, calloused hand. "Let me help you up."

"Oh. *Ja.* Of course." She had been so thrown by the moment that she had forgotten to get up from the ground. She must look ridiculous as they all stood over her, staring down at what a mess she had made of herself. The humiliation faded as Johan's warm hand closed on hers. The touch sent a jolt down to her stomach. She stared into his eyes and he responded with that disarming smile of his. That grin could melt snow on a winter day. He pulled her to her feet without any effort, and she felt herself gazing at him for a few beats too long. But how could she pull herself away from those sparkling gray eyes? Oh, if only everyone weren't watching. His presence made her feel so right, so new and alive! But, dash it all, they had an audience and it would not do to show her excitement over an eligible young man.

With great effort, Christina dropped Johan's hand and lowered her eyes. She could still feel the heat of his skin on her palm. Her face flushed with heat as well, and Christina cleared her throat. She needed to distract the onlookers from her obvious state of flustered admiration. "What happened? Wilhelm, Hilda, and I were sitting and talking, and the next thing I knew there was smoke everywhere. And then it was all over and . . ." She wanted to say, *I found Johan again*, but she did not. "Everything happened so fast," she said instead. "I couldn't tell what was going on with all the smoke and confusion."

Wilhelm shook his head. "Nobody could. Turns out it wasn't so bad. The boys lost control of the brush fire and it spread into the woods, but the trees didn't catch. Only the ground litter. The fallen leaves were damp, so they created a great amount of smoke, but not a lot of fire." He scanned the row of massive oaks at the tree line. "Trunks that big don't catch fire right away. They've stood here for hundreds of years. Half a millennium, even."

"A mercy," Jacob said.

"*Ja*," Hilda murmured in return.

"To think what might have happened!" Catrina said and leaned closer to Eli. "If the leaves had been dry . . ."

"But they weren't, so there's no need to fret after the fact," Hilda said in her ever practical way.

"Thanks to Hilda," Wilhelm said.

"Oh, it was nothing." Hilda frowned at the attention.

"She put out the fire?" Jacob asked. He gave Hilda a respectful nod.

"I thought *you* put it out," Christina said as she looked at Jacob. "You and Eli and Wilhelm." Her eyes slid to Johan, and she couldn't help but smile. Hopefully no one noticed. "And Johan, of course."

"Oh, no," Jacob said. "We had just arrived when you came tumbling out of the smoke. In fact, we don't know much more than you do."

"Hilda saved the day," Wilhelm said. "She had the presence of mind to run to the campsite, douse the quilts with a bucket of water, and smother the fire. I could only think of the boys. Had to make sure they were out of harm's way."

Jacob ran his fingers through his beard as he studied Hilda. "Quick thinking. Most people would have thrown the bucket of water on the fire. But if you'd done that, we would have run out of water. Who knows what might have happened before we could make it down to the creek and back again?"

"Oh, it was nothing," Hilda said and gave a dismissive wave. "The entire crisis was no more than a pile of smoldering leaves, really."

"Well, if you hadn't smothered the flames we would be dealing with a lot more than that right now."

Hilda shrugged. "All's well that ends well. Although I am sorry about the quilts. It did not end as well for them."

"A small price to pay," Wilhelm said. "A few scorch marks won't hurt."

"Quilts are replaceable, but the seed crop . . ." The words died in Johan's throat as the situation dawned on him. "When we told Felix to run, we didn't think about anything but protecting him. He was the one watching over the seed!" The color drained from Johan's face. Everyone whipped around to stare in the direction of the campsite.

Wilhelm began to jog toward the spot where the burlap sacks had been. The earth looked charred and bare where Christina had battled the small fire. "The fire spread to the campsite," Wilhelm shouted. "It's burned the seed to ash."

"No," Christina shouted after him. "It's all right." She glanced from Hilda to Johan with a satisfied grin. She might be covered in soot and wearing a handkerchief on her head, but she had saved the seed crop.

Wilhelm stopped and swiveled around to face her. "It is?"

"*Ja*. I moved the seeds."

"*You* moved them?" Hilda asked.

"*Ja*."

"You did?" Hilda looked surprised. No, surprised was too mild a word. Shocked seemed more accurate.

Christina waved her hand in the direction of the hand-cart. "I ran the bags of seed into the woods and returned just in time to see a patch of weeds ignite. A spark on the wind must have done it." She gave a satisfied smile. "The burlap sacks had been in that very spot."

Wilhelm jogged back to Christina. "You saved our seed crop. The bags would have gone up in flames in an instant."

"You are a treasure," Johan said. "We'd be destitute without next year's crop." He looked at her in a way that made Christina's toes curl with delight. No man had ever looked at her quite like that. It made her feel admired for who she was—for her efforts and talents, and not just for her pretty face and sparkling giggle.

A murmur of agreement rippled through the group.

"Oh. Well." Christina's cheeks reddened. "You make it sound rather more heroic than it was." An image of her exposed legs and undignified stomping flashed through her mind. "Truly."

"A lesser woman would have run from the fire," Johan said. "But you plunged right into it. To think that your skirts might have caught fire." His expression sharpened to concern. "You're sure you're not burned?"

Christina avoided his eyes. "Oh, my skirts were quite safe." She cleared her throat and hoped that Johan did not put an image to her words. "It was not nearly so heroic as you describe. I hadn't time to think. That's all."

"Well done." Hilda nodded at Christina with a look of approval. Christina rarely received such a look from her older sister, and she beamed with satisfaction.

It had been a most memorable afternoon.

Chapter Eight

Christina stayed on Johan's mind long after she left. Her heroics seemed out of character with the giggly, shallow woman that he had perceived her to be. Perhaps there was more there than he had realized. Or perhaps she had done something out of character. Either way, he was unaccustomed to having a woman stay on his mind. It wasn't that he didn't think of women—they were lovely creatures, no doubt—but he never focused on any *one* of them for too long. He had no desire to settle down with one, so he had no need to keep one on his mind.

Johan noticed that he was rubbing his temples. He closed his eyes and sighed.

"Uncle Johan." Fritz tugged on his elbow. "Do you have a headache?"

Johan's eyes reopened. *Did* he have a headache? Or was he just trying to rub out all thoughts of Christina Dresser? Johan sighed again. "I don't know."

"How can you not know if you have a headache?"

"I don't know."

"You already said that."

Johan rubbed his temples harder. "I guess." He closed his eyes again. "Does it matter?"

"I should think so."

"You'll understand when you're older."

"You and Papa are always saying that."

Johan grunted and leaned forward to stir the campfire. A shower of sparks shot upward as he stoked the charred logs. The sight reminded him of the fire that Christina had put out, which reminded him that she had saved his seed crop, which reminded him that he was in her debt. In her debt! What an odd thought. He was not a man who allowed himself such emotional entanglements. He had thanked her and that ought to be enough. Johan frowned and stoked the fire again. He *had* thanked her, hadn't he? Dash it all, he couldn't remember. He owed her that much, at least. In truth, he owed her much more . . . but acknowledging that could lead to feelings, and feelings could lead to a world of trouble. Best to keep things brief and businesslike between them. Otherwise, he could find himself lawfully wed with a family to feed by the next harvest.

Not that he had developed feelings for Christina Dresser. Not at all. She simply . . . intrigued him. That was all. He nodded to himself, set down the poker, and leaned back into his hands. He was quite safe—for now, anyway.

"Uncle Johan."

Johan had forgotten Fritz. He cleared his throat. "*Ja?*"

"We were talking."

"Right."

"Why are you so distracted? Is it the headache?"

"What headache?"

"The one you said didn't matter."

"Oh. Right." Johan rubbed his temples again. "That one."

He did not tell his nephew that it was, in fact, an intriguing young lady causing his discomfort.

"You look cross." Fritz frowned and sat down on the log beside his uncle.

"Do I?"

"*Ja.*" Fritz inched closer and stared up at Johan with wide, concerned eyes. "Is it because Franz and I failed at the job you gave us?"

"Failed?"

Fritz nodded. His eyes stayed big and solemn.

"Oh, I wouldn't put it quite like that."

"You wouldn't?"

"Why don't you tell me what happened? Then I'll tell you what I think."

Fritz poked out his bottom lip. "It was Franz's fault."

Johan raised an eyebrow and stared down at Fritz.

"All right. It was both our faults. But he saw the fox first."

"A fox, was it?" He had suspected the boys had been distracted by something.

"As big as a wolf, it was!" Fritz spread his arms apart. "You should have seen it!"

"Ah. I see."

"No, you didn't. That's the problem. If you had seen it, you would understand why we forgot our job."

Johan tried very hard not to smile.

"We only chased it for a moment. And when we turned around, the leaves in the forest were smoldering. Then smoke filled the clearing, and you and Papa ran and got us."

"I understand. It isn't easy for a boy to keep his focus on his job. But do you understand how important it is to try your best?"

Fritz looked down. "*Ja*." He began to pick at the bark on the log beneath him.

"Thanks be to *der Herr* the leaves were damp. But they might not have been. Let this be a lesson to you for next time. You must always keep your focus." Johan knew he'd do well to keep his own advice. He reminded himself to keep his focus on what mattered—building a new life and enjoying the adventure of a new world. Not getting entangled with eligible young ladies ready to snare him in matrimonial monotony.

Fritz perked up. "Next time?"

"*Ja*. Of course."

"But, I thought . . ." Fritz's brow furrowed. "I didn't think you would trust us again."

"Oh, I think the only thing to do is to put you back on the job. How else will you learn to do it right? Life is about learning lessons—not being defeated by them."

"Really?" A smile transformed Fritz's face.

"Really." Johan returned the smile and tousled his nephew's hair.

The boy leapt to his feet and galloped toward the forest.

"Where are you going?"

"To find that fox!"

Johan smiled and shook his head. To be a child again! If only life could be so simple and straightforward now. Johan stared into the campfire and rubbed his chin. In all honesty, life *was* pretty simple and straightforward. He had everything that mattered right here, in this camp, and years of work ahead of him clearing the land and building a farm. There was no need to complicate anything. No need at all. Especially with women who fancied themselves heroes and intruded into one's mind at the most inconvenient times.

Johan yawned and leaned forward to rest his elbows on his knees. He had not realized how tired he felt until now. They could have lost everything today. The thought weighed heavily on his mind. Worse, one of the boys could have been hurt. Christina could have been hurt.

Dash it all! There he went again, thinking of *her*. Johan scowled. He needed to get up and put on the corncakes for supper. He needed to clean the Jaeger rifle and sharpen his ax before the morrow. Johan's scowl deepened. What he really needed to do was thank Christina. It was the gentlemanly thing to do. He would call on her at first light, give a quick thanks, and be on his way. That should relieve him of his debt. He would take care to maintain his distance and not to dillydally.

Johan's resolve against dillydallying evaporated as soon as he stepped through Christina's threshold the next morning. The savory scent of an apple and meat pie rose to meet him in a most welcome greeting.

"Oh!" Christina leapt up from the hearth when Hilda opened the door. Her cheeks matched the color of the coals that covered the Dutch oven. "I didn't expect to see you here . . . now . . ." She smoothed her prayer *kappe* and brushed ash from her white linen apron. He had to admit that the flustered look on her face was simply adorable.

"Forgive the intrusion."

"Not at all." Christina beamed. "You must stay for breakfast."

"I couldn't—"

"You must. I've just made a pie with dried apples and currants and rabbit. We can't possibly eat it all. What a crime it would be to let any go to waste. Besides, it's the last of the currants, and who knows when we will have any again?"

Johan breathed in the rich, warm flavors of salted meat, tart apples, and juicy, plump currants. It would indeed be a crime. Savory-sweet pies were his favorite. Besides, the sisters' cabin felt so snug and cozy that he didn't want to leave. A fire crackled in the hearth and cast dancing shadows across the rough-hewn log walls. Bright, cheerful quilts lay folded in the corner, where the sisters' sleeping pallets had been neatly stacked for the day. The dirt floor looked freshly swept and the scent of pine and earth mingled with the wood smoke and roasting meat. Everything felt pleasant and right. Resistance was futile.

"Thank you. It is most appreciated." Johan's eyes twinkled as his lips curled into a half smile. "Although it might be injurious to my health. I am not sure you can be trusted at the hearth. We might find ourselves enveloped in smoke for a third time."

Christina laughed and motioned to the bench beside the hand-carved table. "Be good or you'll go home with an empty belly."

That was enough warning to quiet Johan. He did not want to push his luck too far. He sat and watched Christina rake the coals off the top of the Dutch oven. She hummed a tune to herself as she lifted the heavy metal lid and a wave of steam billowed into the cabin.

A man could get used to this. Especially after months of corncakes, salt pork, and limited company. Oh, Wilhelm was a fine man, but conversation with him always focused on hunting, trapping, and the likelihood of a good crop. Conversation with a lovely young woman with a lively wit was quite different. Not that he noticed.

Johan frowned and promised himself that he would only

stay long enough to wolf down breakfast. It was the polite thing to do, after all. No woman would want to see her pie go to waste. Johan let out a happy, satisfied sigh as he watched Christina at the hearth. He felt warm and contented.

No, dash it all! This was exactly the trap he was trying to avoid. The trap tightened a little more when Christina filled his plate and settled beside him to stare into his eyes with dreamy admiration. He tried his best to disengage himself from conversation during the meal, but Christina kept asking him questions as if she were genuinely interested in his life and well-being. For pity's sake, did she have to be so considerate on top of being a good cook and a lovely girl?

Johan worked harder to remain aloof. Christina made it easier for him to do so when she mentioned Wilhelm. She set down her pewter spoon and leaned forward. The weak spring sun shone through the open window and highlighted her rosy cheeks and the golden curls that showed beneath her prayer *kappe.* "And how is Wilhelm faring?" she asked with a furrowed brow and concerned voice.

Johan felt his stomach tighten. Not that again.

"We've been frightfully worried. Haven't we, Hilda?"

"About Wilhelm?"

"Naturally." Christina glanced at Hilda.

Hilda didn't respond.

"Haven't we, Hilda?"

Hilda did not look concerned. But then she jumped in her seat and glared at Christina. "Don't kick me."

Christina gasped. "Kick you?" Her cheeks went from rosy to a fiery crimson. "Oh! Was that you?" She cleared her throat. "Apologies, sister mine. The room is crowded. The table was built for two, not three."

Hilda raised her eyebrows. She did not look amused. "Indeed. I would say three *can* be a crowd."

"Oh!" Christina fumbled with her spoon and it fell from her hands to clatter against the tin plate. "Whatever has gotten into me?"

"I can't imagine," Hilda answered in a deadpan voice.

It seemed plain to Johan that Christina wanted Hilda to back Christina's pursuit of Wilhelm. Hilda wasn't having it, and Johan could not blame her. Meddling nonsense! He pushed his empty plate away in a quick gesture. The tin made a louder noise than he had intended as it scraped the wood surface. He had not meant to signal his annoyance, but dash it all, how much could a man take? Christina was such a lovely girl—a perfect girl really. All he wanted was for her to feel the same about him.

A perfect girl! The same about him! Had he really thought those things? This was going from bad to worse. Not only did Christina prefer Wilhelm, but Johan was struggling to deny his feelings. How could he pretend he had no affection for her as she fixed those adoring, sparkling eyes on his?

Johan shot up from the bench. "I really must be going."

"Oh." Christina looked down. She cleared her throat and hesitated, then looked back up at him with wide doe eyes. "Must you?" She gave her best smile and added a soft little giggle. "You've only just arrived."

Now she acted as though she wanted his company. It was so dashed confusing! Perhaps she only wanted to pry out more information about Wilhelm. Regardless, Johan knew he had best be on his way. No good could come of this. None at all.

* * *

Christina watched Johan dash out of the cabin as tears stung her eyes. Where had she gone wrong?

"Well, he could not get out of here quickly enough," Hilda said in a flat voice.

Christina threw up her hands. "And no wonder—you accused me of kicking you under the table! What must he think of that?"

"That you shouldn't kick your sister under the table?"

"No! That I am—" Christina wanted to say, *That I am conspiring to set you up with Wilhelm!* The words almost flew from her mouth before she could stop them. But she clamped her lips shut and stared at Hilda with narrowed eyes. The morning was going from bad to worse.

Hilda cracked her knuckles and leaned back to rest her shoulders against the cabin wall. "That you are what?"

Christina swallowed. How could she dig herself out of this pit? It was vital that Hilda not suspect her plan. If Hilda suspected, she would refuse to cooperate and make some excuse about how she was too old to find love. Christina had to protect Hilda from herself.

"That you are what?" Hilda repeated.

Christina opened her mouth, but no words came out. She had never been quick on her feet.

"It's all right." Hilda leaned forward and patted Christina on the shoulder. "I know you feel affection for Wilhelm."

"What? No! We've been over this—"

"*Ja*, and we will keep going over it until you admit the truth. There's no need for secrets with me. I know what it is to fall in love and never . . ." Hilda straightened and cleared her throat. "Never mind." She glanced out the open window. "My goodness, is it that late in the morning?" She stood, brushed off her skirts, and began to clear the table.

"No. You must understand I have no interest in Wilhelm."

Christina stared at her sister and debated coming clean about her entire plan. If Hilda thought Christina held affection for Wilhelm, Hilda might not consider Wilhelm for herself. On the other hand, if Hilda felt pressured into a match, she would dismiss the possibility without giving Wilhelm a chance.

The situation was getting too complicated.

Hilda hesitated as she hovered beside her sister, the stack of pewter plates balanced in her hands. "Christina. I only tell you for your own good. I don't want to embarrass you, but it's my job to make sure you do well in life. I'm the closest thing to a mother you have, so . . ."

"Oh, Hilda."

"No. Not 'oh, Hilda.' You know I'm right."

Christina could feel the frustration burning through her skin. She loosened her neck cloth with fumbling fingers.

"And the truth is, you are embarrassing yourself. You mustn't throw yourself at a man in such a way. You must find something else to talk about, especially to poor Johan." Hilda picked up the pie tin and balanced it atop the plates. "It's just too forward. You don't want to be seen as a wayward woman, do you?"

This was too much. Christina squeezed her eyes shut and took a deep, deep breath. She let the air out slowly. *Don't give in*, she repeated to herself. *Hilda will see soon enough. Just hold out a little longer—even if she does think you are throwing yourself at a man.* Christina pushed her frustration into the pit of her stomach. She opened her eyes and forced a smile. "Fret not, sister mine. This situation will resolve itself soon enough, I am sure. And, in good time, you will see your concerns are unfounded."

Hilda shrugged and carried the dishes to the hearth to rinse in the water bucket. "You always have let your emotions get the best of you. But you always mean well. That's why everyone loves you."

Emotions getting the best of her! Ha! If only Hilda knew.

"But, as you say, I'm sure it will be resolved in the end." Hilda kneeled on the dirt floor in front of the hearth, then glanced up with a knowing grin. "And my guess is that it will end with wedding bells."

Christina smiled. That was a statement with which she agreed. "More than you know, sister mine." Double wedding bells for a double wedding, if all went well.

Hilda gave her a quizzical look before turning back to the dishwater. She scrubbed a pewter spoon for a moment, then paused. "You do know I love you, don't you?"

"Of course I do."

"I don't say it enough, I suppose." She resumed her scrubbing, harder this time. "It isn't my way. Not that that excuses it." She set the spoon atop a clean cloth laid over the stone hearth. "You are a treasure. I just worry. . . ." She frowned and dried her hands on her apron. "You can take to such fanciful notions sometimes. Some things just aren't meant to be."

"Like falling in love with the perfect man and living happily ever after?" Christina asked.

Hilda hesitated. "Well . . . yes. Like that."

"Oh, Hilda. It's *you* who has fanciful notions. I shiver to think that you have no faith in love. What a dreary world you inhabit."

"Reality is not dreary. It is simply . . . realistic."

Christina rolled her eyes. "You tire me so. But fear not, sister mine, your day will come!" Christina skipped across the room, leaned over, and planted a firm kiss atop Hilda's head.

Hilda frowned and straightened her *kappe*. "Don't you have work to do?"

"Oh, yes, I have plenty of work to do." If only Hilda knew. Christina smiled to herself as the next step in her plan began to form within her mind.

Chapter Nine

Christina thought about her matchmaking scheme as she milked the sheep. In the springtime, anything could happen. Dreams and hopes bloomed alongside wildflowers in the sun. She pondered her new strategy as she patted the soft, wooly side of a ewe and shifted her milking stool to the next one. Bruno circled and barked occasionally to remind everyone who was boss. The sun shone from a brilliant sky and the scent of violets wafted on the wind. Christina's cloak lay discarded in the grass and her bare arms felt warm and free where she had rolled her linen sleeves up to her elbows. Spring had come. Soon, it would be time to shear the sheep and process the wool.

Christina stood up from the milking stool and stretched her back. She hoped that Hilda would be settled by then. Spring was far too busy a season for matchmaking. She needed to bring those two together as quickly as possible. The only question was how. Christina hoisted the wooden bucket and milk splashed over the side. She reminded herself to take more care. Bruno barked and galloped over to lap the milk before it soaked into the earth.

"Good boy," Christina murmured absentmindedly as

she scratched behind his ears. She was too distracted to pay attention to anything but Hilda's fate. "It will all work out in the end," she said to Bruno. "But a little help couldn't hurt." She sighed as she headed toward the cabin. The sheep did not move aside—poor docile creatures that they were—and Christina had to weave her way through the flock. Pigs were wonderfully clever and knew how to fend for themselves all year, alone in the forest. Even cows knew to fear the wolves. But sheep! "What we would do without you, Bruno, I do not know. The wilderness would make lamb chops of them all."

And without their sheep, Hilda and Christina would have no way to make a living. After their parents had died in Germany, the sisters had learned to survive off the bounty of the flock. Milk, cheese, wool, meat—sheep were a wonderful resource, especially for two women alone in the backcountry. Christina had heard grumblings and rumors that sheep did not thrive in the Colonies, and perhaps it was true. But she and Hilda only troubled themselves with their small corner of the world, and the success of their own flock. Sometimes they wondered whether other settlers let their sheep graze free alongside the pigs and cows, or penned them in. They knew that, throughout the backcountry, settlers only fenced in the crops—keeping the livestock out, rather than in. But sheep—the silly, foolish creatures—were a unique matter.

There was no one to ask about the best way to raise sheep in the backcountry. No one else in New Canaan kept sheep, and there was no way to get word from anyone else, unless a traveler knowledgeable in the subject happened upon the settlement. That had yet to occur. So the sisters simply made their way the best they could. As with every aspect of their new lives, they took what they knew from Germany and tried to adapt.

So far, they had done well enough. Although not even Bruno could protect the newborn lambs from the chicken hawks that circled overhead with sharp, predatory eyes. Wolves threatened the flock from time to time, but Bruno stayed ready. And, remarkably, the delicate Catrina Webber had once saved the flock from a roving wolf in a remarkable—and quite uncharacteristic—display of bravado. All in all, they had done well enough.

Too well, perhaps. For Hilda did not see the need for a man! Oh, independence was all well and good—and Christina did not want to see her sister settle for anything less than true love—but enough was enough. Hilda needed to stop being so independent and realize life could bring more than the satisfaction that came from a solitary life of self-reliance.

Christina pushed open the cabin door and set the heavy bucket by the hearth. Milk splashed over the lip of the wooden bucket, and Hilda frowned. "Careful."

"*Ja.*"

"You know the milk would stay in the bucket if you moved more slowly."

"*Ja*, and life would be more boring."

"You mean more predictable."

"You would be bored to tears without my unpredictability."

"I would have fewer spills to clean."

"A small price to pay."

Hilda smiled. "Indeed." She tossed a rag to Christina, who caught it and patted the hearthstones dry. "Sometimes

I wonder how two sisters can be so different," Hilda added as she watched Christina.

"Oh, that's an easy answer. One of us refuses to be boring. I believe we just covered that."

Hilda laughed and shook her head. "I'll get started on the week's bread while you make the cheese, *ja*?"

"*Ja*." This would be the perfect opportunity to encourage Hilda to open her heart. The question was how. Her sister was not free with her feelings. Christina would have to tread carefully. She reached for the strainer and the big wooden bowl, worn smooth from years of use, as she pondered how to approach the subject.

"I need to mix the dough in that," Hilda said.

"Oh. Right." Christina picked up the Dutch oven instead. The sisters had had to carry their belongings in a handcart when they'd traveled through the wilderness to their new home. Roads to New Canaan were footpaths at best, nonexistent at worst. A horse could barely make it. A loaded wagon simply could not get through. So they had to make do with little. The Dutch oven would have to double as a bowl today. Perhaps one day they would have a fully stocked kitchen like the one they'd had in their quaint, thatch-roofed cottage in Germany's Rhine River Valley. But for now, a single mixing bowl, an iron spider, a cauldron, and a Dutch oven would have to do.

Christina lifted the bucket and poured a steady stream of rich, frothy milk through the strainer and into the Dutch oven. She had to work fast, while the milk was still warm from the sheep. "I've been thinking. . . ." She turned up the bottom of the bucket to drain the last of the milk. The liquid made a happy splash as it poured.

"You've been thinking? Oh dear," Hilda said as she shook flour from a burlap sack into the mixing bowl.

"Very funny." Christina set down the bucket and picked up a clay jar filled with whey from last week's cheese making. That was the marvelous thing about cheese: Each batch created a new stock of whey, so they could go on making cheese forever with nothing but a fresh bucket of warm milk. One needed rennet and cheese culture for one's very first batch of cheese, but after that the process became completely self-propagating. Christina unclasped the lid of the clay jar. "I'm being serious."

"So am I."

But when Christina glanced at Hilda, her sister was smiling. "Ha, ha, ha," Christina said in a deadpan voice as she poured a measure of whey into the strained milk. "I'm serious about being serious."

"Is that possible?"

Christina made a face at her sister and slid the lid onto the Dutch oven. It settled into place with a satisfying clang. The strained milk and whey needed to sit in a warm place for an hour, so she pushed the Dutch oven to a corner of the hearth.

"All right," Hilda said. "I'm listening. No more jokes."

"Indeed." Christina tried to frown at her sister, but her lips fell into a smile instead. She couldn't help that. It was in her nature to smile, and she never stayed irritated for long. After all, being teased for being too cheerful was hardly a cause for offense. "I noticed that you and Wilhelm enjoyed a fine conversation last you spoke."

"Ah, Wilhelm again." Hilda leaned her body weight into the wooden bowl as she kneaded the dough.

"No. I mean, yes. What I mean to say is that you two seem to get along."

"I should hope so. I do try to get along with all our neighbors."

"I mean that you get along better than with other neighbors."

"Mmmmm. Do we?" Hilda did not take her attention off the dough.

"I noticed a glow in your cheeks when we called on them the day of the fire. Why, I even caught you smiling when he spoke to you."

"Well, I never. Any glow was from the warm weather." Hilda punched the dough down one more time before placing a cloth over the top and sliding the bowl to the back of the hearth, alongside the milk and whey. "I'm sure we have something better to do with our time while the dough rises than talk about Wilhelm."

"Why, you seem uncomfortable with the subject, sister mine. Which doesn't make sense—unless you feel some affection for the man."

"Affection! Certainly not."

"I would not suspect it if you were not so quick to deny it."

"Humph." Hilda stood and shook out her skirts. "I believe there is water to fetch and weeding to attend to."

"A lovely idea. We can continue our conversation in the kitchen garden."

"Heaven help me, Christina. You will not leave this be, will you?"

"Of course not."

Hilda made an irritated noise in her throat and marched outdoors. Christina followed and kneeled beside her on the damp earth, along the rows of vegetables and herbs. "Now, as I was saying. I cannot help but notice your . . . proclivity toward friendship with Wilhelm."

"Proclivity toward friendship?" Hilda shook her head and pulled a weed from the ground. "What a way with words you have, sister mine."

"If only you took my words seriously."

Hilda frowned and tugged a weed harder than necessary. The plant broke in half, rather than popping out of the earth, and Hilda's frown deepened.

"I've also noticed how his children take to you."

"Ah, I see what you are doing."

"What?" Christina grinned. Perhaps her sister would admit the truth now.

"Trying to deflect my attention from your own interest in Wilhelm. Well, it won't work."

Christina released a sharp puff of air. Hilda was not going to make this easy. She decided to try another tactic. Denials—even when truthful—never worked with Hilda. "All right. Let's forget about Wilhelm."

"An easy task."

Christina sighed. "As I was saying. Let's forget about Wilhelm and speak purely hypothetically."

"Mmmm." Hilda ran her fingers over a carrot leaf. "I do think the carrots are coming along nicely. Don't you?"

"*Ja*. But that is hardly the point."

"Isn't it? We are in the garden, gardening at this very moment."

"Yes. But we are also, at this very moment, speaking hypothetically about your romantic prospects."

"Humph."

"So if, speaking hypothetically, a nice, eligible man moved to New Canaan, shouldn't you pursue that man?"

"Oh, I should say not."

"No?" Christina's eyes jerked from the weed in her hand to Hilda's face. "Why not?"

Hilda hesitated. She ran her fingers along the soft, purple leaf of a cabbage. A flicker of emotion passed over her face.

"Hilda?"

Hilda's eyes stayed on the plant.

"Why are you so troubled by what I've said?"

"I pursued a man once and will not make that mistake again."

Christina sucked her breath in through her teeth. "You what?"

"Oh, you heard me." Hilda's vulnerable expression transformed to hardness. "And there's nothing more to say on the matter."

"I beg to differ."

"Beg all you want—there is nothing more to share." Hilda stood up and brushed the dirt from her apron.

"Hilda. Why haven't you mentioned this man before?"

"There was no point."

"Of course there was—*is*." Was this the real reason for Hilda's stoic determination to remain single? "Please, tell me. What happened? Who was he?"

Hilda opened her mouth, then closed it again. She shook her head. "It was a lifetime ago and an ocean away. It no longer matters."

"Clearly it does." Christina spoke in her softest, most careful voice. She sensed a vulnerability behind her sister's tough veneer that she had never seen before.

Hilda stood for a long moment without speaking. The sun shone above her solitary figure, and the wind whipped her skirts. She stayed as still as a statue while fabric rustled around her and the sun lit the honey-colored flecks in her brown eyes. Her gaze focused on something far away, beyond the tree line.

Christina waited, but Hilda did not respond. "Hilda?"

The word broke the strange mood. Hilda shook her head and cleared her throat. "No, it does not matter." She strode across the yard and disappeared into the cabin.

Christina stared at the empty doorway. There was more to her sister than she had realized. And a greater need than ever to find her love—love that Hilda had been denied in the past. What had happened? The question ate at Christina as she studied the empty doorway. What was Hilda feeling? What was she thinking? Christina had always seen her sister as the tough one, the serious one, the one who didn't dream of a charming man coming to rescue her from a life of monotony.

Had she been wrong about her sister all these years?

Christina wanted to dash into the cabin and breathlessly demand to know everything. That, of course, would not work. So she spent the next hour weeding and biding her time. But the mystery of her sister's lost love invaded her every thought. By the time she finished the job, Christina could bear the wait no longer. In addition, she had begun to feel more than a little hurt. Why had Hilda not confided in her all these years? Were they not the closest of sisters?

Christina pulled the last weed from the dirt and pushed herself off her knees. The damp earth had left a wet stain on her apron, and her knees felt cold. The mud had soaked through her apron, skirts, shift, and woolen hosen, all the way to her skin. The harder she worked, the more laundry her efforts created, which only led to more work. Ah, well. Work was a worthy pursuit—all good Amish knew that. But enough about skirts and mud and cold knees, Christina reminded herself. She had a mystery love affair to uncover.

Christina marched into the cabin with her head held high with purpose. She would pry the secret from her sister—for Hilda's own good, of course. No one should keep pain locked away inside. Shadow fell across her face as she passed from the bright, spring day into the dim, smoky interior of the cabin. Hilda stood at the table, punching down the risen dough. A long ray of sunlight reached through the open door to highlight the dust motes in the still, warm air.

Christina debated how best to approach the subject as she pulled the Dutch oven from the corner of the hearth. She lifted the lid and nodded with satisfaction. The cheese had come along nicely. Over the past hour, the milk and whey had congealed into a firm, jiggly substance called junket.

"I did not know you had been in love."

"Love!" Hilda punched the dough with a firm fist. "Bah!"

Christina reached for the knife and began to slice the junket into squares. "Love is nothing to mock," Christina said in a gentle voice. The cabin fell into an uncomfortable silence. Hilda stopped kneading the dough. She stared into the wooden bowl. The only noise was the scrape of Christina's knife against metal.

"I know that better than you," Hilda finally said in a low voice.

Christina did not know what to say. She hesitated, then said the only thing she could think to say. "I'm sorry."

Hilda pursed her lips and began to knead the dough once more. "Let's not speak of this again."

"Hilda, please don't keep this pain to yourself. You'll feel better if you let me share the burden."

Hilda pushed the bowl away. "No, Christina. There are some things you should not know. So I will say no more."

Hilda wiped her floured hands on her apron and flexed her jaw. "I ask that you do the same."

"But, Hilda!"

"I've the baking to do. And I hear the Widow Yoder has caught the fever and ague. I'll pay her a visit on the way back from the bake oven, so don't expect me before dinner."

"Hilda."

Hilda did not respond to her name. She did not look at Christina. She tucked the dough into a square of cloth, knotted the bundle, and passed the empty mixing bowl to Christina. "You'll need this." She acted as if they had been speaking of nothing important—as if it were an ordinary moment in an ordinary day. Christina took the bowl from Hilda's hand and watched her sister stride across the cabin.

Christina felt rejected and confused. All she wanted was to be close to her sister. But Hilda's emotional walls were impossible to breach. "Hilda," she repeated, more softly this time. "Hilda."

Hilda paused in the doorway and spun around to face her sister. "I love you more than anyone else in this world. Know that, Christina." Hilda stared into Christina's eyes with an intense gaze that communicated more than words ever could. "Know that."

And then she turned on her heel and hurried out the door, into the sunlight. Christina let out a sharp hiss of air. She had not realized that she had been holding her breath. She had been balanced on her heels, leaning over the junket, and she sat down hard on her backside. She felt as if all the energy had drained from her body. That had been more than she had expected. Far more. Hilda's past held some secret that Christina had never envisioned. She could not imagine her sister young and vulnerable, untainted by the disappointments of life. And yet, Hilda must have been that young, innocent girl once. And her heart had been broken.

But why keep it a secret to this day?

Christina shook her head as she rinsed the flour from the mixing bowl, then secured a linen cloth across it. She wanted to collapse onto her sleeping pallet and have a good cry. Unfortunately, collapsing onto one's sleeping pallet for a good cry never solved anything—although it sure did feel good, sometimes.

But life in the backcountry did not allow for such luxuries. Christina had to get the cheese made, then draw the water and start dinner. She had already decided on pudding, which would take hours to boil after she made the pastry crust, rolled it out, and filled it with spiced apples. Yes, she had better stay on task.

Christina poured the junket onto the linen cloth to let it drain into the bowl. She felt too distracted to concentrate and nearly knocked over the bowl when she set the Dutch oven aside. She tried to be more careful as she folded the linen cloth over the junket and tied it into a secure bundle. Christina stood and hung the bundle from the wooden rafter above the table, alongside the dried herbs and a side of salt pork. The cabin had a low ceiling, but she had to stand on her tiptoes to tie the cloth. She set the wooden bowl directly beneath the linen bundle and watched the remaining liquid drip into it with a steady pitter-pat. The junket would turn into cheese overnight, and the liquid would turn into whey to save for the next cheese making.

Christina wiped her hands on her apron and nodded as she surveyed her work. That was one job finished. Now if only her matchmaking job could be so simple and straightforward! If only the human heart could be molded as easily as a block of cheese. Surely, the heart was the most complex of all *der Herr's* creations.

And yet, Christina would not be deterred. Her heart was set on Johan. And after seeing Hilda's pain, Christina was more determined than ever to heal her sister's broken heart with Wilhelm's love.

Chapter Ten

Johan had been out of sorts ever since he'd left Christina's cabin the day before. It irked him to no end that she preferred his brother to him. The very idea! Wilhelm studied Johan with raised eyebrows as they rose before dawn to light the fire and send the boys to the river for water. Johan scowled as he fastened his knee breeches and pulled woolen hose above each knee. "What's gotten into you?" Wilhelm asked as he shrugged into his loose, linen shirt. Johan just scowled harder. He secured each hose with a strip of cloth and refused to answer.

"You've been in a state ever since you returned from Hilda and Christina's homestead yesterday."

"Bah!" Johan stormed to the firepit and threw a log onto the coals. The wood landed with a mighty crash. He hadn't meant to toss it so hard.

"What did that firewood ever do to you?" Wilhelm looked amused. He was used to his brother's passionate emotions. Johan's family knew he gave himself fully to whatever caught his fancy. So far, his passions had been limited to passing interests—like the time he took a notion to learn the cobbling trade before realizing how tiring it was to squint over a length of leather all day. That pursuit had ended after a fortnight. His latest and most notable passion had been to leave everything behind to start a new life in the Colonies with his brother. "Heaven help him when he finally falls for a woman," his mother used to say, shaking her head. "If he has this much passion for adventure, can you imagine how he will react when the right woman comes along?"

Johan and Wilhelm had left their parents and sisters behind when they made the journey and did not know if they would ever see them again. The brothers dreamed of sending for the rest of their family someday. But first, they had to survive the wilderness. Johan frowned and jammed another log onto the campfire. Surviving his feelings for Christina Dresser felt more difficult than surviving the wilderness at the moment. Did she really prefer Wilhelm? Was that possible? She had given every indication that she did.

Johan glared into the flames as he stoked the fire. He could not dismiss the connection he had felt between Christina and him. Those moments had been so exhilarating, so full of life and excitement. . . . Johan's frown deepened. Bah! He did not even want to settle down. Why should he care about any so-called connection—or lack of one?

"You have to stop this," Wilhelm said as he laced his waistcoat and pulled on his black linsey-woolsey jacket.

"Stop building a fire? There is a distinct chill in the air. I wouldn't want the boys to catch cold."

Wilhelm rolled his eyes. "You know what I mean. Stop acting like a child who hasn't gotten his way."

"Hasn't gotten his way?" Johan's eyes flashed. "What is that supposed to mean?"

"Yes, Papa," Franz said from his sleeping pallet. "What is that supposed to mean?" The boy looked warm and rumpled from sleep, and Wilhelm reached down to tousle his son's messy hair.

"Time for you to fetch the water, *ja*?"

"Mmmm." Franz snuggled deeper under his quilt. "But it's so cozy under the bedcovers."

Wilhelm gave Franz his sternest look, which was not very stern at all.

"All right. All right." Franz shook his brothers awake and they dragged themselves from their pallet.

"First one to the creek wins," Johan said as he stoked the fire.

The boys leapt up as if a whip had cracked across the clearing. "I'll win!" Fritz shouted and raced toward the yoke and buckets in his long, linen nightshirt.

"You've forgotten your breeches," Wilhelm pointed out while trying not to smile. The boys jumped into their knee breeches and tucked in their nightshirts—the long linen shirts doubled as sleepwear and daywear.

Wilhelm waited until the boys' shrieks faded into the pines, then turned his attention back to Johan. "I think you know what I meant."

"Humph."

"You've been a beast to live with ever since you returned from the Dressers' yesterday."

"Humph."

"Come now, Johan. You can't keep secrets from your brother. I can always tell, you know."

Johan released a long, frustrated breath and sank onto a three-legged stool he had built since they'd arrived in New Canaan. The stool shifted under his weight, and he frowned. He hoped the shift came from sinking into the soft earth and not from the stool's construction. He had never been handy at carpentry.

"Johan."

"*Ach*, Wilhelm. Let a man be, won't you?"

"No."

Johan threw up his hands. "Fine. I'll come out and ask you. Are you interested in Christina Dresser?"

Wilhelm looked surprised. "Christina?" He shook his head and gave a short, dry laugh. "That girl isn't the one for me, Johan. She's too young and too . . ." He searched for the right word and shook his head again.

"Too what?" Johan's brows drew together, and he leaned forward.

"Too flighty," Wilhelm said. "Too prone to daydream."

Johan's eyes flashed. "How can you say that about her?"

"*Ach*, it isn't a bad thing. She's sweet and fun loving too, I'm sure. But she isn't for me. I need a down-to-earth woman who knows how to get things done."

"A woman like Hilda?" Johan asked.

"We are talking about you, not me," Wilhelm said.

"So you don't deny that Hilda is right for you?"

"Oh, I don't know. She's wonderful good with the boys, but I wouldn't expect her to take on a widower with three rowdy sons." He shook his head. "It's too much to ask. Besides, she has never shown any interest. I've never been a charmer, you know. That's always been your department."

"So you don't deny it."

"Wait." Wilhelm grinned at his brother. "How did you manage to turn the conversation around on me? This is about you. Now tell me what's gotten into you. If you're afraid I'm interested in Christina, you can put your mind at ease."

"No." Johan sighed and rested his chin in his hands. He looked more like a dejected boy than a robust young man of twenty-three years.

"Whatever you need to admit, you may as well admit it. I'll pry it out of you, you know."

"*Ach*. All right." Johan gave another heavy sigh. It took all his strength to admit his feelings and possible defeat. Could he bear to play second fiddle to his brother? "I fear Christina has set her sights on you."

Wilhelm stared at Johan with an incredulous expression before bursting into laughter. His voice boomed across the clearing and startled a rabbit that had crept from the forest to nibble a patch of clover. Wilhelm did not stop laughing until his face turned red and he sputtered into a coughing fit. "That was a good one, brother," Wilhelm said at last. He coughed a few more times and pounded his chest with a fist. "Christina Dresser interested in me!"

Johan narrowed his eyes. "She has given plenty of hints."

"Nonsense. That girl is too flighty to know how she appears to others."

Johan's face darkened, and Wilhelm held up a hand. "I'm not criticizing the poor dear. She has a good heart, I'm sure. And some men"—he gave Johan a knowing look—"might even find such flightiness endearing."

"Bah." Johan's face relaxed a fraction, but he maintained a hearty scowl. "Endearing, indeed."

"I think you're falling for her." Wilhelm studied his brother with a sly expression.

"Falling for her. Bah."

"Well, there's only one way to prove me wrong."

Johan's eyes narrowed.

"March over there, spend some time with her, then come

back to me and say you aren't interested. Lying is a mortal sin, you know." Wilhelm looked serious, but there was a distinct twinkle in his eye.

"I am not lying."

"I fear you are lying to yourself. You might actually believe what you say."

"The very idea. Why wouldn't I believe what I say? Really, Wilhelm, you are full of nonsense today."

"Hmmm. Well, I'm not the one slamming firewood and stomping about in a sour mood since yesterday afternoon."

"Fine. I'll go back and I'll prove to us both that the only emotion I feel right now is wounded pride."

"Wounded pride, is it?"

Dash it all, Johan had not meant to let that slip.

Wilhelm's lips curled into a smile. "You think your old, un-charming brother has gotten the best of you?"

"No. Of course not." But Johan's expression spoke the truth.

"You waste your time on nonsense," Wilhelm said. "She has not set her sights on me, so you needn't worry. Although I should make you stew in it. It would give me great satisfaction to see that pride of yours brought down to earth."

"Pride. Bah. Amish aren't prideful."

"Amish aren't *supposed* to be prideful. Those are two very different things."

Johan's scowl stayed on his face. This conversation had gotten away from him.

Wilhelm's smile softened into a look of concern. "Pride cometh before a fall, you know. I'd hate to see you fall, brother."

Johan shook his head. "I am quite all right, thank you."

"A prideful answer if ever there was one."

Johan stood up. "You would drive the most patient man crazy."

Wilhelm smiled and gazed up at his brother from his place by the fire. "Ah, on your way to Christina's to prove me wrong?"

"*Ja.*"

Wilhelm's smile widened. "This could become a most interesting day."

Christina untied the linen bundle from the rafter as soon as she awoke. She unfolded the cloth to reveal a rich, buttery ball of white cheese. The liquid drippings had turned to whey in the bowl, and she poured the liquid into the clay jar, fastened the lid, and set it aside for the next cheese making. What could be better than fresh cheese and bread for breakfast? The day had begun very well indeed.

"How was the Widow Yoder faring when you visited yesterday?" Christina asked as she spread the creamy, crumbly sheep's cheese over the bread Hilda had baked the day before.

Hilda stoked the fire, stood up, and stretched. "Well enough. She is recovering."

"I ought to take her some cheese."

"They have Greta's milk cow."

"Ah. True." Christina shrugged. "But with the adopted twins to feed, I'm sure they run short of milk, even with a good cow. Besides, Jacob bagged us that rabbit the other day. I should do something and the cheese is all we have, so the cheese it shall be."

Hilda nodded and stoked the fire again. The flames danced higher, and Christina held her palms to the heat from her place at the table. The cabin still held a chill in the mornings, despite the spring weather.

"I'm sure it will be appreciated," Hilda said. "No one has enough of anything in the backcountry." Hilda poured a bucket of water into the big iron cauldron that hung above the fire.

"We have enough wolves, trees, and mud."

"Indeed." Hilda laughed. "But I hope you will not be making a gift of those."

A knock at the door stopped Christina from answering.

"Who could it be at this hour?" Hilda asked and headed to the door. Night still clung to the woods and sky, bruising everything a soft, purple color.

"Oh!" Christina dropped her slice of bread and leapt up from the table. "I'm not decent!" She had on her shift, skirts, bodice, pinned-on sleeves, woolen jacket, neck cloth, and prayer *kappe*, but had not bothered with her hosen yet. "Tell whomever it is to hold on for a moment!" she said in a loud whisper.

"This is why I tell you not to lounge about the cabin without your hosen on, like a common strumpet."

"*Ja. Ja.*" Christina balanced on one leg as she yanked a woolen hose up her other leg. She hopped twice and hit the wall with her shoulder.

"Really, Christina."

"Almost ready!"

The knock sounded again.

"Just a moment," Hilda said in a loud but calm voice. She watched Christina struggle into the second hose with raised eyebrows.

Once she had the hose on, Christina grabbed two strips of linen and tied each hose above her knee. Then she pushed her shift and skirts down, smoothed the fabric, and exhaled. "Ready." A bolt of excitement zipped up Christina's spine. What if Johan had come calling? There was no reason for it . . . and she must keep her distance for Hilda's sake . . . but still . . . She fought to remain calm and reasonable. It was probably Jacob Miller, come to give them another rabbit.

But when Hilda opened the door, Johan slouched against the doorframe. He looked casual and in control, as if he owned the place. His signature grin flashed when he saw Christina. "Hello, there."

"Hello!" The bolt of excitement shot all the way from her toes to the top of her head. Johan Lantz *had* come calling!

Hilda gave her a look, and Christina recognized that her voice sounded too eager. She cleared her throat and lowered her voice to a soft, detached tone. "What I mean to say is, we did not expect you." She nodded toward the hearth. "But do come in."

Johan held a fat turkey by its feet. He lifted his arm to show off the bird. "Bagged it before dawn." The morning sun filtered through the trees and made the feathers glisten in shimmering shades of purple, brown, and indigo.

"Oh!" Christina clapped her hands together and skipped across the cabin. "It's as big as Bruno."

Johan laughed. "Not quite. But big enough, anyway. It should keep you two fed for some time."

Hilda nodded. "Your generosity is much appreciated, Johan. It's a fine bird."

"Eli and Abram deserve credit as well. They told me they had sighted a flock near the village green."

"A village is only as good as its neighbors."

Johan grinned and let his eyes rest on Christina. His

stare felt warm and full of possibilities. "Then I am blessed to have such good neighbors," he said.

Well! Johan's words sounded vague, but his gaze told the rest of the story. Christina felt the blush travel from her throat to her cheeks, until she looked very red indeed. She hurried to take the bird from Johan before he noticed her reaction to that intense, masculine gaze. That had been a gaze of interest and delight, of dreams and longing. That was a gaze she would not soon forget. It had seared her soul.

She cleared her throat and hung the turkey from a rafter beside the hearth. She noticed that her fingers shook as she struggled to knot the twine around the cool, scaly feet. Christina swallowed and forced her stomach to settle. "I'll dress it after breakfast and we will have a hearty feast for dinner, *ja*?" She stated the fact in her smoothest, calmest voice. She must not let Johan see her interest in him. Then where would poor Hilda be? Left all alone, that's where!

Johan eyed her with thoughtful but amused eyes. "You can invite me to dinner as thanks," he said in a deep, arresting voice. He sounded very much in control.

Christina did not feel in control at all. She turned away to busy herself at the fire. Her heart thudded in her ears. Everything she had dreamed and hoped for stood in her cabin, at this very moment, inviting himself to dinner. Oh, it was too good to be true.

And, of course, it was. Because there was one dream that could not be fulfilled in this moment. Christina's mouth went dry. She swallowed to push her heart back down into place. Loyalty to a sister had to come first. She had to see Hilda settled with a man before she, Christina, ran off with one. Christina swallowed again. She took a deep breath, steadied herself, and set her heart like a stone. That was exactly what it felt like—a stone.

"Oh." Christina smiled a distant smile.

Johan's expression changed. He looked confused by the sudden coolness in her expression.

"What a lovely idea."

Johan's grin returned.

"But you must bring Wilhelm as well, *ja*? We would welcome him at our table."

Johan's grin disappeared and did not return. The stone in Christina's chest felt sharp. If this was the right thing to do, then why did it feel so wrong?

Johan had arrived at Christina's cabin before the sun had fully risen, filled with a sense of purpose. He had good reason to call on the sisters, for any good Amish man should remember the widow and the orphan—or any neighbor in need—and he had bagged a fine, fat turkey after his conversation with Wilhelm. But Johan had more than charity in mind. He needed to prove to himself that he didn't feel any affection for Christina Dresser. He wanted to be able to look his brother in the eye and tell him honestly that Christina was no more to him than a sister in the faith.

But, dash it all, she had gazed at him with those big, blue eyes in such a charming way that he had felt a tug on his heartstrings. And then she had flitted about the cabin as light and graceful as an angel. *An angel?* He was glad Wilhelm couldn't hear his thoughts. But how could he resist? Christina had practically danced across the cabin to greet him. Her eyes had shone, and he saw the blood rush to her cheeks when he grinned down at her. She had been so flustered that she'd turned away.

Or so he had thought. Now, he was not sure. Just when he was convinced there was a connection between them, she had said that word he had come to dread from her lips: Wilhelm. *Wilhelm?* Why on earth should she ask for Wilhelm at a time like this? Couldn't Christina see that Wilhelm had no interest in her? That he was all wrong for her?

The strange thing was, the more Christina rejected Johan, the more he felt compelled to pursue her. A terrible realization struck him as he watched her at the hearth. He wanted her to return his affection. No, he *needed* her to return his affection. She wasn't like other women—they all doted on him and fought to win his favor. Christina did not dote on him. She did not fight for his favor. She was her own woman, with a strength that her giggles and flightiness nearly hid.

Nearly.

The room became too hot, his collar too tight. A burning disbelief invaded Johan's chest. He was falling for Christina Dresser. Dash it all, this was not how things were supposed to go. His jaw began to ache, and he realized he had been clenching his teeth.

"Johan?" Christina stared at him with a strange expression. "Are you quite all right?" Dash it all, that was the second time someone had asked him the same question in as many days. And both times over a woman! And not just any woman. A woman with the innocence and cheerfulness of an angel . . .

This simply would not do. Johan set his jaw and straightened his spine. "I am well, thank you." He let his gaze shift back to Christina. Her expression looked strained and distant. It was the face of a woman who does not return a man's affection.

He did not know what to do. It was an unfamiliar and unsettling experience. Johan Lantz always felt sure of himself. Had he really misread their earlier connection? Hadn't they locked eyes just moments before? He had fallen into her gaze, reached through those clear blue eyes and touched her soul in that moment. Or at least he felt he had.

Now, instead of a connection, all he felt was the sting of rejection. Johan mumbled a hasty good-bye and stumbled outside. The chill spring air met him with cool indifference. Even the sun felt more distant and aloof than before. Christina's rejection had upended his world. A small voice reminded him that she had not rejected him outright. But a louder, bolder voice told him she had been clear enough.

He had no idea what to do now. His emotions warred within him. One half argued to move on and forget the enchanting Christina Dresser—he didn't want her if she didn't want him! But another, deeper part of him fought his pride and whispered to be patient.

Patient! Ha! How could he ever face Christina again? Much less pursue her? Besides, hadn't he promised himself to stay single? Hadn't he always valued his freedom above all else? Why should he change his plans now, just because a woman tugged at his heartstrings?

Christina's mind whirred. Johan had brought a fine gift! Of course, other men of the settlement did too—out of neighborly concern and nothing more. But other men of the settlement did not stare into her eyes in a way that burned her soul and made her toes curl with delight. She could barely focus. That moment was all she could think about. The rest of the day passed in a whirl of activity as she rushed from one mindless job to the next to distract herself.

"They will come, won't they?" Christina asked as she turned the spit above the fire. Turkey grease dripped onto the hearth and sizzled against the hot stones. The cabin smelled of roasted meat, wood smoke, and pine. Christina inhaled deeply and smiled. Johan would get a fine home-cooked meal when they arrived. *If* they arrived! "Won't they?"

"Well, they must be starved for a good meal."

Christina laughed. "They had naught but salt pork and corncakes on the trail."

"Burnt corncakes," Hilda added.

Christina laughed again. "And I doubt they're eating much better now. It's one thing to bring down a turkey or a deer. It's quite another to cook it right."

Hilda chuckled. "Indeed."

"So they will come." Christina said the words more to herself than to her sister. She could not bear the thought that she might not see Johan that evening.

Hilda hesitated and her smile disappeared. "I fear you did not make Johan feel welcome this morning."

Christina flinched. She turned her attention back to the fireplace. "It was the neighborly thing to do to invite the entire family."

"But you did not invite the entire family. You only invited Wilhelm."

"It goes without saying that the boys are invited."

"And it goes without saying that your sights are set on Wilhelm. Really, Christina, you must not declare your intentions so openly. It is most unbecoming."

Christina felt a surge of righteous indignation flash

through her. The very idea! She bit her tongue to keep from blurting out the truth.

"We've been over this before, you know." Hilda shook her head in a slow, disappointed manner as she swept the homemade broom across the dirt floor.

Christina bit her tongue harder. Was there any injustice so great as being falsely accused when trying to help someone? There most certainly was not. If she did not escape the conversation, Christina knew she would tell her sister everything before she could stop herself. "I'm going to check on the sheep." Christina did not wait for a response. She shot out of the cabin and through the door before she lost her self-control. Bruno galloped out of the woods, bounded across the clearing, and leapt up to greet her. He rested his paws on her shoulders as he balanced on his back legs and met her eye-to-eye with a goofy expression of adoration.

"At least someone appreciates me!" Christina wrapped her arms around him and squeezed until he dropped back to the ground. "I've made a mess of things, I'm afraid. If Hilda thinks I'm interested in Wilhelm, she won't pursue him herself. But if I tell her my plan, she'll clamp down on her emotions and refuse to fall for him." Christina scratched behind Bruno's ears absentmindedly. "Which means I have to try even harder to throw those two together." Bruno whined and wagged his tail. "I'm sorry. I can't play fetch today. I've too much work to do. I have a match to make." Christina gave a quick, decisive nod. She had better get back to it.

"That was fast," Hilda said as Christina swept through the doorway with a set expression. "You had time to see to the sheep?"

"Mmmm." Christina had to up the game. She would

create a situation so romantic that Hilda and Wilhelm could not resist one another. "I had a lovely idea for the meal," Christina said.

"I'm afraid to ask."

"This one is much better than the last."

"Your last idea left us eating bread in the rain."

"This one is foolproof."

Hilda glanced upward with a longsuffering expression. "And what, exactly, is this idea of yours?"

"A picnic." Christina flashed an enthusiastic grin. Hilda did not.

"A picnic? Why go to the trouble? We've everything we need right here."

Christina knew a lovely spot alongside the river that was so peaceful and beautiful at sunset that even Hilda—killjoy that she was—would have to feel a romantic spark. Christina paused as she considered her answer. There had to be another, reasonable excuse. . . . "Because the children will run wild inside our cabin."

"Mmmm."

"The poor dears are quite uncivilized. You have said so yourself."

"Indeed . . ." Hilda frowned. "But it is rather unorthodox to ask guests to traipse through the woods before they are fed."

"Traipse through the woods! I would call it a lovely walk before dinner."

Hilda threw up her hands. "Oh, Christina. You'll have your way regardless, so I may as well give in now."

"I'm glad you see reason, sister mine."

Hilda raised her eyebrows.

"You'll have a lovely time, I promise."

"If you say so."

"I do."

"Mmmm. Well, I've enough to do without transferring a meal to the wilderness. If you want it done, you'll have to do it yourself." Hilda shook her head. "It is most unusual. What will Johan and Wilhelm think?"

Romantic thoughts, if all went well. Christina smiled like a satisfied cat after a bowl of cream. "It's all in hand, sister dear. It will be a most memorable day."

"Yes. That is what I'm afraid of."

Christina did not rise to the bait. This time, her plan would be a success—a wonderful, romantic success.

Chapter Eleven

The Lantz family arrived with growling stomachs.

"I could eat a horse," Johan announced in a gregarious, booming voice.

Christina beamed. "I hope a turkey will do."

"A turkey will do very well indeed," Johan said. Their eyes met, but his did not linger this time. Christina's heart hammered against her throat as she watched him frown and lower his gaze.

Christina did not lower her eyes. She could not think clearly enough to tear her attention away. Instead, her knees felt weak as butter and her stomach warmed with butterflies. She reminded herself not to show her interest, but her body would not obey her mind. The fact that he would not hold her gaze made her crave his attention more than ever.

Christina felt a tug on her skirt.

"Christina."

The child's voice sounded far away. She continued to stare at Johan until his eyes came back to meet hers. He rewarded her stare with a smile, though it looked weak and uncertain. She smiled back at him and thought her knees might give way. She had connected with him again. Oh, he seemed reluctant, but that was all right. He had still gazed into her eyes and given her that charming smile.

"Christina!"

She felt the tug again, stronger this time. The moment broke and suddenly she was back in her own yard, surrounded by a group of people, with a young boy pulling on her skirt. "Oh. Franz." She cleared her throat and smoothed her skirt. How long had she been staring at Johan? What a complete fool she must look!

She glanced around to see Hilda watching her with a strange expression on her face. Christina looked away and frowned. She wondered what Hilda was thinking. No matter. There was no time for regrets or worries. She had a marriage to arrange. And it would begin with a perfect picnic. . . .

"Yes, Franz?"

"Hilda says you are sending us into the woods to eat."

"Will we see a bear?" Fritz asked as he hopped past on one foot.

"Or a wildcat?" Franz asked. He ran to follow Fritz and slammed into his brother's back when Fritz stopped short.

"Papa, tell Franz to stop following me! He's imitating everything I do."

"Mmmm." Wilhelm rubbed his eyes. "They do say imitation is the sincerest form of flattery."

"I don't know what flattery is," Fritz said. "But whatever it is, I don't want it. Not if it comes from Franz."

"Franz, stop following your brother," Wilhelm said as he continued to rub his eyes with a thumb and forefinger.

"Look, I can go as fast as he can!" Franz said. Then he tripped over his feet, fell forward into Fritz, knocked his brother to the ground, and bounced backward to land on his backside. Franz howled and Fritz gave a yelp of surprise.

"That's why I told him to stop following me!" Fritz said and rubbed his elbow. "He's hurt me!"

"Now, now, boys." Hilda stepped between them, crouched down, and looked them both in the eye. She took a moment to look at Fritz's elbow. "You'll be all right."

"What about me?" Franz asked.

Hilda looked him over and smiled. "You will be all right, as well." She patted his shoulder, then dropped her smile for a no-nonsense expression. "But if you had been hurt, it would be no one's fault but your own."

Franz's mouth dropped open in protest, but he didn't speak. Instead, he stared at her with big, sorrowful eyes.

"Your father told you to stop, didn't he?"

"*Ja.*"

"Then you should have stopped. This is what happens when we don't listen to our fathers."

Franz looked as if he wanted to argue, but he did not.

Hilda gave him a quick, serious nod, then turned her gaze back to Fritz. "Now, the best thing for a hurt elbow is the privilege of leading the way. Would you like to go ahead with Bruno and break the trail for us?"

Fritz leapt to his feet. "*Ja!*" He jumped up and down. "You can all follow me!"

"Wonderful good," Hilda said. "There is one catch, however."

Fritz stopped jumping up and down. "What?"

"You have to take Franz with you."

Fritz hesitated, then shrugged. "All right. I don't mind."

"Hurray!" Franz bounced up and took off for the tree line.

"Wait just a moment, young man," Hilda said.

Franz skidded to a halt and turned around. "*Ja*?"

"There is a catch for you too."

"There is?"

"You have to apologize to your father and to your brother."

Franz scowled.

"Or you can stay with us while Fritz and Bruno run ahead."

"Oh, all right." He heaved a dramatic sigh and looked up at his father. "Sorry I didn't listen, Papa."

"You're forgiven. But see that you do, next time."

Franz nodded and started for the woods.

"Franz. Aren't you forgetting something?"

Franz heaved another sigh, even more dramatic this time. "Fritz, I'm sorry I wouldn't stop imitating you."

"That's all right. Come on. Let's beat everyone else to the river!" The boys raced to the tree line as Bruno circled and barked. Felix watched his older brothers run ahead and pulled at his father's waistcoat. Wilhelm scooped him up, planted a kiss atop his head, and swung him onto his shoulders. "I wasn't sure about your plan, Christina. I'll admit it seemed . . . strange. Never heard of carrying dinner into the woods when there's a perfectly good table to use in the cabin. But I have to admit you had a fine idea. Those boys would have torn the room apart, they've so much energy."

"And that's after a day's work clearing brush," Johan said. "You should have seen them when I returned from the hunt this morning. I don't know how they keep going."

Wilhelm laughed. "Those two have endless energy. Especially when it comes to quarrelling."

Christina motioned toward Hilda and smiled. "It was Hilda who settled the quarrel."

Wilhelm glanced down at Hilda with appreciation. "Well done."

"Nonsense," Hilda said. "There's nothing to it but a firm hand and plenty of love."

Christina hung back as Hilda and Wilhelm strode into the woods side by side. She could hear them talking, although she couldn't make out the words. Hilda even laughed at something Wilhelm said. *Laughed!* The outing was off to a very fine start indeed.

"I'll get that," Johan said as he swooped in to grab the quilt and basket before Christina could.

"Thank you." His thoughtfulness put a soft, fuzzy feeling into her stomach. "Although it's light enough for me to carry."

"Nonsense." Johan tucked the quilt beneath his arm and swung the basket carelessly as they followed the rest of the party into the woods. "Anything's too heavy for you."

"Oh?"

"I mean . . ."

"You mean what?" Christina had never seen Johan look flustered before. Did she make him feel uncomfortable?

Johan frowned. "I mean you are such a little thing. Not that you aren't strong. I'm sure you're strong. Not that you seem strong in a manly way. You don't seem manly in the least."

"I should hope not."

"I meant, it wouldn't be right for you to carry something heavy. You're too . . ."

"Too what?"

"Too . . . lovely?" Johan puffed out his cheeks and let out the air. He laughed and shook his head. "I don't know what's gotten into me."

Christina watched his expression carefully. She hoped she knew what it was. Oh, how she hoped!

Johan wanted to give himself a good shake. How foolish he sounded! He needed to keep his mouth shut. But the presence of Christina Dresser turned his mouth to mush and shook his confidence. He'd never experienced such a thing. Being tongue-tied over a woman! Preposterous. And yet, here he was, babbling on about her seeming manly, or some other nonsense. Perhaps he should clarify . . . and say what? That she was the ideal woman—captivating, spirited, and full of life? No, he had best quit while he was ahead. Or not any worse off than he already was, anyway. She was only interested in his brother so he would not be interested in her. It was as simple as that.

Wasn't it?

Johan had sworn off Christina Dresser after their last visit. Until he saw her today. Now, she had gotten under his skin again. It simply would not do.

"You are in quite a state, by the look of you," Christina said and giggled.

Johan loved that laugh. The sound reminded him of the chime of the village church bell back in Germany. Or the warble of songbirds in the spring. Church bells? Songbirds? Oh dear. He really had lost it. He frowned. "The fever and ague is in the air, I hear. Perhaps that is why I am not myself."

"My goodness! Have you taken ill?"

Now he had done it. He had caused her worry. That adorable crease in her forehead showed her concern.

"No." His frown deepened, and he shook his head. "I'm sure I'm fine. It's just we've been camping out in the

night air and . . ." He let his voice trail away before he
made matters even worse.

"Mmmm." The furrow on Christina's brow deepened.
"I've often wondered about that."

"About my camping out?" Had he really asked her that?
What a bizarre question. Why would she give any thought
to such a mundane thing? Dash it all, he was only trying
to make small talk.

Christina laughed again. "I meant I've wondered whether
or not the night air really does cause the fever and ague. It
seems more likely to come from some warm-weather pest.
I know not what. Insects or humid bogs or something of
that nature."

"Ah." He cut her a sidewise glance.

She smiled. "What is that look for?"

"What look?"

"The one you are giving at this very moment."

Johan shrugged and grinned.

"Do you find my thoughts amusing?"

He did. Very much so. Johan shrugged again. "*Ja.* I
suppose."

"You are making fun of me."

"No." Johan dropped the grin. "I am . . . intrigued by
what you said."

"Because I do not seem like a deep thinker. You're
surprised."

"I didn't say that."

Christina giggled. "No, you just thought it."

Did he think that about her? She was quick to smile and
quicker to fall into trouble. She acted before she thought,
but laughed at her own mistakes. She giggled and gasped
like a young girl, but held a depth behind her eyes that
spoke of dreams and hopes beyond the reach of many

minds. No. He did not think her shallow. "I've always admired your depth of thought."

Christina gave a doubtful smile. "That would make you the first."

"I find that hard to believe."

"Johan, I am not known for my intellect or wit. Come now, be serious or you will hurt my feelings. I am quite sensitive, you know."

Johan studied the emotion that lurked beneath her bright blue eyes. He could tell she meant what she said. He could also tell that she did not realize he saw a side of her that no one else did. Perhaps that was why he felt himself falling for her; he could see all of her—the vivacious, childlike playfulness as well as the thoughtful, introspective dreamer. Why couldn't anyone else? It was just plain wrong that her qualities should go unrecognized.

"Christina, I think you are one of the deepest thinkers I know."

Her face changed, and she looked away. "Now I *know* you are making fun of me." She readjusted her prayer *kappe*. "That's quite enough."

Johan wanted to touch her face and smooth away the hurt with his fingertips. He wanted to whisper to her everything he admired about her. He wanted to make her see her worth. But all he could do was shake his head and murmur her name. "Oh, Christina."

Her eyes shot back to his, and her frown deepened. "What?"

He tensed. There was no way to tell her, no way to explain what he recognized. "Nothing," he said. "It's nothing."

But it was everything. And yet, for the first time in his life, Johan had no idea how to put his feelings about a woman into words.

* * *

Johan could not keep his eyes from Christina. For the rest of the walk, he snuck sideways glances, then averted his gaze before she noticed. He grimaced when he realized he was acting like a young boy with a crush. Dash it all, that was how women felt about *him*, not how *he* felt about women.

He snuck another glance.

He could not help himself. She looked radiant. Evening light slanted through the trees and painted her face gold. A wisp of blond hair curled from beneath her prayer *kappe* and glowed in the sun. They passed beneath thick, low-lying branches, and her profile slipped into shadow. He studied the slightly upturned nose and the gentle curve of her cheek before she stepped back into sunlight. The yellow rays made her white prayer *kappe* look bright and crisp against the brown trees and damp earth. She glanced upward, noticed him staring, and smiled. She held his gaze boldly for a long, exhilarating moment before Johan came to his senses and jerked his eyes away. He rubbed the back of his neck in an awkward motion, as if he had been caught doing something he ought not to be doing.

Well, he ought not to be staring at Christina Dresser.

This would not do. This would not do at all. He was a man of action, after all. He should either give up and run now, or charge forward, unafraid. *Charge forward, unafraid?* She wasn't a bear for heaven's sake. She was a lovely, captivating woman. But he knew that. He knew that very well indeed.

Even so, he couldn't charge forward and pursue Christina. He didn't want to marry. He didn't want entanglements. He should just enjoy her company and leave it at that.

Besides, she had given hint after hint that her heart was set on Wilhelm. But she had also hinted that she had feelings for Johan. Didn't she stare at him as if he were the only man in the world? Dash it all, what was he to think?

His thoughts were interrupted by a shout ahead of them.

"Felix! You'll get your breeches wet!" Wilhelm's words were followed by a splash.

"Too late, I imagine," Christina said as they emerged from the woods and onto the riverbank. She laughed when she saw she was correct. Felix stood knee deep in water. The surface sparkled around his woolen hosen as he splashed and grinned. The two older boys rushed across the muddy bank and plunged into the water after their brother.

"Didn't you hear what I told Felix?" Wilhelm asked as he ran his hand through his hair. He looked as if he'd given up.

"Yes, Papa," Fritz shouted as he splashed Franz in the face. "But you didn't tell *us* not to get our breeches wet."

"Actually, you didn't tell Felix not to get his breeches wet either," Franz added. "You simply said he *will* get his breeches wet." Franz presented a smile of pure innocence. "So we aren't disobeying you."

"Oh, *ja*!" Fritz flashed his own smile, though his looked naughtier than his brother's. "Franz is right. In fact, we are just fulfilling your words! You predicted it, and it came true. How wise you are, Papa."

Wilhelm groaned and sank onto a patch of clover. He drew up his knees, rested his elbows on them, and let his head sink onto his arms.

"You know very well what your papa meant," Hilda said as she settled onto the ground beside Wilhelm. "But since he did not outright forbid you to go in, we will leave it at that. I dare say you will find the natural consequences of your actions punishment enough. You'll be chilled to the bone for the rest of the evening."

None of the boys looked concerned about Hilda's warning. They were too busy splashing. As Johan and Christina strolled toward the patch of clover, an arc of water shot up the bank and sprayed her gray woolen bodice. "Oh!" she gasped. "That *is* cold!"

Wilhelm's head lifted from where it rested on his arms. "Boys! Apologize to poor Christina."

They grinned and managed to shout an apology between giggles.

"It's quite all right, Wilhelm," Christina said as she darted to the edge of the water. "They shall reap what they sow."

Johan watched with amused eyes. Would she dare? Oh, she would. He smiled as she gathered her skirts, stooped down, and splashed Fritz and Franz until their wool waistcoats looked thoroughly soaked. Christina beamed. "I win."

The boys glanced down at their wet clothes, then back up at Christina with open mouths.

"You didn't think an adult would come after you, *ja*?" she asked with an innocent smile.

Johan's smile spread into a grin. He hadn't thought she would either. Christina certainly knew how to have fun.

The four adults took some time basking in the gentle, evening sun and watching the children play. Johan couldn't remember the last time he had just sat and done nothing. It felt delightful. He watched the sunlight ease through the branches and paint the river shades of orange and yellow as dusk approached. The sky above the tree line turned purple, and the birds began to chirp and dart from branch to branch. Johan leaned back in his hands and closed his eyes. The children laughed in the distance. Christina sat beside him, her warm shoulder brushing his. He could feel her body rise and fall with each breath. They didn't speak for a moment, just listened to the sound of running water and the murmur of Wilhelm's conversation with Hilda.

"I suppose we ought to eat," Christina said at last. Johan didn't want the moment to end. "*Ja*," he said without enthusiasm. "I suppose so."

Christina shot him a playful look as she rose to her feet. "You don't sound as if you are looking forward to my cooking. You didn't enjoy the first meal I made you?"

Johan frowned. "Oh. Well. It was burnt beyond recognition so . . ." He cleared his throat. Everything had been going so well. He didn't want to hurt her feelings. Johan shifted uncomfortably. "The truth is, I was enjoying sitting beside you. It was . . . pleasant."

Christina paused. "Pleasant?"

Johan cleared his throat again. His face grew hot and he tugged at his collar. "Most pleasant."

"Mmmm." A happy smile spread across Christina's face. "Most pleasant, indeed." Her cheeks reddened to match his and her eyes dropped. "I really should see to supper." She glanced back at him as she reached for the picnic basket. "I was joking, you know."

"It wasn't pleasant?"

"No. I mean yes." She shook her head and laughed. "I was joking about the first time I cooked for you. Of course, it was terrible."

"Ah." Johan felt a contented glow in his chest as he watched her push a stray curl beneath her prayer *kappe*. Her gaze flicked to Wilhelm, who sat beside Hilda. Christina bit her lip and studied the pair with great interest. Johan felt his contentment evaporate. Not that again.

Hadn't they just spent a lovely time together? She had agreed it had been pleasant, although friends could have a pleasant time together, he supposed. Pleasant wasn't necessarily romantic.

Dash it all, it had certainly felt romantic to him.

Christina shifted her attention from Wilhelm to the picnic basket. She pushed aside the linen cloth and let out a yelp that made Johan jump to his feet. The boys stopped splashing and stared with wide, startled eyes. Wilhelm's and Hilda's attention jerked toward her.

"What is it?" Johan scrambled to her. "A snake? A spider?"

"It's nothing!" Christina wailed.

"Then why the fuss? If there's nothing there, there's no cause for alarm."

"No. You don't understand. There's nothing there!" She turned the basket upside down and shook it.

Oh. *Oh.* "You mean . . ."

"No supper!"

Hilda closed her eyes and pinched the bridge of her nose. "You forgot supper?" She sighed and repeated in a quieter voice, "She forgot supper."

Johan should stay out of it. If he rushed to her defense, he would be one step closer to pursuing her. And he did not want to pursue Christina Dresser. He wanted to enjoy her company and leave it at that. He did not need to complicate his life with romantic entanglements. But the words came out before he could stop them. "This is what makes you special, Christina."

"I can't believe I forgot . . ." Christina looked inside the basket again, as if the food might have appeared since the last time she'd checked. "The basket did seem light, but . . ." She leaned her face closer to the basket, until her nose was nearly inside.

"It isn't going to magically appear," Hilda said.

Johan gently took the basket from her.

"I can't believe . . ." Christina shook her head. Her bottom lip quivered in the most adorable way.

"You aren't listening to me." Johan tipped her chin up with his finger so that he could look her in the eye. He gave her a tender smile. Christina hiccupped. "This is what makes you special."

"What?" She hiccupped again, but her lip stopped trembling.

Johan let his gaze penetrate deep into hers. "You were so intent on giving us the perfect outing that you forgot the food. It just shows how preoccupied you are with others' happiness."

"*Ja.*" She nodded slowly and dabbed the moisture from her eyes with the corner of her apron. "*Ja*, that's it exactly. How did you know?" Her expression brightened. "It's as if you could read my mind."

"And yet, reading minds does not bring us any closer to dinner," Hilda muttered.

"That's all right," Fritz said and splashed out of the river. He skipped to Christina and wrapped his cold, wet arms around her. "We had fun anyway."

"Oh!" She gasped, then laughed. "You're so cold!" She hugged him back, buried her face in his damp hair, and shivered. "But thank you, Fritz. How nice of you to say."

Johan reached down and patted his nephew's head. "Fritz is right. It's been a lovely evening. And the disaster is easily averted. It isn't far to the cabin. We'll eat in no time."

Christina beamed at Johan, and they all marched back

to the homestead to enjoy a hearty dinner of cold roasted turkey and brown bread. Throughout the meal, Christina smiled at Johan with appreciation. She did not stare at Wilhelm—not one time. It was as if she had forgotten all about Wilhelm. Johan felt a warm glow in his chest for the rest of the night.

Everyone—even Hilda—seemed to have a splendid time. Everyone except perhaps the boys, whose lips had turned quite blue by the time they reached the cabin. Hilda warned them not to chatter their teeth so loudly or they might wake the sheep. They boys erupted into laughter when they realized she was joking. Wilhelm grinned at her. "But she was right, you know," he reminded his sons as he turned his gaze from Hilda to give the boys a no-nonsense look. "The water has chilled you." The boys spent the meal huddled by the fire, stripped to their underclothes and wrapped in quilts. The indignity of the situation did not seem to spoil their appetites whatsoever.

Chapter Twelve

Christina and Hilda sewed by the fire after their company waved their good-byes and strode into night with satisfied smiles and their Jaeger rifle for protection. "I do hope they manage to avoid the night predators," Hilda said as she bit off a length of thread.

"And I hope you stop biting the thread when we have a perfectly good pair of scissors."

Hilda laughed. "You sound like me."

"Mmmm. Well, not even *you* can be perfect all the time."

Hilda paused and lifted her eyes to Christina. "Is that what you think? That I'm perfect?" She looked surprised.

"No." Christina frowned and felt her cheeks turn scarlet. She cleared her throat. "The fire grows too hot, *ja*?"

"You never could deceive me, Christina. Your cheeks give you away. And we both know it isn't the fire putting that blush on them."

"All right, fine." Christina pushed her mending away. She was too distracted to work anyway. All she could think of was Johan. "It's not that I think you're perfect. Not exactly. It's that you always seem so proper. I can tell you think me frivolous. You rarely laugh or joke. You just look at me with that no-nonsense look of yours. You never make mistakes. You just keep plodding forward like an ox, sure-footed and certain of its path.

"Well." Hilda poked the needle through the linsey-woolsey cloth in her lap and pulled it taut. "I never."

"See! That's what I mean. You never do anything out of line. You never even say anything out of line!"

"Well, I don't call my sister an ox, if that's what you mean."

"You know what I mean."

"Do I?" Hilda raised her eyebrows, but kept her focus on the needle and thread. "Because it is not a flattering image."

"I'm sorry. I just meant you have no passion, no *spark*."

"Ah. So poor, boring Hilda just keeps plodding along like a beast of burden."

Christina put up a hand. "No. I'm sorry. That's not what I meant. I meant . . ." Christina looked upward as she concentrated, as if she could pull the right words out of the ceiling. "I just meant that you seem so competent and serious. You don't show any emotion. You don't make mistakes. You don't spill things or burn supper until the cabin fills with smoke, or forget to pack dinner when we go on a picnic."

"I don't forget to pack dinner because I don't serve dinner in the middle of the wilderness."

"*Ja!* That's what I mean. You don't come up with crazy schemes like I do. I can't seem to do anything right."

"Oh, Christina. I like your crazy schemes."

Christina flinched. "You do?"

"*Ja.* I do. Not all the time, mind you. But you bring a

breath of fresh air to a life of hard work. We would have little excitement without your schemes."

"Is that really how you feel?" Christina grinned and straightened in her seat. "I should scheme more often then, *ja*?"

"Absolutely not. You bring quite enough excitement as it is."

"Oh." Christina deflated a little. "Excitement annoys you, doesn't it?"

"I wouldn't put it that way, but I suppose so."

"What a tiresome life you lead, Hilda. I wish you could be more like me."

"Then we'd get nothing accomplished."

"That isn't very nice. I do plenty around here."

"*Ja*. You fill the cabin with smoke, forget lunch, spill the milk. . . . Shall I go on?"

Christina frowned, but Hilda gave a soft smile. "It isn't funny," Christina said. "I try so hard to be like you, but it never works."

"You shouldn't be like me. You should be yourself."

"No. Nothing ever works out when I do that."

"You made everyone happy today. Especially Johan."

Christina pressed her palms to her cheeks. "Oh! You think so? Do you really?"

"Ah. That's some response. I can certainly hear the emotion in your voice."

Christina tried to look calm, but she could hear her heartbeat in her throat. "You think Johan seemed happy with me?"

"*Ja*. But I don't know why you care. Aren't you set on Wilhelm?" Hilda shrugged. "Although heaven knows your mind changes as often as the weather. Have you set your sights on the younger brother now? I did notice you ignored Wilhelm most of the evening."

"I already told you that I feel no affection for Wilhelm. I've never felt any affection for Wilhelm."

"Mmmm." Hilda rummaged through her mending basket and pulled out a woolen hose with a hole in the knee. "So it *is* Johan now."

Christina furrowed her brow and looked down at her hands. She didn't want to lie to her sister. "You have managed to turn the conversation from being about you to being about me. We are supposed to be talking about how serious you are. Can't you ever relax? You make me feel as if you are always annoyed with me—as if I can never live up to your expectations."

Hilda stiffened. "Do I really?"

"*Ja.*"

"Then I'm very sorry." She shook her head. "That's not what I wanted."

"Oh." Christina leaned closer. "Then you're not always annoyed with me?"

"Well . . ." Hilda hesitated. "You do annoy me sometimes. But that's all right. I'm sure I annoy you sometimes too. We can't help that. We live together and have very different natures. It's only natural. It isn't personal."

"I suppose." Christina would rather hear that Hilda was never annoyed, but the truth would have to do.

"But I have never, ever been disappointed in you. I have never felt that you didn't live up to my expectations."

"Oh." *Oh.* Christina's eyes shot to Hilda's. "Truly?"

"Truly."

"Then why do you act like it?"

"I don't know. I don't mean to. I'm sorry if I have. I

suppose it's because . . ." Hilda let the words die. "It's getting late. We ought to retire for the night."

"No. We ought to finish our sentences."

"Well, I don't think you'll like the answer."

"If it's the truth, then it doesn't matter if I like it. It will still be the truth whether or not it pleases me."

"All right, then. The truth is that I have to be hard. I have to be serious and no-nonsense. I was so young when our parents died, and I had to learn how to take care of you. I couldn't be young and free anymore. I had to learn how to survive for the two of us."

Christina did not know what to say. The words died in her throat. She knew Hilda had sacrificed for her. But she had not realized how much it had hardened her sister's personality. She turned her face to look into the fire. Memories drifted through her mind. She remembered how Hilda had stood up to the wealthy owner of the farm next to theirs in Germany. He had tried to pressure her into selling their small plot of land and all their sheep to him. After Hilda refused, he had threatened. And still Hilda refused. She would not give in. Christina also remembered how, during a particularly hard winter, they ran out of food. Hilda traded the candlesticks for a bag of wheat and managed to drive a hard bargain. She'd never complained that it had cost them the only heirloom their parents had left them. And she had skipped meals so that bag of wheat lasted until spring. Why hadn't Christina seen it before? Of course Hilda's personality had hardened over the years. She had fought tooth and nail to survive as a woman alone. And now, she had led them to a better life in the wilderness, where she would have to keep on fighting. . . .

"Now I'm the one who is sorry," Christina said after a long pause.

Hilda put a hand on Christina's shoulder and left it there for a moment. It felt strange but comforting. Hilda never touched Christina. She wasn't the type to show affection through hugs or smiles. Instead, Christina realized, Hilda showed her affection through sacrifice. And it had drained the life out of her.

Well. Christina would have to put that life back in Hilda. She would try even harder to bring romance into her sister's dreary existence.

"No," Hilda said and dropped her hand. "You should not be sorry. I am not. I am glad that things have been as they were. I love you, you know. And love makes everything worth it."

Christina closed her eyes. She tried to steady her thoughts and organize her words. A difficult realization began to spread through her mind. "It is true—love makes everything worth it. But I fear you have sacrificed love for me." Christina opened her eyes and turned to see her sister's reaction. Hilda sat still as a stone. "You gave up the man you loved because of me, didn't you?"

Hilda did not answer.

"Didn't you?"

Hilda's jaw flexed. "What makes you think that?"

"Because of what you said the other day in the kitchen garden. You said you pursued a man once and never would again. And then you refused to tell me why you lost him."

"I also told you never to speak of it again."

"You lost him because of me, didn't you? That's why you won't tell me."

Hilda hesitated. "You certainly are astute for someone who acts so flighty."

"I am correct, then?"

Hilda nodded her head in a slow, hopeless motion. She looked away. "*Ja.*"

"What happened?"

"I told you, it does not matter now."

"Why not?"

"Because he was not worth loving."

"But you said . . ." Christina frowned. "You did love him, didn't you?"

"*Ja.* I did." Hilda looked defeated. "I did not want to hurt you with this story, Christina."

"I know. But it's too late now."

"He asked me to marry him—but only if I left you behind. He said he could not support a child who was not his."

"Your own sister!"

"*Ja.* My own sister." Hilda smoothed her apron and lifted her chin. "So, you see, he was not worth loving."

"And yet, you *did* love him."

"*Ja.* But I did not marry him."

"No. You did not."

Hilda stared into the fire with a hardened expression. Christina understood that her sister would say no more about it. She studied Hilda with new eyes. Christina had known her sister had sacrificed her youth for them, but she had never realized she had sacrificed love. Even if the man was not worth loving, Hilda had still loved him and she had given him up. For *her.*

A warm, complicated feeling bubbled into Christina's chest. She thought it might be gratitude—and hope. Don't all things work together for good? Wouldn't it all be worth it if Hilda found a better man in the end? Never had Christina felt so determined to find Hilda a husband. And *this* man would be worth loving.

* * *

Johan thought about Christina as he cleared land the next morning. He had plenty of time to think about her, for no matter how many trees he took down, there was always another one. He remembered that she had forgotten all about Wilhelm by the end of yesterday's dinner. The memory made Johan whistle while he worked, until Wilhelm pointed out that they had run out of ammunition for the Jaeger rifle.

The brothers made their own lead balls, but they'd run out of metal too, so there was nothing to melt down to fill the molds. The Pennsylvania backcountry was no place to be caught without ammunition. The Blue Mountains teemed with hungry predators eager to find a man alone. Johan's gaze wandered to the dark, shadowy tree line, where the wilderness loomed around their small clearing. Bears roamed those woods on big, lumbering feet. And last night he'd seen a row of yellow eyes that glowed in the moonlight and circled the campsite. The night had erupted in a chorus of howls that had woken the children and sent shivers down Johan's spine. In the Rhine River Valley, wolves existed only in the old fairy tales. The ancient forests had been cut down and transformed into rolling farmland centuries ago.

But here, at the far edge of the Colonies, a man did not know what he might meet in the darkness of the night. Johan tossed down his ax. He would not wait for that ammunition. If not for himself, then for the sake of his neighbors. Did the Dresser sisters own a musket or a Jaeger rifle? Did they even know how to shoot one? What if they fell under attack from a bear or wolf?

No, it would not do to leave this side of the settlement

unprotected. Thankfully, Christina had a trusty guard dog. Otherwise, he could not bear to think of her alone. But even a guard dog as large and loyal as Bruno could fall to an angry bear.

Johan wiped his forehead and straightened his black beaver felt hat. His mind had drifted to Christina once again. Even the thought of ammunition—a most unladylike subject matter—brought his mind back to her. He pushed her from his thoughts and headed toward his nearest neighbor. One of the best things about being Amish was that neighbors gave freely and expected nothing in return.

Johan trekked through a stand of trees to the narrow footpath that led to Eli and Catrina Webber's homestead. He heard high, carefree laughter drifting through the open window as he reached the door to the cabin. A loud guffaw followed. The door swung open before he could open it and an enormous man with a bushy beard and twinkling blue eyes stared down at him.

"You must be one of the Lantz brothers." The bear of a man leaned against the doorframe and assessed him. "The younger one, *ja*? Johan?"

"*Ja*. How did you know?"

The man laughed in a deep, rumbling way. His ample midsection jiggled, and his eyes danced with amusement. "Because you don't have any children hanging from your waistcoat. I hear your brother is a father three times over."

"*Ja*. That is the truth of it."

The man gave Johan a hearty slap on the back, and Johan shifted forward to catch his balance. "Don't fret, my boy—the backcountry is the best place to find a bride." The man grinned and glanced inside the cabin. "Isn't that right, Gertrud?"

"Don't listen to a word that man says!" a female voice shouted back in a gleeful tone.

"Ah, but where are my manners?" the man asked as he turned back to Johan. "I'm Abram, Eli's brother-in-law. Married his sister, Gertrud. I suppose you met everyone else at the last worship service, but we were down with the fever and ague."

"I hear the Widow Yoder and the Witmers are ailing as well."

Abram nodded. "Strange country, this is. The fever and ague doesn't strike in the winter, as with other fevers. It comes when the weather warms and lingers until fall."

Johan nodded. "We'll all do well to stay out of the night air."

"Indeed." Abram motioned to the door. "But enough gloomy talk. Come in, come in."

"Hello," a stout, serious-looking woman said as Johan walked through the door. "I'm Gertrud. And pay no mind to my husband's teasing. He'll have a little one hanging onto his waistcoat soon enough."

Abram beamed, picked Gertrud up, and spun her around in a circle.

"Put me down, you big oaf!" she said in a firm voice, but her eyes were shining.

"Ah." Johan grinned. "Congratulations."

Gertrud landed on the dirt floor with a thump, straightened her bodice, and wagged a finger at her husband. "I hope this baby is as full of mischief as you are. Then you will finally get what you deserve."

"Two of me. How marvelous!"

Gertrud shook her head. But her smile said she could not get enough of him.

"It's good to see you again." Eli Webber stood up from

the table and offered his stool. Catrina cut a slice of pie before Johan could ask for one. "You must have some dessert."

"I came at the right time."

"Abram agrees," Eli said and laughed. "He always knows when to appear. Arrived for a visit just in time for a meal."

Abram shrugged. "Once you've had one of Catrina's pies, you'll understand."

"And she always manages to have some sugar stored away, somehow," Eli said. "It is remarkable." He gazed down at his wife and rested a hand on her shoulder. "*She* is remarkable."

Johan could make himself at home here. Between the pie and the company, the cabin seemed a very nice place to be. He wondered what it would feel like to be Abram, with a wife at the table and a child on the way. What would it be like to see himself in his own son's face?

Whatever had come over him? It must be the heat of the cabin. A fire roared in the hearth, and the room felt overly hot. He tugged at his collar and frowned. Had he really just daydreamed about being a husband and father? A settled man, deprived of his freedom?

"My goodness, Johan. You look as if you've seen a ghost." Catrina swept across the room in a whirl of skirts and set a plate before him. "Are you quite all right?"

Johan picked up a pewter fork. "*Ja*. Of course. A good slice of pie after a good day's work. What else could a man ask for?"

"A fine, plump wife?" Abram said and grinned at Gertrud.

"Plump. Humph!"

"I should hope so. Who wants a skinny wife? We don't want you wasting away."

Gertrud could not keep the frown on her face and she smiled before turning away to help Catrina scour the dinner pots with sand.

Eli ran a hand through his red hair and left it standing on end like a rooster's comb. Johan wondered if he should tell the poor man, but he thought better of it.

"You *are* looking unwell," Eli said. "Could it be the fever and ague?"

"No, no." Johan shook his head. Had he really looked that aggrieved by thoughts of marriage? Were his feelings that transparent? "I'm hale and hearty, thank you. My only concern is that I've run out of scrap metal to melt into lead balls. I hoped you could help. Hate to be caught alone in the backcountry without a loaded rifle."

"Or a way to catch your supper," Catrina added. She glanced up from her scrubbing and laughed. "Eli. Your hair."

Eli pressed a hand to his head. "Ah. Right." He looked sheepish, but his wife flashed him a dazzling smile that put a grin back on his face.

"I'm sure we can find enough scrap metal to spare," Abram said.

Eli nodded. "We'll find something." His expression shifted to seriousness. "But something more is troubling you, *ja*?"

"Oh." Johan stuffed a fat forkful of pie into his mouth. He shook his head. "Mmmffh hummh."

An amused expression spread across Abram's face. "Ah. I see."

Johan frowned and swallowed. "See what?"

"What's her name?"

"Her name?"

"There's only one thing that gives a man the look on

your face. Who is she? It's a narrow list, to be sure. I could just start naming names. There are only so many eligible young ladies in the wilderness."

"No." Johan frowned and shook his head. "You're quite mistaken. I've no interest in taking a wife just yet."

"Who said anything about taking a wife?"

"You did."

"No. I suggested you have a lovely young lady on your mind. Whether or not you see a future with her is a different matter altogether. But your own words have given you away." Abram flashed a sly smile. "Some men are too afraid to pursue a woman, you know."

Johan's eyes bulged at those words. Too afraid? Bah! He'd never been afraid of a woman's rejection. Granted, he'd never cared about a woman before, but that was irrelevant. Wasn't it?

"Leave him alone, dearest," Gertrud ordered from the hearth. "He looks ready to jump out of his skin. You must stop tormenting the poor man so."

Abram shrugged and gave a dramatic sigh. "If you insist."

"I insist."

"Ah. She insists."

Gertrud laughed and shook her head. "Don't mind him, Johan."

Johan was more than ready to make his escape. "Thank you for the pie, Catrina. It was the best I've ever tasted." He stood up from the table so fast he nearly knocked over a tin cup of water.

"In a hurry to leave?" Abram gave a sly half-smile. "Going to call on a certain young lady?"

"Abram." Gertrud did not need to turn around.

Abram pressed a finger to his lips and winked. "Not another word."

"That was another word," Gertrud said.

"Alas. She wins every time."

"Thank you again. But I must be going." If he didn't escape soon, Abram might drag Christina's name from his lips. And he wasn't ready to admit his true feelings to himself, much less to Abram Zeigler. "Really. My brother expects my hasty return. We have much to clear before the planting."

Johan hurried out the door before anyone could say another word. He was already out of the Webbers' clearing and on the footpath before he realized he had forgotten to collect the scrap metal. Dash it all. Since when had he become such a sniveling lovestruck fool of a man?

Lovestruck? *Love*struck? Had he really said that forbidden word inside his mind?

Yes. He had.

Johan had already admitted to himself that he fancied Christina. He had even admitted to himself that he held *affection* for her. But love? Well, that was going too far. Hadn't he promised himself to enjoy her company and leave it at that? Love would make things far too complicated. He had too many adventures ahead of him to settle down now. He wanted to *live,* dash it all!

And yet, Johan thought of Christina as he doubled back to retrieve the scrap metal. He thought of Christina as he hacked down an oak tree and dragged the limbs to the brush fire. He thought of Christina as he listened to Wilhelm read the boys a Bible verse and a passage from the *Martyrs Mirror* at bedtime.

Johan leaned back on his bedroll and stared into the sky as he listened to his brother's deep, comforting voice. Each star twinkled and winked like a familiar friend looking down on the family. Johan thought about how safe and secure his nephews must feel, tucked into their quilts, watching the stars shimmer above the clearing, hearing the crackle of the campfire, knowing they could trust their father.

Would a family of his own really be such a burden? Were his nephews a burden? No, of course not. Each one was a precious gift—a rowdy, unpredictable gift, but a gift nonetheless. Johan readjusted his pillow and rolled over. Why was he fighting a commitment to Christina Dresser? What was so wrong with letting go? What was so wrong with settling down?

Nothing. Nothing at all. Could it be that Abram was right, that beneath all his bravado, all his self-confidence, Johan was afraid of rejection? What if he finally chose a woman and she didn't want him in return?

Bah! Nonsense! Johan sat up, punched his pillow, and lay down again. The very idea. Of course, Christina would return his affection. Women always melted when he smiled at them. Christina would be no different. *If* he decided to pursue her. And that was a very big if.

Chapter Thirteen

Christina laid the buckets and yoke beside the stream. She should hurry back to the cabin with the morning's water, but the day dawned so bright and beautiful she wanted to breathe it in. Sunlight sparkled across the clear water and lit the silver scales of tiny, darting fish. Wildflowers covered the riverbank in a white carpet and tickled her nose with pollen. She wanted to lie down and sink into the beauty. She imagined it would feel like collapsing into a white snowbank, but without the cold. Spring was surely the most glorious of all *der Herr's* seasons.

A distant voice pulled Christina from her daydream. She stood still and strained to hear the low murmur above the rushing river. Christina smiled. That was a man's voice, and she felt sure she knew which man. What's more, he was singing. The settlement's men often hunted along the edge of the stream, since deer gathered there in the morning. If Johan was nearby, singing loudly enough to wake a sleeping bear, he must have already bagged his dinner. He was probably heading home in a happy mood. Christina left the bucket and yoke by the water and followed the sound of his song. The day was off to a lovely start, and she was sure it would get even better.

Christina hitched up her skirts to hurry toward Johan. The lush, green ferns that grew along the riverbank whispered against her woolen hosen as she walked. Johan must be across the meadow, behind a grove of pines. Christina wondered what she would say when she reached him. She smiled as she wandered along the damp ground, toward Johan's distant voice. Her fingers trailed over the soft petals of wildflowers as she walked. The stalks rippled in the wind like a bright, billowing sea.

A mighty roar tore Christina's attention from the wildflowers. Her chest dropped, and her body tensed. A bear. What else could it be? A loud, confused shout echoed along the riverbank, followed by another terrible growl.

"Johan?" Christina ran toward the shout. "Johan!"

"Stay away!" Johan's voice reached her through the wall of pines that edged the meadow. She hesitated, then plunged forward. Johan, alone with a bear. *Her* Johan! Christina's heart thudded inside her throat as she ran. Her pulse slammed against her temples. Her mouth felt dry as dust. "Johan!"

"Stay away, I say!" She heard a strange, wild panic in his voice. "Stay away!"

Christina did not hesitate this time. She continued to run toward him. Her feet crushed the wildflowers as she left a trail of broken petals behind her. She did not notice. All she knew in that moment was the sound of Johan's voice and the growl of an unseen predator.

A shot rang out. The sharp explosion reverberated across the meadow and echoed through her chest. "Johan! Johan!" Christina froze and strained to hear an angry growl or the heavy movement of a predator in the underbrush. A Jaeger rifle took three minutes to reload. An injured bear could charge and kill a man in seconds. If Johan's first shot had missed its mark. . . .

"Christina!"

Christina realized she had been holding her breath. She sucked in air and shouted Johan's name again. "Are you hurt?"

"No."

Christina's knees felt weak. She had not realized how tense her body had been. Her muscles melted as the adrenaline drained from her. "Where are you?"

"Here. Beyond the pine trees."

Christina hurried to the tree line and plunged into the forest. The cool, piney scent of sap mingled with the sharp smell of gunpowder. White smoke rose toward the sky and faded into the silence of the canopy. Johan stood tall and alert, his eyes hard. "You should not have come."

"Should not have come?" Christina felt a pang of indignation.

"What were you thinking, girl? You could have been killed."

"I run to your aid and that is all you can say?" Christina fired back. "*And* you call me *girl*? We're practically the same age!"

"Ran to my aid?" Johan stared down at her with narrowed eyes. "And just how were you planning to aid me? You've no musket. Did you think you would have a nice chat with the bear and convince him to move on?"

"Well . . ." Christina cleared her throat. When he put it

that way . . . She cleared her throat again and raised her chin. "It's the thought that counts, *ja*?"

"Not when the thought could have gotten us both killed."

"Hardly. There is no need for such dramatics. I can handle myself."

"Can you? Because you just charged into the path of a rampaging bear."

Christina's face tightened as her eyes moved to the bear. The animal lay still on the forest floor. "The poor dear." Christina shook her head. "The poor, wild dear."

"The poor, wild dear charged me without warning."

"Mmmm." Christina looked unconvinced.

"It tried to kill me." Johan threw up his hands, the Jaeger rifle still clenched in whitened knuckles. "And he might have killed you too, had you reached us a moment sooner."

"It was hardly a fair fight."

Johan looked at her with disbelief. "Are you listening to anything I said? That bear charged me. And it would have charged you too. Thanks be to *der Herr* that you don't run any faster than you do."

Johan had a point. But Christina did not like being reprimanded for rushing to his aid. Shouldn't he be thanking her? Or at least acknowledging her courage? Why, most women—most *people*—would have fled. But not her! She had run into danger.

"Thank you would suffice."

"Thank you!" Johan's eyes lit with what looked like fire. His jaw clenched so hard it trembled. "What would

I have done if you had been hurt or killed? How could I live with that?"

"Oh." *Oh!* Christina felt a victorious smile soften her face. Johan cared for her. She had suspected it—felt it. But to hear him say it gave her a thrill of joy. "You couldn't live with that, you say?"

Johan's brows drew together. "No," he said in a harsh voice.

"Mmmm. I see." She understood why he was angry. It was adorable, really. Men always flew to anger when they were afraid. It made them feel braver, she supposed. Christina let out a lovesick sigh. He had been afraid for her. Oh, happy day, he was *beside* himself with fear for her!

"Why are you looking at me like that?" Johan's brow relaxed a fraction.

Christina smiled and shrugged. "Oh, I don't know." But her eyes said she did.

"First, you risk both our lives, then you look at me like *that*."

"Like what?" Christina blinked at him through long, thick lashes. She could hear her heartbeat. Johan stared back at her. Christina knew he could not ignore the moment between them. The connection felt as real as the danger had an instant before.

Johan cleared his throat. His face softened, and the anger melted into a sheepish expression. Christina's knowing smile widened. That was a look of fear on his face— an entirely different kind of fear than he had shown earlier. This was a fear of commitment. Only a man who feels affection for a woman but doesn't want to admit it would look like that. Which could only mean one thing. Johan

Lantz returned her affection. She had suspected, but now she knew for certain.

Christina stared into his eyes and wondered if she should tell him everything. A scheme always worked better with a partner. And what better partner could there be than the man she wanted to marry? Christina felt such a thrill of hope and excitement that she did not know if she could contain herself.

Johan felt the frustration drain away. He had been beside himself with fear when he'd seen Christina throw herself into danger. What had she been thinking? Would she fight a bear with nothing but her bare hands and sweet disposition? Had his first shot missed its mark, Christina would have been a dangerous distraction at best. He did not want to think of what she could have been at worst. The backcountry was no place for the foolhardy. He ought to give her a lecture. He ought to warn her never to set foot in the forest again. Had the girl no common sense?

Clearly, she did not. She had even carried on about the poor bear. The bear that had wanted to rip him apart! Johan glanced at the bear and frowned. He did not want to admit it, but he almost agreed with her. It was a shame he'd had to shoot the bear. This was not the season for it. Bears ought to be left alone to raise their cubs in the spring. Dash it all, he was going as soft and dreamy as Christina. Bears couldn't be allowed to rip one apart, and that was that.

Johan felt his frustration reignite. This girl understood nothing about survival. A small voice reminded him that he did not either. He was just a farmer from a green, settled valley who'd crossed an ocean and plunged into a strange, unfamiliar land.

Except for bears. He knew bears were dangerous. Anyone could see that. He started to tell Christina so. She ought to listen to common sense. But her eyes locked on his and the words got lost in his throat. Her gaze melted him and warmed something deep inside his chest. He could not form a sound. Johan swallowed. He had never frozen like this before, not even when the bear stood on its hind legs, towering over him, and roared. He had seen the glistening teeth and yellow claws—and held steady.

He could manage a bear, but not a woman? Bah!

But those eyes continued to bore into his. He felt his frustration soften. She had reached a place inside him that no other woman had before. He tried to keep his gaze steady. "Why did you come when I told you not to?"

Her chin raised a bit, but she did not break eye contact. "I was afraid for you. I could not bear to think . . ." She cut herself off and looked away. Johan watched the vein in her throat flutter. He wanted to touch her face. He wanted to draw her close and tell her nothing would ever hurt either of them. He would not allow it. Christina hesitated. She glanced into his eyes, then down again. "Nothing else mattered but you."

"Not even Wilhelm?"

Christina frowned. "Why . . ." She shook her head and looked confused. "Of course not. I told you, nothing else mattered but *you*!"

Nothing else mattered but him. Those were the words of a woman in love. She did return his affection. Of course, she did. Women always returned his affection. Or more accurately, they held far more affection for him than he did for them.

But no other woman had risked her life for him. True, it had been a foolish risk—there was nothing she could have done. But, somehow, that made it all the more poignant. She had been consumed with fear for him, consumed with the need to go to him. Other women had fallen for him, but no other woman had done *that*. An unarmed woman against an angry bear? Preposterous. And yet, she had run toward it.

Johan felt a long puff of air escape his lips. What now? This was not a connection he could ignore. He remembered the warmth of Eli Webber's cabin. Would it be so bad to settle down with a woman who would fight a bear for him? A small smile flickered across his face. No, it would not be bad at all.

Christina looked concerned. "Have you no response?"

Oh, he had a response, all right. He wanted to scoop her into his arms, lift her up, and spin her around while she laughed. He wanted to tell her how daring and beautiful and remarkable she was. "It was terribly foolhardy," he said instead.

Her face crumpled, and he wished he could take back the words. Why had he said that? It was true—she had done a terrible, foolish thing. And he loved her for it. He loved her brashness. He loved her act-first, think-later bravado. He had never met a woman quite like her. But could he tell her that? Was he really ready to tie himself to one woman for life?

Christina met his gaze with courage even though he knew the words stung. "Perhaps." She kept her eyes on his. "Although a gentleman would thank me regardless."

"I am not a gentleman. I am a poor farmer who would rather not find himself in the jaws of a hungry bear."

"Well!"

"Or find a lovely woman in the jaws of a hungry bear."

"Mmmm." She hesitated, then set her face in a firm expression. "A lovely woman, you say?"

"*Ja.*" Now it was his turn to hesitate.

"Go on, then."

Johan cleared his throat. "A lovely, bold woman who has—" Johan was about to say "captured my heart" when a rustle in the underbrush drew their attention. The ferns trembled, and a furry face peeked up from the leaves. Wide, black eyes stared up at them.

"Why, it's a cub!" Christina dropped to her knees and scooped up the brown, fuzzy creature. "Oh, you poor darling. You poor, poor thing." She pressed the small, wriggling body to her chest and whispered soothing words into its little round ear.

Johan wondered if he should finish his sentence. He had been about to make the announcement of his life.

"The poor thing is an orphan now. What has Johan done to you, poor darling?"

Johan sighed. He would not finish his sentence. The moment to declare his affection had disappeared. Christina was back to blaming him for saving his own skin. Would she rather he had lain down and offered himself up for breakfast? "You have a way of making a man feel less than appreciated, my dear." He felt a little relieved that the cub had interrupted him. He should stop and think before telling a woman—even the captivating Christina—that she had captured his heart.

"Oh! Forgive me, Johan. One can hardly help defending oneself. But just look at him!" Christina pressed her face into the cub's fur. He nibbled the edge of her prayer *kappe* and she laughed. "You see, he likes me. What shall we name him?"

"Oh no, Christina. We are not naming him."

"But we must."

"Naming him means forming an attachment. And we do not need to form an attachment with a bear." Johan frowned. *Or with lovely young women . . .*

"Don't listen to that grumpy old Johan." Christina kissed the cub on the top of its soft, furry head. "You are coming home with me."

"Think this through, Christina. Although I know that is against your nature."

"Really, Johan." Christina stood up and wrapped her apron around the cub as she pressed him against her chest. "Are you always so tiresome?"

"Yes. Always."

"I thought you were more fun than this."

"Forgive me. Being nearly killed by a bear drains one of good humor for the day."

"Mmmm." Christina's attention stayed on the little cub. "Fuzzy is a fine name for a fuzzy bear, *ja*?"

Johan knew when he had been defeated. "A fine name."

"It's the least we can do, the poor darling."

"We could let nature take its course."

"Never."

"The woods are full of orphaned animals. You cannot save them all. You cannot change the world."

Christina turned her eyes from the cub to look up at

Johan. Her gaze felt sure and strong. "No, but we can change the world for this one little bear."

Johan felt himself smile. He wanted to tell Christina it was preposterous to save a bear. But he could not argue with the sincerity in those clear blue eyes. "Very well then." Johan reached out and scratched behind a velvety brown ear. "Come along, Fuzzy."

Christina and Johan paused outside the cabin door.

"Hilda won't like this."

"No, she won't like this at all." Johan grinned. "But I'm sure that has never stopped you before."

Christina furrowed her brow. "I only do what's best for her."

"But of course."

"No. Really."

"I did not argue that."

"Not with your words. But I saw the look in your eyes."

"Christina, you are incorrigible, you know."

Christina's eyes sparked. "*I* am incorrigible!"

"So you admit it?"

"No! I was denying it!"

"And yet, you did say *you* were incorrigible."

They both laughed. Johan felt warm and full as he watched Christina's eyes sparkle. She laughed freely, without any self-consciousness or pretense, and yet she managed to remain so feminine, so delicate and charming. Christina pressed a finger to her lips. "Shhhh. We have to think of a plan before Hilda hears us. I can't imagine how she'll react—"

The wooden door rattled. "Too late," Johan interrupted. This was going to be quite a show. Hilda did not seem the type to welcome wild animals into her snug little home. Christina set her face in a firm, no-nonsense expression— or at least what she must think was a firm, no-nonsense expression. Johan thought she looked like a child pretending to be serious. She wore a funny-looking frown and that adorable crinkle between her eyes.

The door swung open, and Hilda stood before them with narrow eyes, hands on her hips. "Well, if you two aren't loud enough to wake the dead. I thought you'd never get back with the water." Hilda looked at Christina, and her eyes narrowed further. "You did bring back the water, didn't you?"

"No."

Johan leaned into Christina's ear and whispered, "Relax. You look like you've swallowed a fly. Or something bigger. A goat, maybe."

"What?" Christina looked confused. She lowered her voice. "I'm trying to look serious."

"*Ja*. I know. That's the problem."

"Christina." Hilda's eyes continued to narrow. "I'm standing right here. I can hear you."

"*Ja*."

"And Johan's right. You look ridiculous."

"Oh." Christina relaxed her face.

"And I know you're up to no good whenever you try to look that serious."

"Oh."

Hilda waited, but Christina said no more. "The water?" Hilda asked after a long pause.

"*Ja*. I brought something better."

"Where are the buckets and yoke?"

"Oh, that. I forgot all about them. I told you, I've got something so much better."

Hilda sighed. She did not look convinced. Christina's apron covered the cub, but he stirred and the linen cloth shifted. Hilda's eyes moved downward. "What are you hiding?" As she said the words, the cub poked his head out of the apron and stared at Hilda with wet, black eyes. His mouth opened into what looked like a mischievous grin. Then his mouth snapped shut and he began to chew on the hem of Christina's apron. "Oh, for heaven's sake! What have you done this time?"

"Isn't it wonderful!" Christina stared down at the cub with adoring eyes.

"Wonderful?" Hilda's face fell. "Wonderful?" She shook her head. "What are you thinking? That is a wild animal, not a pet. You must take him back to the forest immediately. The very idea! Treating a wild thing like a puppy. You're doing that animal no favors, you know."

"Fuzzy."

"What?"

"I'm doing Fuzzy no favors."

Hilda closed her eyes, took a deep breath and opened them again. "So you agree."

"Of course not. I'm merely correcting your sentence. You called him 'that animal,' but he's much more than that."

"A bear is a bear. That is all there is to it."

"Not this bear. He is a friend in need." Christina met Hilda's stare with a dignified expression. "And you always say that, as Amish, it is our duty to help a friend in need."

"I mean people, Christina. People! Bears don't count." Hilda's lips tightened. "You know that. For heaven's sake."

Christina's eyes held a take-no-prisoners spark. "Well, you never specified."

"I shouldn't have to. You are being ridiculous."

"Mmmm. I see. So you are not true to your word when it comes to hospitality?"

Hilda flushed red. Johan could see the heat of exasperation flare beneath her skin and cover her cheeks. "Of course, I am."

Christina shrugged. "I suppose I will have to rethink all the lessons you've taught me. After all, if friends are not always welcome at our door . . ."

"A bear is not a friend!"

"Ah, but *this* one is." Christina pulled the cub from her apron and held him aloft. His legs dangled as he stared eye to eye with Hilda. Johan could not help but smile at the sight.

"I suppose you are behind this too, Johan Lantz."

"What, me?" He dropped his smile and assumed his most innocent expression.

Hilda put on her most severe expression.

Johan shrugged. "I'm just a poor farmer, trying to make my way in the wilderness."

Hilda snorted.

"It's only until he grows up, Hilda." Christina lifted Fuzzy a fraction closer to Hilda's face. He kicked his legs and turned his head to try to nibble at Christina's hand. Christina laughed. "I wouldn't try to keep him when he's grown."

"What happens after you let him go and he wanders back and takes a sheep for his supper? Have you thought of that?"

"He isn't a wolf."

Hilda looked upward and threw her hands in the air. "Well, thank heaven for small mercies."

"And anyway, I've never heard of bears taking sheep. They keep themselves to themselves, it seems."

Johan cleared his throat and looked down.

"Oh, except for Fuzzy's poor mother. She did charge Johan. But that was his fault, really."

Johan raised his eyebrows.

"You never should have come between a mother and her cub. What did you expect?"

"Ah. The next time I am alone in the forest, minding my own business, I will have to remember not to accidentally stumble upon a mother bear and her cub."

"Precisely."

"All right, you two. That's enough. I have plenty to deal with aside from your bickering."

"Oh, I'm so glad you agree with me," Christina said and beamed. "Fuzzy will be a lot to deal with, but I'm sure we will manage just fine."

"No, that's not what I meant."

"But you wouldn't accuse a good Amish man of bickering. That would be quite uncharitable, dear."

"I didn't mean—"

Johan smiled. "And yet, you did say . . ."

"Oh, don't you try to trap me."

"Trap you? I'm not the one who accused someone of bickering." Johan tried to keep a straight face, but seeing the exasperation in Hilda's expression was too much. He was enjoying playing along with Christina. He couldn't remember the last time he had gotten along so well with a woman. It was as if they had planned the conversation.

Hilda's face turned a deeper shade of red and she shook her head. "Fine." Her eyes narrowed and she shook her head again. "Fine. You win."

"Oh, Hilda. You have won too. I am sure you and Fuzzy will become fast friends. You'll thank me one day."

"Humph!" Hilda crossed her arms and glared at Johan.

"And I suppose you will be traipsing off and leaving me to deal with this . . . this . . . *creature*?"

"Ah, well. Now that you mention it, I do have a full day's work ahead of me. Plenty of trees to clear." He shrugged and gave his most innocent smile. "A pity, that."

"His name is Fuzzy," Christina cut in. "Not creature. Do try to keep up, Hilda. And you've always been so good with names."

"Arrrghhh!"

"Are you all right?" Johan switched his expression to one of concern. "Something caught in your throat?"

Hilda closed her eyes, covered her face with her hands, and shook her head. "Oh, you two make quite a pair. Quite a pair indeed." Johan did not want to imagine how red her face must be behind her hands. Fortunately, he did not have to, for Hilda whirled around, marched back into the cabin, and shut the door firmly behind her.

"Well, that went well," Christina said to the closed door.

Johan thought she would be flustered, but when he looked at her, Christina's face was as placid as a lake. She pulled Fuzzy to her chest and buried her face in his fur.

"Oh, you're being serious?"

"*Ja*. She barely put up a fight. She's given up, I think. She knows I'll win in the end anyway."

Johan shook his head. "I suspect there is more to you than shows on the surface."

Christina grinned. "Perhaps I am not so silly after all?"

Johan's smile faded, and he studied her thoughtfully. "Perhaps not."

"Mmmmm. One never knows." She kissed the cub's head, then shifted her attention to Johan. "Thank you for defending Fuzzy. I thought you were against keeping him."

Johan shrugged. He *had* been against the idea. So why

had he defended Christina's plan? Johan began to feel hot and stuffy. He cleared his throat and tugged at his collar with a finger. There was no answer but the truth. He cleared his throat again. He had no problem telling women sweet nothings—after which they would giggle and go on their way. But he didn't want this woman to giggle and go on her way. He wanted to form a connection with her. Heaven help him. A connection!

Johan hesitated. "Because I wanted to make you happy."

Christina gazed up at him with a soft expression that spoke more than words. He could see the adoration in her eyes. He swallowed hard. There was no turning back now. He was hooked—and so was she.

Johan was not a patient man. Once he made up his mind that he wanted something, he saw no point in waiting. He wanted to connect with Christina. No, more than that. He wanted a lasting relationship with Christina. He wanted to hear her delightful giggle every day. He wanted to see the willful spark in her eye and the sheepish blush in her cheeks. She was such a mesmerizing contradiction— soft and feminine as well as strong-willed and independent. He had thought her rather shallow at first, but the more they interacted, the more Johan realized she had a depth to her thoughts that other people overlooked. And when he thought of her with that bear cub! What an adorable, ridiculous, intriguing woman she was.

As he headed home from Christina's cabin, the full force of his emotions hit him. It felt as if all the feelings he had withheld from other women had combined and struck him with an irresistible power. Johan had buried any desire for commitment so deep within him that he'd thought he would never want to marry. But Christina had dug and dug through his defenses until she hit home—and his heart burst to the surface as water pours from the ground after the digging of a good well.

Johan threw up his hands and looked upward, into the sky. "All right. I give up. I can't stop thinking about her. I can't stop imagining having her by my side every day, until we both grow old together. It isn't enough to love her from afar. I want to spend the rest of my life with her." And that was that. There was nothing else to do but ask her to marry him.

Marry him?

Now this really did seem like the fever and ague. Fever, chills, hallucinations. He didn't have the first two symptoms—but mayhap he had the third? Could he be imagining his love for Christina? Johan shook his head and laughed out loud. He startled a flock of birds, and they took to the sky in a whirl of feathers and beating wings. No, he was not hallucinating. He was in love.

He had no experience with such things, of course. But if love meant he couldn't get a woman out of his mind, he wanted to be with her every moment of the day, and he would do anything for her, then this was love.

Oh, it was rash of him to jump to love so soon. Plenty of couples married without ever reaching that stage. Affection and companionship were reasonable expectations. But love? Johan laughed again. What had come over him? Could a man fall in love this fast?

Yes, he realized. That was why they called it falling. And that was precisely what he had done. He had fallen so hard, he still had not caught himself.

And suddenly, it all became clear. Johan had always wanted to squeeze out every adventure life could offer him. He had always wanted to live—really *live*. He never thought he could be contented if he were tied down with a wife and children. But now he realized love *was* his next adventure. Life without love was not really living. If he loved, and was loved in return, then—and only then— would he live life to the fullest.

Chapter Fourteen

Wilhelm stared at his brother with a strange expression as Johan entered the clearing. Fritz ran to Johan, stumbled to a halt, and furrowed his brow. He stared up at his uncle with a confused look.

"What?" Johan asked. "What's the matter with everybody?"

"It isn't us," Fritz said. "It's you! What's the matter with *you*?"

"What do you mean?"

"You look so . . . so . . . ." Fritz's frown deepened as he searched for the word. "So funny."

"I look funny, do I?"

"It's your smile," Wilhelm said from across the clearing. "Can't you wipe that silly grin off your face?"

"Sure can't."

"Ah." Wilhelm stoked the fire. "So you *are* in love."

"Love!" Fritz made a face. "Yuck!" He shook his head and dashed off to find his brothers.

Johan shrugged, widened his grin, and began to whistle as he loped across the clearing.

"*Ja.* You're in love, all right."

Johan just shrugged again.

"And does Christina Dresser return your love?"

Johan dropped onto a log and leaned into the campfire to warm his hands. "I never said I was in love."

"You didn't have to."

"Mmmmm." Johan stared into the fire with a distant, dreamy look.

"Oh, for heaven's sake, Johan. Get a hold of yourself."

Johan pulled himself from his thoughts. He grinned at his brother and ran his fingers through his hair. "I think I'll propose. As soon as possible. Not today. I've just left there. Might seem pushy. Tomorrow morning. First thing."

Wilhelm's mouth fell open.

"Oh, you don't agree? You think I should go back there tonight? Is tomorrow too late?"

"Heaven above, brother. What's happened? Where has Johan gone, and who is this poor, lovestruck creature left in his place?"

"So tomorrow morning sounds good?"

Wilhelm made a sound in his throat and shook his head.

"Tomorrow it is."

"Johan. Listen to yourself. You've just met this girl. And now you're talking marriage! You! Marriage! It's impossible. You always say you want to be free and single."

Johan smiled and sighed dreamily. "All things are possible."

"Is it possible that she'll say no?"

Johan laughed and slapped his brother on the back. "Now that *is* impossible."

"Ah, I see." Wilhelm did not look convinced.

"When you go through your whole life with no thought of love, it catches up to you eventually." Johan flashed a goofy grin. "It catches up to you in an instant."

"And has it caught up to Christina in an instant?"

Johan jerked his attention to his brother. "Of course, it has." He furrowed his brow and cleared his throat. "Anything else is impossible."

"But you just said all things are possible."

Johan's frown became a scowl. "Dash it all, Wilhelm. Can't you just relax and celebrate a man's impending marriage?"

Wilhelm raised his hands with an innocent expression. "Let me be the first to congratulate you then." He paused for emphasis, then leaned forward. "*If* a marriage truly is pending."

"What's the matter with you?" Johan's face flared with frustration—and a twinge of fear, though he would never admit that. Christina did return his affection. Didn't she? Sure, he had thought she had eyes for Wilhelm, but he had been mistaken. Hadn't he? Hadn't he connected with her over the last few days?

"Easy, now." Wilhelm put a hand on his brother's shoulder. "I'm on your side."

"Are you?"

"*Ja*. I just want you to think about this. It's rather sudden, isn't it? Don't you want to give it a little more time? Overnight, you have shifted from disavowing marriage to jumping into one."

"I know what I want, and I can't see any reason to wait, dash it all."

Wilhelm shrugged. "All right, then. I wish you all the best. And I'll miss you. So will the boys."

"Don't worry. We'll keep working the land together. Christina is wonderful good with children. She'll make a perfect stand-in mother until you remarry."

Wilhelm's face looked carefully expressionless. Johan felt too excited to notice. Everything was going his way.

Johan headed to Christina's cabin before the sun had fully risen, filled with a sense of purpose. After a good night's sleep, he felt as sure about his plans for marriage as he had the day before. He had denied his feelings since the night Christina had found him trapped atop the wood-pile. But the truth had kept at him, like the steady drip of rain through a leaky cabin roof. The more he tried to push Christina from his mind, the more she invaded. That lively giggle, those rosy cheeks and dancing, blue eyes. Every-thing about her was seared into his mind. She had snared him, all right.

He had no peace. No recourse. There was nothing to do but march over to her cabin and invite himself into her life.

It shouldn't take much effort. More than a few women had fallen head over heels for him in the past. More than a few fathers had hoped to snag him for a son-in-law. He was handsome, rugged, and capable. Not to mention charming. His only weakness was pride.

As an Amish man, pride was absolutely forbidden. The one character trait he must resist above all else. He was a Plain man, committed to Plain ideals. And yet, could he help that women enjoyed his company? Or melted when he flashed his signature grin? Dash it all, he would have to work harder to be humble.

But he would not worry about that today. Today was a day for joy and celebration. He had finally come to grips with his feelings for Christina. He *did* want to settle down. He *did* want all that his brother had—and more. He wanted Christina Dresser in his life, and he could hardly wait to burst through her door. They had not known each other very long, but in the backcountry men and women often married out of practicality, and remarried quickly after a spouse passed away. Surviving the wilderness was easier with a partner.

He knew he loved Christina, and he believed Christina loved him—if he ignored that little, nagging worry inside that told him she might reject him. He ignored it. Johan took a deep, cleansing breath of pine and fresh morning air. A slow, easy smile spread across his face. He would be engaged by nightfall.

Johan leaned against the threshold and waited for the door to open. The smell of fresh cut wood and damp earth felt familiar and comforting. He could hear whispers inside the cabin and the thump of a stool hitting the wall. Fabric rustled. He wondered if he should have some words prepared. He frowned when he realized that he had no idea what to say. Could he just rush in and ask her to marry him? Of course, he could! What else would he do? She would say yes. She had to say yes.

But what if she didn't?

Johan gnawed on the edge of a cuticle as he waited. His stomach churned and his throat felt tight. He had never felt this way before. He had never even *thought* of feeling this way before. How could a marriage proposal throw him into a panic? Oh sure, he looked calm enough as he leaned against the threshold ready to flash an easy smile. But on the inside he felt as if he might explode.

Dash it all, he was not supposed to feel this way. He was supposed to make *women* feel this way. Hadn't they always fawned over him, hoping for a proposal? And now, here he was, on the other side of the table. Impossible. Inconceivable.

There was only one solution. He had to remind himself who he was. He was Johan Lantz, the man who had never been rejected. He squared his shoulders. Why would he be rejected now? He wouldn't be. *Couldn't* be. He was not a man who got rejected. He was a man who rejected others.

Johan nodded. He felt better already. Christina Dresser would melt in his arms when he proposed. She would cry tears of joy and then ask how quickly they could marry. *Why not this week?* he would ask, and she would nod as she dabbed her eyes with her apron and gazed at him with adoration. Johan chuckled. How foolish he had been to doubt. He knew who he was and how to get his way. He should have this wrapped up in no time.

The door opened, and Christina stood in the sliver of light from the oil lamp on the table behind her. Her lips slid into a soft smile. So far so good. He really had been foolish to doubt himself. Look how her eyes sparkled to see him!

"Johan! How good of you to come." She motioned inside. "I've got to do the milking soon, but we've got breakfast left if you'd like some." Fuzzy bounded across the dirt floor and skidded to a stop beside Christina. He huddled against her ankles and stared up at Johan.

"How's the little fellow doing?"

"He's a little angel." Christina stooped down and whisked the cub into her arms. She kissed his wet black nose and smiled. "Aren't you, Fuzzy?"

"He's eating?"

"Oh, *ja*. He laps sheep's milk from a bowl just like a puppy."

"But he isn't a puppy, Christina." Hilda's voice carried across the cabin.

Christina gave a sly smile. "You know you love him, Hilda. Even though you'll never admit it."

"Love a bear? Bah! I'll do no such thing. And you ought not either if you know what's good for you. He'll be grown up and gone by winter, and you'll be left with a broken heart."

Christina kissed the cub on the head. "Winter is a long way away, *ja*?" She scratched behind a soft round ear. "And don't listen to that mean old Hilda. She doesn't understand that love is worth everything."

"I heard that."

"Good. That was my intent."

"Humph."

Christina turned her attention back to Johan. "Do come in."

"Oh." He cleared his throat. "Actually. I thought we might sit outside. I'd like to talk to you."

"Oh?" Christina looked surprised. "All right. I suppose it's light enough now." Dawn spread over the tree line and painted the forest in pale pinks and blues. She gave Hilda a quick glance over her shoulder as she followed Johan outside. "Be back in a moment, Hilda."

"You can milk the sheep while you—" The door shut before Hilda finished her sentence.

"Hilda's right. I ought to do the milking while we talk."

Johan frowned. He wanted this to be a momentous experience for Christina. He didn't want to propose while her attention was on her milking pail. That would be most unromantic. "I had hoped to sit for a moment." He led her toward the hand-hewn bench that rested against the side of the cabin. "There's something you'll want to hear."

"Is there?" Christina's face brightened. "He's got news for us, Fuzzy." The cub wriggled against her chest, and she let him leap out of her arms as she settled onto the bench beside Johan. "Let me guess. Someone new has come to the settlement?" She clasped her hands together. "Or perhaps Greta is with child? Or Catrina? I hear that Gertrud will have a little one before fall arrives. Oh, she was a bitter one before she met Abram. You didn't know her then, but she's like a different person now, the poor dear. Although she still has a rather severe streak. I always thought that she and Hilda should have been sisters. They are rather alike, though Hilda is not quite as severe perhaps. I think—"

Johan laughed and held up his hand. "No. It's nothing like that."

"Oh. Well, I suppose it would have been strange for you to rush over first thing in the morning to tell me a neighbor you've barely met is with child." Christina laughed. "I am silly, aren't I?" She cocked her head and looked at him with a curious expression. "Why *are* you here?"

"That's what I've been trying to tell you."

Christina smiled again, but it faded quickly. Johan realized that he was scowling. He must look annoyed with her, although he was not. He simply couldn't wait to hear her answer. The wait was unbearable. What if—he cut off the thought. No. She would not say no. He would make sure she said yes, if it took all the charm he had to give.

Christina sat still with her hands folded in her lap. Her face looked uncertain. Johan realized he was still scowling.

Charm her, dash it all! *Charm her!* He inhaled and exhaled to steady his nerves. He let an easy smile spread over his face. He relaxed and leaned back against the cabin's rough log wall. It was important to look at ease when wooing a woman. Women like a man who is sure of himself. Johan stretched out his legs, crossed his boots at the ankle, and began.

"I have good news."

"*Ja?*" Christina still looked uncertain. "Are you sure? You looked rather severe a moment ago."

"Ah." He let his smile widen into a reassuring grin. "Not to worry. I was distracted by a passing thought. But now"—he leaned a bit closer and let his gaze penetrate deep into her eyes—"I want to talk about you." He heard a little intake of air and her eyes widened.

"About me?"

"*Ja.*" He let the grin slip back into his signature, casual smile. Women had always loved that smile. It made him look dashing and unobtainable. He had perfected it over the years.

Christina swallowed. "What about me?"

"I know what you need."

"What I need?" Her eyes began to narrow. "I don't understand."

"What's best for you."

"Best for me?" Her eyebrows began to rise even as her eyes narrowed.

Johan took her hand and held it between his own. The skin felt warm and soft beneath his calloused fingers. Christina looked surprised, then confused, but she did not let go.

"I have it all figured out."

Christina did not answer. She just kept staring at him.

"You'll marry me."

She flinched. "I'll what?"

Johan frowned. Had he said the wrong thing? Perhaps she hadn't heard him clearly. "You'll marry me," he repeated.

Christina's cheeks began to redden. But her face did not look flushed with shyness or excitement. Her face looked flushed with frustration. Johan felt confused. Christina was not crying tears of joy. She was not dabbing her eyes with the corner of her apron and gazing up at him with adoration.

"So that's a yes?" he asked and stared at her with a growing sense of concern.

"Oh." Christina's eyes dropped. She slid her hand from his and began to pick at the folds of her apron. "I'm afraid it's not so simple. I have to think of—"

"No." Johan shook his head. Cold, undeniable panic slid down his throat and spread through his stomach. "You don't understand." He cleared his throat and plunged forward. He would convince her. He would show her that everything would be perfect if she would only say yes. "You'll marry me and I'll take care of everything. We can live with Wilhelm until other arrangements can be made. Don't worry, I have it all worked out. You'll be glad you said yes. Just trust me."

"Until other arrangements can be made? You have it all worked out?"

Christina's gaze moved from her lap to his eyes. Her brow furrowed in an expression between confusion and exasperation.

Johan could not read her face and decided to double

down. "*Ja*. Just trust me to take care of everything. You don't need to worry your pretty little head about anything."

"Worry my pretty little head?" Christina's expression was definitely one of exasperation now. Johan frowned. He slipped off his black beaver felt hat and scratched his head. She was annoyed with him, but he couldn't understand why. Didn't she want a dashing man to sweep her off her feet and take care of her? He studied her face for a moment without speaking. She stared back. He had forgotten to get down on one knee. Maybe that was it.

Johan lowered himself to the ground. He could feel the damp earth soak through the knee of his woolen breeches. "I'm the man for you," he said and flashed his best, most practiced smile. Surely she couldn't resist that. Women never resisted that smile.

But she did not burst into tears of joy. She did not gaze at him with adoration. Her face hardened and she raised her chin. Johan felt the situation spin away from him. His mouth went dry and his heart pounded in his throat. He wished he were any place but here. His worst fear had come true. The woman he loved was rejecting him. It was unbearable. He had to show her they were meant to be together. The words poured from his mouth in a desperate tangle of need. "You know, a lot of women have dreamed of being in your position right now. More than a few women have been heartbroken because they wanted to marry me. But you are the only woman I've ever asked to marry me! Can't you see how special you are? How special *this* is?" He gestured from him to her then back to himself again, trying to show her they had a once-in-a-lifetime connection. She had to see. She *had* to.

She did not.

* * *

"A lot of women have dreamed of being in my position right now?" The nerve! Christina wanted to fly off the bench, run into the house, and slam the door shut. Instead, she raised her chin and met his gaze. A marriage proposal from Johan Lantz should have been a dream come true. But not when he had the audacity to tell her she should be grateful for his affections. Grateful indeed! Oh, it was insufferable.

Christina opened her mouth to explain why she could not marry him yet. Then she closed it again. Humph! He did not deserve an explanation. Johan kept staring at her with that arrogant smile. Christina began to feel hot and sweaty beneath her neck cloth and wool bodice. She swallowed hard. How dare he tell her what she would do with her life! He had it all planned out—as if her *pretty little head* could not think for itself. He stared down at her with that arrogant smile. As if she ought to thank him for the gift of his proposal! The very idea!

Well. She would not succumb to such a proposal. That would show him. He could marry one of those other women if they liked him so much. Christina straightened her posture. This would take willpower. She must not give in to Johan's charms. Not when he made it clear that he saw her as a silly little woman who needed a man to sweep in and solve her problems. She and Hilda had been doing just fine, thank you very much. And they would continue to do just fine without Johan Lantz!

Christina knew what she had to say. She did not look away. She drew a deep breath and tried to speak calmly, even though her heart trembled inside her chest with disappointment and frustration. In her daydreams, this was the moment when she imagined she would share her matchmaking plans for Hilda with him. The plan would be wildly successful, and they would have a double wedding before the end of the planting season. Her daydreams did not account for Johan's arrogance. So she said the opposite of what her heart felt and offered no explanation. "I will not marry you, Johan Lantz."

His eyes flickered with an emotion she could not read. Somewhere, far beneath his smooth self-confidence, she sensed vulnerability and desperation. But her frustration was too strong to consider his feelings. She heard her next words tumble out of her mouth before she could stop them. "Why don't you ask one of those other women? I'm sure they would be grateful to win a proposal from the great and mighty Johan Lantz!"

Johan's face crumpled. He scrambled to his feet, slammed his beaver felt hat on his head, and backed away. "Good day, then," he said in a flat, distant voice. He stared at her for a moment, opened his mouth again, closed it, and shook his head. His face no longer looked arrogant or self-assured. He almost looked like a crushed little boy. But that would be impossible. Wouldn't it? Christina felt her frustration weaken and she almost apologized, but he whirled around and stalked away before she could say anything. Christina watched him until he disappeared into the forest. She kept staring at the tree line for a long time.

Chapter Fifteen

Christina did not move from the bench. She replayed the proposal over and over in her mind. She did not know how much time had passed when Hilda swung open the door of the cabin, rested her hands on her hips, and peered around the threshold. "There you are. This is no time for daydreaming. There's the milking to do."

Christina did not look up. Hilda paused and studied her sister's profile. Her face softened. "Something's happened, *ja*?"

"*Ja*." Christina's voice sounded flat and faraway.

Hilda wiped her hands on her apron as she walked outside. She settled onto the bench and leaned against Christina's shoulder. The wood creaked under her weight. They sat without talking for a while. Christina liked the warm weight of Hilda's shoulder. It made her feel that she was not alone. When she finally turned to speak to Hilda, Christina's eyes and nose were red.

"You've been crying," Hilda said.

"*Ja*."

"Something to do with Johan?"

"*Ja*."

Hilda waited, her shoulder still resting comfortably

against Christina. The silence felt safe, and Christina was glad Hilda didn't push for an explanation. A butterfly flitted past on bright, yellow wings. Fuzzy growled and bounded after it. He tripped over his feet and somersaulted onto his nose. Christina almost laughed. Then she remembered that her life was over. Johan had turned out to be an arrogant imposter. What had happened to the man she loved?

"Your life isn't over, you know," Hilda said at last.

Christina gasped. "How did you know what I was thinking?"

"Because I know how dramatic you are."

"That's not very nice. Especially when my life *is* over."

"Ah. So I am correct."

"About the latter. Not the former. I am not being dramatic. This situation *is* dramatic. Johan, he . . . he . . ." Christina squeezed her eyes shut and turned away. She had to be careful not to say too much.

"He what?"

"He . . ." Christina swallowed.

"Oh, go on now. Spit it out. You'll feel better."

Christina's chin wobbled. She could feel her resolve weakening. She had to tell someone. "He . . . proposed!"

Hilda raised her eyebrows. "The beast."

"No, you don't understand."

"Clearly not."

Christina spun around on the bench to stare into Hilda's eyes. "He said he had it all planned."

"The monster."

"He already had it all worked out."

"Beastly." Hilda looked like she might smile. The amusement showed in her eyes.

"No. You don't understand."

Hilda raised her eyebrows again. She looked as if she understood very well.

"He said I didn't need to worry my pretty little head about anything." Christina narrowed her eyes. "As if I'm just a pretty little woman who can't think for herself!"

"That doesn't sound like Johan. I've heard him compliment your intelligence on several occasions."

Christina's face changed. A flicker of joy passed over her face. "You have?"

"You were there. You heard it too."

"*Ja* . . ." Christina furrowed her brow. "But don't distract me. I was telling you how terrible he is."

Hilda motioned with her hand. "Continue."

"Then he got down on one knee."

"Inexcusable."

"Hilda, stop it. You really must see how impossible he is."

"Do go on."

"Then he said how special I am and how special our connection is."

"Beastly."

Christina scowled. "Oh, it gets worse."

"Worse than telling you that you are special?"

"Much worse." Christina hesitated. "I know you're making fun of me, by the way, and I don't appreciate it. This is a moment of devastation for me."

"Forgive me for making light of your moment of devastation."

"You're still making fun of me. This is serious."

"I'm sorry. I know it feels very serious to you right now.

But it doesn't sound so bad. Mayhap it will blow over and all will be well."

"No, you don't understand. It gets worse."

"*Ja*? Go on."

"Well, then he said that a lot of women have dreamed of marrying him. He said that he had broken all their hearts. He acted as if I should be grateful that he would propose to me." Christina crossed her arms and scowled. "Can you imagine? As if he were *der Herr's* gift to women!"

"Ah. That does seem . . . unromantic."

"To say the least."

"He does have an easy way with women, but even so, that doesn't sound like him."

"And yet he said it."

"*Mmmm*." Hilda paused. She watched Fuzzy scramble across a stone and tumble onto his backside. "You know, people often say things they don't mean."

"Well, they shouldn't!"

"No, they should not."

"Oh, Hilda, don't you see?" Christina grabbed both of Hilda's arms and held on as if she might fall. "It's impossible. All of it is impossible."

"You always say nothing is impossible."

Christina closed her eyes. If only she could believe that now, when everything had fallen apart. How could her life work out now? Even if Hilda and Wilhelm married, Johan would still be arrogant and impossible and Christina would be left alone. Fancy that! Christina imagined Hilda happily married while she, Christina, lived alone in their cabin with naught but the sheep and the wolves for company. How unfair life could be!

* * *

Johan wandered the woods after he bolted from Christina's. His feet kept moving without his mind telling them where to go. He was too distracted by his emotions to think straight. The proposal kept replaying inside his mind like a thunderclap that he could not escape. He had arrived at her cabin brimming with bluster and charm. He was supposed to be engaged at this very moment.

He was not.

The entire situation was intolerable. How many women had hoped for a proposal from him? Too many to count! And now, when he finally did propose, Christina rejected him. Rejected *him*, Johan Lantz!

Johan knew that he shouldn't have been so sure of himself. He was Amish, dash it all. Amish men should be humble. He had not been. Johan kicked a log in his path. The rotten wood gave way, and his boot sank into the soft bark. He hopped to keep his balance and yanked his foot out of the hole it had made. The air filled with the dank smell of damp, musty wood. Johan scowled and marched onward. He had had enough of these woods. He had had enough of cutting trees and hauling brush. He had had enough of the entire settlement. He wanted to go home.

Ah, home. Where a man could rest easy in a sturdy, thatched-roof cottage after a good day of work in the fields. Here, he didn't even have a field yet. Only trees, trees, and more trees. And he most certainly did not have a sturdy cottage. He had the sky for a roof and rain for company. He was tired of camping out in a windswept clearing. He was tired of eating salt pork and corncakes. He wanted to go home.

No. That wasn't quite right, was it? Johan stopped and leaned against a tree. He didn't want to go home again. He wanted to make a new home. Johan inhaled deeply. The scent of pine and cedar filled his lungs. He closed his eyes as he exhaled. He wanted to make a new home with Christina. He wanted Christina to fill his days with merriment and joy. He wanted to laugh with her. He wanted to sit beside her during the long, quiet evenings and know that she loved him.

But she didn't love him. She had rejected him.

Johan opened his eyes and pushed away from the tree trunk. The sun filtered through the canopy and warmed his face in the cool shadow of the pine. He had not realized the sun had risen so high. His stomach rumbled, and he remembered he had not yet eaten. How long had he been stomping through the woods like a petulant child? *Ach*, he was as bad as his nephews. But could anyone blame him? It was not every day that a man has his hopes dashed. He wasn't upset about a skinned knee or broken toy. He was ailing from a broken heart.

Wilhelm waited with a stony face when Johan stalked into their clearing. "When you didn't return, I had hoped you were celebrating. I can see by your expression that you are not."

"No. I am not." Johan threw himself onto the stump beside the campfire. There were no flames, only smoldering coals that seemed to stare back at Johan with red-hot eyes. He leaned his elbows on his knees and rested his chin in his hands. He should get to work, or at least stoke the fire and put on a late breakfast. He did not. He could not make himself move. He felt too defeated. "She said no."

"I am sorry."

He realized that Wilhelm was whispering and had been since Johan's arrival. He had been too dismayed to notice.

"Why are you whispering?" Johan asked.

Wilhelm glanced over Johan's shoulder and frowned.

"Because he doesn't want me to hear!" a good-natured voice bellowed from behind Johan's back. Johan did not bother to look. He recognized the voice as Abram Zeigler's. Johan closed his eyes and slouched even more than he had been.

"Abram came to call while you were gone," Wilhelm said in a voice that sounded too cheerful. "We were just discussing the best time for planting a barley crop in this climate."

Johan did not respond.

"I'm sorry that you caught my brother at a bad time," Wilhelm said as he glanced at Abram.

"Nonsense," Abram said and dropped onto a stump beside Johan. Abram slapped Johan on the back with a hearty clap. "It's the perfect time. We've got a man in need of cheering up."

"You can't cheer me up," Johan said in a flat voice. His eyes stayed closed.

"Because she said no? Couldn't help but overhear."

"*Ja*."

"I knew you were in a bad way when I saw you at Eli's cabin a few days ago." Abram shook his head, but kept the smile on his face. "When you fall for a girl, you fall hard, *ja*?"

"I've never fallen for a girl before."

"Ah." Abram shrugged. "That could be the problem."

"How so?"

"You're out of your element, my boy."

"I've never wanted to settle down before." Johan frowned and ran his fingers through his hair. "It doesn't make any sense. I shouldn't be so torn up about it. What does it matter? It's never mattered before."

"But it matters now."

"*Ja*." Johan's shoulders sagged. "It does."

"All right." Abram rubbed his hands together. "Tell me what happened. Let's hear it."

"I don't feel like talking about it. Anyway, what's the point?"

"What's the point?" Abram chuckled. "To fix the problem, of course."

"You can't."

"Try me."

Johan did not respond.

"You know, my Gertrud was not easy to woo. Indeed, she was irritated by my very existence for quite some time." Abram winked. "But she came around, all right."

Johan rubbed his eyes and shifted on the stump. "All right. Fine. I asked Christina Dresser to marry me. She said no. That's all there is to it."

"Oh, I doubt that. Tell me exactly what you said."

Wilhelm leaned forward expectantly.

Johan shrugged. "I told her I had everything planned out and that I'd take care of everything. What's wrong with that?"

"Mmmm." Abram ran his fingers through his long, dark beard. "That was the first thing you said?"

"No. First, I told her she'd marry me."

"Ah." Abram rubbed his chin. "You told her she'd marry you, did you?"

"*Ja.*" Johan frowned. "But it didn't sound the way it does when you say it."

"Mmmm." Abram looked doubtful. "Then how did it sound?"

Johan considered for a moment. "Dashing."

"And yet, she said no."

"Unbelievable, *ja?*"

Wilhelm pressed a palm to his forehead. He looked as if he thought it were quite believable indeed.

Abram cleared his throat. He glanced at Wilhelm, then back at Johan. "Mayhap your approach could use a little . . . adjustment."

"Nonsense." Johan shook his head. "We're perfect for each other. She ought to see that. She ought to have said yes."

Abram ran his fingers through his long, dark beard as he considered what to say next.

Johan did not wait for Abram to respond. "I told her she'd be glad if she said yes. I told her to trust me." Johan shook his head again. "But she didn't."

"You told her that?"

"Of course." Johan threw up his hands. "I told her not to worry her pretty little head about anything."

"You didn't." Abram and Wilhelm exchanged a quick glance.

"I did."

"And she didn't take it well." Abram looked like he wanted to smile. He forced a frown instead.

"No, she did not. Unbelievable, *ja?*"

Wilhelm looked away so that Johan did not see his smile.

"At that point, I realized she needed convincing so I reminded her that lots of other women have wanted to marry me, but she's the only one I've ever asked. I made sure she understood that what we have is special."

"Oh, Johan." Wilhelm stared at his brother in surprise. "You didn't."

"Why shouldn't I tell her how special she is? Women love to know they are special. And she is! She ought to know that. I wanted to tell her that."

Abram opened his mouth, closed it again, and looked at Wilhelm. Wilhelm shook his head. Abram cleared his throat. "Johan. I'm going to tell you the truth. That's the worst marriage proposal I've ever heard."

"And how many marriage proposals have you heard?" Johan's tone was light, but his eyes were not. They flashed with indignation.

Abram smiled. "What I meant was that it's the worst marriage proposal I've ever imagined hearing."

Johan snorted.

"Women don't want to be told what to do or what to think any more than a man does."

"I didn't tell her what to think. I just . . ." Johan frowned. Had he really come across that way? Dash it all, how could he have bungled it so badly? "Okay. Maybe I did. But it wasn't as bad as you make it sound!"

Wilhelm laughed. "Sorry, brother. I don't mean to make light of your situation. But . . ." He tried to wipe the smile from his face.

"But what?"

"You sound ridiculous. Telling a woman she ought to

be grateful for your affection." He laughed and shook his head. "I'm surprised she didn't chase you away with a broomstick."

"She did nothing of the sort."

"Ah, well. Maybe there's still hope."

Abram shook his head. His eyes twinkled. "So you thought if you marched in there and told her how lucky she was to have you, she would jump at the chance to marry you?"

"Well . . ." Johan frowned and considered for a moment. ". . . yes." He stared at Abram as if daring him to challenge that logic. "Why not?"

"How long do you have? Could take a while to list all the reasons."

"For heaven's sake." Johan scowled and crossed his arms.

"He looks like Felix when he hasn't gotten his way," Wilhelm said with an amused look.

Johan's scowl deepened.

"The problem is that Johan's never been in love before," Wilhelm said. "He doesn't know how to handle it."

"*Ja.*" Abram steepled his fingers and pressed his fingertips to his lips. "That's the root of it, all right."

"Would you both quit talking about me like that? I'm right here. I can hear everything you're saying about me."

"Good," Wilhelm said. "Because you need to hear it. You need help getting this right."

"Bah."

Wilhelm shrugged. "Suit yourself. If you want to let Christina slip away from you, that's your choice. . . ."

Johan made a sound like a growl in his throat. He shot up from the stump and began to pace. "Fine." He threw up his hands as he stalked back and forth in front of the campfire. "Go on."

"*Ach*, where to start?" Abram shook his head, but his eyes looked merry. He looked as if he were enjoying himself. "The boy's dug a deep hole for himself, *ja*?"

"*Ja*." Wilhelm laughed and leaned forward to stoke the fire.

"Have you ever heard of a self-fulfilling prophecy?" Abram asked.

"*Ja*. Of course." Johan did not stop pacing. "Are you telling me that I made her reject me?"

Abram gave an innocent shrug.

"That's outrageous."

"Is it?"

"Why would I do a thing like that?"

"Because you've never been in love before." Abram gave a half smile. "And you were terrified she would reject you."

"Terrified! Bah!" Johan glared at Abram without breaking his stride. "You heard about the bear attack, *ja*? I wasn't terrified of that bear, even while it charged me. I'm not afraid of anything."

Abram chuckled. "Oh, Johan. You have a lot to learn."

Wilhelm smiled knowingly.

"A woman is far more frightening than a bear."

"That's ridiculous."

"Is it?" Abram caught Johan's gaze. "Then look me in the eye and tell me you weren't terrified that Christina would reject you."

"Terrified. Bah!"

Abram and Wilhelm exchanged amused glances.

Johan paced in silence for a few beats. He was not ready to hear this. How could it be his fault that Christina had rejected him? He had tried his best. And when his best wasn't good enough, he had tried even harder. All he wanted was for her to see how much he loved her and how happy he could make her. What was wrong with that? "All right. Maybe I was afraid. Not *terrified*, but afraid. But that's beside the point. The point is that I laid out the facts as to why she should marry me and she said no. She has no affection for me, dash it all."

"She has no affection for your *approach*," Wilhelm said. "She has affection for *you*."

Johan stopped pacing and swung his head toward his brother. "What makes you think she has affection for me?"

"I've seen the way she looks at you."

"Humph." Johan's response sounded like a strangled grunt. He was too agitated to get proper words out.

Abram nodded. "That always gives a woman away."

"And a man." Wilhelm gave a sly smile. "I've also seen the way you look at her, Johan."

"Humph."

Abram stood up and stretched. His ample stomach bulged over his belt as he raised his arms. "Ah, well." He leaned over and picked up his musket from the ground. "He'll come around. Give it time." Abram winked and straightened his beaver felt hat. "Pride cometh before a fall, you know."

"This isn't about pride," Johan muttered. "It's about a woman who can't see reason."

"Is it, now?" Abram smiled with amusement. "It would be interesting to hear her side of the story, wouldn't it?"

"Humph."

Abram's face changed, as if an idea had popped into his head. He grinned and moved his attention to Wilhelm.

"My flax crop has been retted and dried. It's time to process it. Can you lend a hand on the morrow? It would be a great help to Gertrud and me."

Wilhelm nodded. "*Ja*. We'll be there."

"So will the Dresser sisters," Abram said and gave a sly look.

Johan felt a heavy, sticky feeling inside his throat. He would have to see Christina tomorrow. It was too much. It was all too much. How could a man try his best and end up being the one at fault? It simply was not fair.

Chapter Sixteen

Christina lingered over the milking the next morning. She did not want to face anyone. The sheep seemed to understand her mood and stared at her with big, mournful eyes. They bleated and pushed against the milking stool. "*Ja*. I know. Nothing is all right today, is it?" Only Fuzzy seemed immune to the day's sorry mood. He was too preoccupied by the fresh milk in the bucket. He tried to steal a taste whenever Christina turned her attention from him.

She patted the soft, firm side of a ewe. The animal lowered her head and bit into a clump of grass. Christina curled her fingers through the ewe's tangled wool. "Time to shear you, *ja*?" The sun shone bright and full, even though it lay low in the sky. "I don't think you will need your wool coat any longer."

The shearing had been a time for celebration back in Germany. It meant another winter had passed and all the promises of spring were in full bloom. What a lovely excuse for a work party that was. Shepherds came together to lead the sheep through the river to wash the wool and clip each sheep with freshly sharpened shears. There were pies and puddings and roast meats afterward.

Thoughts of the shearing reminded her of today's work party. Christina had to go out amongst her neighbors, and she did not feel up to it. Worst of all, Johan might be there. Her stomach dropped at the thought. The only thing worse than his being there would be his *not* being there. Dash it all, did she want to see him or not?

She did.

She didn't.

She did not know. She only knew she could not stop thinking of him. And the more she thought of him, the more frustrated she felt. Christina tried to focus on anything but him. She listened to the soft swish, swish, swish of milk hitting the side of the wooden bucket. She watched Fuzzy scamper in the grass. She noticed how good the sun felt on her face. Until a shadow blocked the warmth. Christina sighed and looked up. Hilda stood there with her hands on her hips.

"Aren't you ready yet?" Hilda raised an eyebrow. "It's almost as if you're avoiding somebody."

"Humph."

"It will be all right."

"No. It won't."

"You don't sound like yourself," Hilda said. "You always see the bright side."

"I don't feel like myself." Christina pushed back her stool. "Mayhap it's the fever and ague."

"Mayhap it's love."

"Ha! Love!" Christina jumped up from the stool so fast she knocked it over. The ewe swung her head around to give an annoyed look. Christina patted the animal and frowned. "I would never be in love with such an arrogant man."

"Then why are you so upset?"

"I am not upset."

"Even the sheep can tell you're upset." As if on cue, a row of wide, black eyes turned to Christina.

"Oh, not you too!" Christina said to the flock. "You're supposed to be on my side."

"If you didn't love him, you wouldn't care if he was arrogant," Hilda said as she picked up the bucket. "Don't waste time arguing. We'll take the milk to the root cellar on the way. We're already late."

Christina wanted to argue, but she did not. She knew neither her sister nor the sheep would listen.

"And leave that bear at home," Hilda added. "He'll only get underfoot."

Just when Christina thought the day couldn't get any worse.

Bruno helped herd the flock to Abram's clearing. The sheep would graze on the wild grass that grew in the fallow field where Abram had grown the flax. That way, the Dresser sisters could work all day and still keep an eye on their flock. Tending sheep took time and effort, but Christina and Hilda had a small flock, so they did not have to wander far to find enough food to keep the sheep fat and happy. Back home in Germany, shepherds with large flocks had to spend most of their time away from home in search of good grazing. They could not even take Sunday off, for the sheep still needed food and protection, so in some parts shepherds were buried with a lock of wool to remind *der Herr* on judgment day that they had good reason to break the Sabbath.

When they reached Abram's field, Christina saw the stagnant pond where Abram had soaked the flax and the shelter where he had hung it to dry for weeks afterward. She could not see Johan Lantz. She did not know whether to be relieved or disappointed. Mayhap he would rush to her side and explain that it had all been a ridiculous mistake. Or mayhap he would rush to her side and ply her with more arrogant nonsense.

A brilliant blue sky stretched over the field where dried flax lay in neat stacks, waiting to be processed. A bright, clean smell like sun-drenched hay filled Christina's lungs. The air felt warm and fresh with spring. It was almost enough to make her happy. *Almost.* Christina squinted against the sun as she scanned the field. She recognized Abram and his wife, Gertrud. And there, beside a stack of bundled flax, she saw Eli and his wife, Catrina. Wilhelm directed his boys as they fetched more bundles from the shelter. Abram whistled a tune from the *Ausbund* that carried across the field and tickled her ears. Christina began to hum along.

The song died in her throat when she saw a man stroll out of the shelter with a bundle of flax balanced on his shoulder. She knew that confident walk and that familiar silhouette. She lifted the blade of her hand to her forehead to block the sun and stared. Johan Lantz turned his head as he walked and flashed an easy grin in her direction. Christina gasped and averted her eyes.

The nerve!

"Are you coming?" Hilda asked.

"Oh." Christina realized she had stopped walking. She cleared her throat and ran a few steps to catch up with her sister. "*Ja.* I was distracted by my thoughts."

"Your thoughts of Johan Lantz."

"Shhhh. Do you want everyone to hear?"

Hilda gazed upward with a long-suffering look. "I'm sure they already know. Johan looks as out of sorts as you do."

"He does not! Did you see that arrogant smile? Oh, it's enough to make me turn around and march home without even saying hello."

"And yet you are marching straight toward him and not toward home."

"Humph."

"And besides, that was not an arrogant smile, if you ask me. It was much more of a hopeful, sheepish smile."

"Mmmmm." Christina was not convinced. Hilda had not heard his ridiculous proposal. She had no idea how very arrogant Johan could be.

"He looks contrite," Hilda said.

"Shhhh. We're almost in earshot."

Hilda shrugged. "Your expression gives you away."

Christina tried to look natural. She knew it did not work. Her face always showed exactly how she felt. Her only consolation was that she did not know how she felt today—so how could her expression give her away?

"Just put on a happy face," Hilda whispered.

"I am."

Hilda glanced at her and flinched. "Oh."

"That bad, huh?"

"*Ja.*"

"Oh, just forget it. I give up." Christina stopped trying to look happy. She looked miserable and hopeful and disappointed instead. There was no stopping it.

Catrina Webber hitched up her skirts and ran to meet them. "Christina, dear, you look a fright!" Catrina grabbed Christina's hands and held them. "Whatever is the matter?"

"I'm fine."

Catrina studied her expression for a moment and dropped her hands. "All right. If you say so. But do stay out of the heat. Mayhap you've had too much sun. Where's your scoop?"

Christina's hands flew to her head. She had forgotten her straw hat. "Oh, bother."

Catrina shook her head. Her soft, delicate skin looked perfect and pale beneath her scoop. She smiled and winked at Christina. "At least you've got your prayer *kappe* this time."

Christina laughed. "*Ja*." Today she would be sure not to end up covered in soot with a loose mop of hair falling every which way. She would have to try harder to impress Johan.

Impress Johan! Dash it all, that was not what she wanted to do. She should throw all her focus into making a match for Hilda. She should put Johan out of her mind. Johan glanced over his shoulder at just that moment. Christina smiled. He returned the smile. Oh my. That *really* was not what she wanted to do. She would have to work harder to show him that he needed to apologize. She forced a frown, raised her chin, and spun around on her heels. *Take that, Johan Lantz!*

She thought she heard a chuckle. Which man had laughed, she did not know. All she knew was that it had better not have been Johan.

Johan did not know how to act. It was intolerable. He always had an easy smile or quick wit in the presence of women. But today the smile felt false and forced. And he could not think of a single thing to say to Christina. Dash it all, what had come over him?

Rejection, that's what. He tried to ignore the emotion, but how could he? The cold, hard truth permeated every bone in his body. His arms and legs felt heavy with it. His head and his belly ached. He had become as emotional as a child. Johan scowled at the thought and tried to forget all about Christina Dresser.

That was impossible, of course, for she was but a few paces away. Every so often her soft, angelic laughter drifted to him. He wanted to turn and steal a glance at her. He could imagine the sparkling blue eyes, flushed cheeks, and energetic whirl of skirts. Johan did not look. He had work to do and he would focus on that.

Abram had soaked the flax and then dried it for weeks. Now, they had to break the inner stalk to separate it from the flax fibers. Johan picked up a bundle of the long, dried stalks and broke apart the roots with his hands. The brittle fibers crunched and crackled beneath his fingers. He laid the stalks on a tall, sturdy stump, then stretched his back and glanced behind him. Christina stood at her own stump with a wooden club in her hand. She was not looking at him.

Johan sighed, picked up his wooden club, and pounded the flax against the stump. He turned the bundle as he worked, so he didn't miss any part of the stalk. After he finished one section, he slid it over the edge of the stump and started on a new section. He kept pounding until he flattened the entire length of bundled stalks.

The thud of wood against wood echoed across the field. Johan felt the beats inside his chest as the sharp punch of a drum. Tiny plant fibers filled the air like goose down from a torn pillow. The fibers caught the sunlight and hung in the warm breeze. Johan heard a sneeze behind him. He turned and saw Christina at her stump with her eyes squeezed shut. She sneezed again. And again. Every time she sneezed, her body shuddered and she gave a little jump. It was adorable.

"Bless you." Johan spoke loudly enough for Christina to hear.

Christina started and glanced at him. "Oh."

Johan flashed a smile. "Thank you would do."

"I mean thank you." She pursed her lips and turned away, as if she had just remembered she was annoyed.

Johan sighed and watched Christina for a moment. Her brow crinkled in concentration as she brought down the club. The sun highlighted a blond curl that had escaped her prayer *kappe* and tumbled down the gentle curve of her throat. Johan sighed again and turned away. What had gone wrong?

The answer felt obvious. Christina Dresser was impossible. He had made a perfectly good proposal, and it had not been good enough for her. Ha! She should have seen what they had between them. She should have jumped at the chance to be together. Johan raised his club and brought it down hard against the stump. The force of the blow shot up his arm and into his jaw. He grunted and tossed the club onto the ground. He needed to take a break.

Johan felt Christina's eyes on him as he stalked to the water bucket. He picked up the ladle and took a good, long sip of river water. He should have felt refreshed, but he did not. Something nibbled away at his heart. Johan frowned and drank from the ladle again. He still felt hot and agitated so he took off his hat and poured a ladleful of water over his head. He let the cool liquid run down his neck and under the collar of his loose linen shirt. Then he pushed his wet hair back from his face and crammed his hat back on his head.

He did not feel any better. Instead of feeling hot and

agitated, he felt damp and agitated. His shirt stuck to his wet skin and itched.

"You look as though you've just drunk a cup of sour milk." Abram took the ladle from his hand and dipped it into the bucket.

"Oh." Johan sighed. "I didn't see you standing there."

Abram took a sip and dropped the ladle back into the bucket with a splash. He wiped his mouth on his linen sleeve. "You can fight it all day long, or you can get it over with and apologize."

"Apologize!"

Abram gave an innocent shrug.

"She rejected *me*."

"Ah, well. If that's the way you see it."

"There is no other way to see it." But even as Johan said the words, guilt nibbled the back of his mind.

Abram started to walk away. He hesitated and turned back to Johan. "You can either be right, or you can be happy."

Johan frowned. What was that supposed to mean? "You think I should apologize even though I'm right?"

"No. I think you should apologize even though you *think* you are right."

"Humph."

Abram smiled. "Suit yourself. You're not hurting me. Just yourself." Abram held up a finger. "And one other person, of course. But I guess Christina's feelings don't matter to you."

"Of course, they matter. But don't you see that I'm not hurting her? She's hurting *me*."

"Mmmmm." Abram raised an eyebrow. He glanced over at Christina, who was working just out of earshot. Her club hit the stump over and over in a steady rhythm. She did not smile as she normally did. Instead, her face looked frail and uncertain. "She looks hurt to me." He shrugged his bulky shoulders. "But what do I know?" Abram's expression looked as if he *did* know. Johan found that knowing expression intolerable. He wanted to argue how right he, Johan, was and how wrong everyone else was. The situation simply was not fair. Why couldn't anyone see *his* hurt?

But Johan did not argue that he was right. Instead, he watched Christina for a moment. He knew why the situation made him so frustrated. And he knew why he could not plead his case. Somewhere, deep down, he suspected that he was wrong.

The thought was intolerable. He decided to ignore it.

The sun wheeled across the sky in a slow arc. Christina's arm ached. It did not take much force to beat the flax, but repeating the motion over and over exhausted her. Sweat dampened her scalp and forehead. She wished she could fling off her prayer *kappe* and feel the breeze on her bare head. Her body felt hot and sticky beneath the layers of woolen hosen, shift, petticoats and overskirt, apron, linen shirt, stays, bodice, and jacket.

Catrina had invited Christina to leave the field to cook dinner in the cool shade of the Webber cabin. Christina had considered the invitation. But she had always preferred an open field to the dark confines of a kitchen. And so she had chosen the heat of the sun over the heat of the cook fire. Catrina had smiled in a knowing way that made Christina flinch. Were her feelings for Johan that obvious? She did not want anyone to see her affection for the arrogant, impossible man—especially Catrina, who was fair of face and fortunate in love. Could Christina hope to end up as happily married as her friend?

Christina wished she could will herself to stop feeling affection for Johan. She could not. She still had feelings for him, regardless of the arrogant nonsense he had told her the day before. And, if she were perfectly honest with herself, she hoped he would apologize. She still believed in happy endings. She wondered if she was a fool.

They finished beating the last stalk around noontime. By then, Christina longed for the dark confines of a kitchen over the blazing sun and aching arms. She wanted to feel relieved to break for lunch, but did not. She had never felt so miserable at a work party. Oh, it should have been lovely, especially when Catrina arrived with meat pies still hot from the hearth and they all sat in the field to eat together.

Christina wondered why Abram had invited her and Hilda to help. It almost seemed that he had an ulterior motive—but surely Abram could not be playing matchmaker! And yet, the rest of the work party had an interest in the harvest, while she and Hilda did not. Catrina and Eli spun and wove the flax into linen cloth. Gertrud helped with the work since she was Abram's wife and shared in his labors. And, since Gertrud was Eli's sister, the gathering had the feel of a family reunion. Especially when Abram teased Gertrud, and Eli laughed his shy, good-natured laugh. Everyone was having a grand time—everyone but Christina and Johan.

The small group sat in the grass and enjoyed a good meal while a hawk circled the sky and field mice scampered along the edges of the clearing. Sheep bells clanged in the distance. Christina pushed away her empty tin plate and leaned back into her hands. The earth felt soft and damp beneath her palms. She closed her eyes and let the sun heat her face. She heard the gentle murmur of Catrina's voice, followed by another round of Eli's laughter.

Johan did not speak throughout the meal. He sat as far from Christina as he could. She willed herself not to open her eyes and steal a peek. What was he doing? What was he thinking? She opened her eyes. He glanced up and met her gaze. Their eyes locked for a moment. She did not know what to do, and she suspected he did not either. They broke the gaze at the same time. He frowned and plucked a blade of grass. He peeled it into strips until there was nothing left to peel. Christina felt a small surge of satisfaction. He looked as agitated and miserable as she did.

The satisfaction did not last. He let the shredded grass drop from his hand and glanced up at her again. She locked onto his gray eyes and felt that familiar connection. Her stomach leapt into her throat. She swallowed and pulled her gaze away. She did not want him to be miserable. She wanted him to be happy. She wanted both of them to be happy, together.

But how could she be happy with a man who allowed pride to rule his heart? A good man would have apologized by now. Did that mean that Johan was not a good man? She frowned and pulled her knees under her chin. She adjusted her petticoats and overskirt to cover her legs. The layers of wool and linen stuck to her sweat-dampened skin. Hilda had always warned Christina that she thought with her heart and not her head. Had she raced into love without realizing Johan's true nature? Had she misjudged him? Perhaps he was not the gentle, loving soul she had taken him for. Oh sure, he was as carefree and fun loving as she, but was he as thoughtful? Did he care more about his pride than about her?

She did not have time to consider that thought. A bright, happy laugh caught on the breeze and carried to her. She straightened her spine in surprise. That was Hilda's voice. She swung her head around to see Hilda and Wilhelm sitting side by side in the grass. Why hadn't she noticed them? She had been so busy agonizing over Johan that she had forgotten all about her matchmaking plans for her sister. Was it possible that Wilhelm and Hilda had connected on their own?

Interesting.

Christina strained to make out their conversation. She could only hear the low murmur of voices and the occasional laugh. But Wilhelm's eyes spoke louder than words. They shone with contentment, especially when Felix yawned and leaned against Hilda's shoulder. Soon, the little boy was fast asleep in her lap while the two older boys lay on their bellies in the grass and kicked their feet in a careless, lazy motion. Hilda looked like part of Wilhelm's family.

The observation made Christina feel warm and satisfied inside. She could drift off to sleep beneath the sun, just like Felix. Until she heard Johan's voice behind her. The thought of him shot a pang through her chest that shook her awake. Why did men have to be so complicated? Why couldn't they just be themselves? Why did they have to try so hard to impress everyone with their manliness? It left her truly vexed.

She twisted around and looked up. His silhouette blocked the sun as he stood over her. "What do you want?" Christina asked, then flinched. She had not meant to say it like that. She was just so vexed. She had been almost content—even if for just a moment—when he'd barged over and reminded her that she was upset.

Johan frowned. He hesitated.

Christina wished she could take back her words. She started to apologize for snapping at him, but thought better of it. If she apologized now, he might think yesterday was her fault too. She couldn't have that. Better not to apologize at all. So she sat with pursed lips and stared up at him.

Johan's expression shifted. His face hardened and his jaw clenched.

"*Ja*?" she asked. Oh, it was rude of her, and she knew she should soften her tone. She did not.

"I was going to say . . ." Johan shook his head. "*Ach*, it's nothing. I was going to say you look overly tired."

Christina could tell that was not what he had planned to say. But, whatever he had been about to say was lost. She had pushed the words away with her cold demeanor.

Johan flashed his signature grin. Christina realized that he wore that smile like armor. Was it his protection against hurt? Perhaps there was more to him than there appeared to be. . . .

"A little thing like you shouldn't work a whole day in the fields, *ja*? You look about to collapse. And we've done no more than beat the flax thus far."

About to collapse, indeed! Oh, now he had done it! All sympathetic thoughts flew from Christina's head. "I am quite capable, thank you very much!"

Johan gave a teasing half smile. "Quite capable of launching a defense."

Christina stiffened. "You are one to talk."

Johan's smile faded. "What is that supposed to mean?"

"You launched quite the defense when you proposed yesterday."

The color drained from Johan's face. He looked like a boy who had been caught and scolded. In that moment, he looked so vulnerable and hurt that Christina wanted to leap up, scoop him in her arms, and tell him that she loved him anyway. She did not. She maintained her resolve and stared up at him.

Johan returned the stare without speaking. The moment hung in the air. It was agonizing. Finally, Johan shook his head and looked away. "I only thought to tease you. You used to like that."

"Oh." Christina frowned. She did not know how they had gotten to this place. Everything felt so wrong. She studied Johan's strong jaw and broad shoulders. His gray eyes flashed with emotion that he tried not to show. She wanted to tell him everything would be all right between them. But he turned away before she could say anything. She shielded her eyes from the sun and watched him walk to the stack of beaten flax. His body looked strong and confident as he strode away from her. He did not turn around. She did not know if she wanted him to or not.

Johan could not believe what had happened. He had tried to speak with Christina, and she had pushed him away. He did not know if he would have gone through with the apology, but he had decided to try. Or to test the waters, at least. Abram's words had haunted him all day. If he had hurt Christina, he wanted to make it right.

And she had pushed him away.

Johan gathered an armful of beaten flax and laid it across a stump so the fibers hung over the edge. He picked up a wooden scutching knife and scraped the dull blade across the hanging flax in a long, sweeping motion.

Johan wanted to steal a glance at Christina. He did not. He focused on scutching the flax. He had a job to do, and he would do it. There was no need to feel distracted by a woman. He would not be distracted.

But he was. He had never been so distracted in his life.

It was intolerable. Johan had tried to force down his pride and offer an apology. She did not want it. She did not want anything to do with him at all. Had he bungled the proposal that badly? Did she really think him such an oaf?

She did.

Well, it was her loss. Her loss! He would not make the mistake of attempting an apology again. Clearly, with an attitude like that, Christina was in the wrong, not him. Mayhap Abram and Wilhelm were wrong too. Mayhap he hadn't bungled the proposal at all. Mayhap Christina was simply unreasonable.

Or mayhap she simply did not love him.

Johan scowled as he swept the scutching knife across the flax. The sounds of the work party drifted around him, but he ignored the laughter, shouts, and conversation. He could only think of Christina Dresser and the way she had shut him down. He had never been rejected before. His entire life had slid past like a pleasure boat on smooth waters. The fear of rejection had always lurked just beneath the surface as he slid along, but he had always managed to avoid it. Until now. His greatest fear had just splashed to the surface to strike him in the face.

With any other woman he would have been able to grit his teeth and get over it. Sure, the rejection would have stung, but his heart would not have been torn from his chest. Johan shook his head as he tossed his bundle of scutched flax and picked up a new bundle. As ridiculous as it sounded, he truly did feel as though his heart had been ripped out of his body. The feeling sat in the center of his breastbone as a burning, pressing pain. He had never understood what people meant by heartache before. Now he did. He felt it as a physical pain. It *hurt*.

Bah! What had come over him? He ought to toughen up and get on with life. He tried to convince himself that his feelings were just that—feelings. They weren't real. And yet, that physical pain sat in the center of his chest, as real as anything he'd ever felt.

And every time he turned his head, he saw her standing there, just a few paces away. She bent over her flax with a strained expression on her face. Her bottom lip trembled. The movement was so slight that no one else would notice. But Johan did. He noticed everything about Christina. He noticed the way she used the back of her hand to wipe the sweat from her eyes and the way she sneezed when the flax fibers floated in the air. He noticed the way she squinted into the sun as she worked and the pink flush on her nose and cheeks where her skin had burned. He wondered why she wasn't wearing her scoop. He wondered why her bottom lip trembled and why her forehead creased in a troubled frown. Did she feel the same angst that he did? Did she regret her harsh words to him? No. Probably not. But it felt good to hope. Hope was all he had right now.

The afternoon sifted past. Hilda and Wilhelm began to gather the bundles of scutched flax to run the strands through the hackle, a board lined with nails like a giant comb. They stood shoulder to shoulder as they pulled the long, silky flax through the nails. After the hackling, the fibers would be smooth and polished, ready for spinning.

Johan noticed that Hilda and Wilhelm chatted and smiled as they worked.

The boys ran back and forth to carry the scutched flax to the hackle. Every time they wandered from their task, Hilda gently reminded them to mind their work. When Felix slowed his pace, she promised him pie. "Catrina is in her kitchen right now, baking our supper. And there will be a fine dessert for little boys who earn it. If we finish by sunset, I will see you each have an extra serving." The incentive worked. Felix, Fritz, and Franz raced one another to see who could carry the flax the fastest. Wilhelm gazed at Hilda with appreciation. Johan took notice of the look, especially when Hilda blushed and lowered her eyes. She looked as flustered and shy as a young girl. It was strange to watch. Hilda Dresser was not the type to blush or stammer. Mayhap Johan was not the only one with longing in his heart.

Chapter Seventeen

Hilda looked stony as she and Christina walked back to their cabin. She did not speak, not even to complain about Christina's slow pace. Christina trailed her fingers along the pine needles that lined the forest path. The soft, whispery needles tickled her fingers and filled the woodlands with a spicy, piney scent. Sheep bells clanged and hooves plodded against the forest floor as the sisters drove the flock ahead of them.

"You are not yourself, Hilda." Christina paused and considered. "Well, you are serious as usual. You are always slow to smile and quick to frown. But there's something more."

"Really, Christina. Is that all you can say about me? That I am slow to smile and quick to frown? You make me sound like an old hag with no chance for affection."

"Oh." *Oh*. Christina's spine straightened as a realization shot down to her toes. "I'm sorry. I only meant that you seem . . . distracted." Christina wondered how much to pry. She broke off a bundle of pine needles and let them sift out of her fingers. She decided to pry as much as she could. After all, Hilda's comment had given away her feelings. "You fear that Wilhelm holds no affection for you."

Hilda's face tightened. "Really, Christina. The very idea."

But Christina noticed the slight sigh that escaped her sister's lips and the way her step faltered.

Hilda glanced up at the sun and quickened her pace. "We should not tarry. Dusk will soon be upon us." The thick, shadowy woods darkened sooner than the open fields and meadows.

"Don't change the subject." Christina jogged a few steps to catch her sister. "If I didn't know any better, I'd think you were running away from me."

"Only from your nonsense."

Christina laid a hand on her sister's shoulder. "Hilda. Stop."

"Haven't time."

"Of course you have."

Hilda walked faster.

"Hilda!" Christina grabbed her sister's sleeve and tugged. Hilda skidded to a stop. She looked heavenward and let out a long, exasperated breath. Her shoulders sagged and suddenly she looked five years older. "Fine. You win. You guessed it. I fear that Wilhelm holds no affection for me."

"I knew it!"

Hilda narrowed her eyes. "Well, don't look so pleased!"

"No, you don't understand." Christina tried to suppress a grin. She wondered how much to say. "It's just that . . . I think you make a splendid couple."

"So do I. And that is the problem."

"I suspected you had been developing feelings for him. I've been watching, you know." She had been doing more than that, but perhaps now wasn't the time to admit how much she had been meddling. Hilda did look very cross.

"I fought it for as long as I could." Hilda rubbed her temples. "What a mess I'm in now."

Christina clasped her hands together and drew them under her chin. "But don't you see, this is marvelous!"

Hilda stared at her sister.

"We can have a double wedding, just as I've always wanted!" Christina felt breathless with anticipation.

"Christina. Really. Aren't you listening? First of all, Wilhelm does not return my affection. How could he? Second, you no longer want to marry Johan, remember?"

"Oh. Right." She had been so excited that she had forgotten how annoyed she was with Johan. "There is that."

"It's best if we just go on as before, as if nothing has changed."

"Go on as before! Hilda, really. You can't be serious."

"Of course, I'm serious. I'm quick to frown and slow to smile, remember? Among other faults that you so often point out. And you are put off by Johan's arrogance. We should give up before we get hurt."

"Oh no, Hilda." Christina shook her head. She had been so caught up in her own drama with Johan that day that she had forgotten to focus on making a match for Hilda. Now was the time to focus. She had to finish the mission.

And, to finish the mission, she had to recognize that Hilda was not made of stone. "I'm sorry." Christina frowned and pushed a branch away from her face. "You just act so serious all the time. It feels as though you disapprove of everything I do." Christina shrugged. "So I criticize you before you can criticize me."

Hilda sighed. She hesitated before speaking. "It's true.

I am quick to criticize. And it's true I am serious minded."
Hilda glanced at Christina. "But don't you understand why?"

"No."

"Because I fear for you. After our parents died, you
became my life. I couldn't bear for anything to happen to
you. If anything happened to you, it would be my fault."
Hilda reached for Christina's arm and gripped her sleeve.
"Don't you see? I only want to protect you."

"By criticizing me?"

"By curbing your wild nature. You are a free spirit. And
free spirits fall into all sorts of mischief. It is the nature of
a free spirit."

Christina crinkled her brow. "You think I should be
more like you?" The idea felt terribly unnatural. Could she
be more serious if she tried? It seemed a sorry way to live.

"Oh, I don't know." Hilda pressed her lips together. She
shrugged. "Sometimes I wish I could be more like you,
truth be told."

"Oh, Hilda. I never thought I'd hear you say that!" They
emerged into their clearing. Bruno circled the sheep and
bounded back to the sisters. He leapt, muddied Christina's
apron with his paws, and ran back to the flock. His mouth
opened in what looked like a proud, energetic grin as he
dashed away. "Good work, Bruno. You kept them safe
another day." Christina turned back toward Hilda. "I will
always be a free spirit. And you will always be serious
minded. There is nothing you or I can do about it. It is our
nature."

"I suppose so." Hilda looked thoughtful. The low evening
sun filtered through the tree line and bathed the clearing in
a soft, orange glow. The light brightened Hilda's eyes,
and Christina could see flecks of gold in the brown. "Unlike

me," Hilda said at last, "you have a personality that men adore."

"Do I really?"

"Oh, *ja*. It's one reason I've been harsh with you. I feared you would run away with the wrong man. I thought it would be easy for a girl like you—who thinks with her heart and not her head—to go astray."

Christina shook her head so hard that a strand of hair flew from her prayer *kappe*. "Never. I would never leave you."

"But you must. When the time comes."

Christina did not answer for a moment. She decided to test the waters. "Not until you have a proposal from Wilhelm."

Hilda laughed, but her voice held no humor. "That day will not come."

"It will. We will *make* it come."

Hilda gave another dry bark of a laugh. "And how would you do that? I am not like you, Christina. I do not captivate men with my giggles and youthful exuberance."

Christina stared at her sister for a long, thoughtful moment. A plan began to form in her head. "Then perhaps you should."

Christina's thoughts stayed on her sister for the rest of the evening. After they banked the fire and lay on their pallets on the dirt floor, Christina could not sleep. She shifted beneath the heavy quilt and watched the shadows cast by the fire. They danced across the wood beams until the coals died and the red glow disappeared from the hearth. She punched down her pillow and rolled over. Christina could make out Hilda's profile in the thin, white moonlight that filtered through the wooden shutters. Her eyes were open.

"Hilda," Christina whispered.

Hilda sighed and turned her head. "*Ja*?"

"You awake?"

"*Ja*."

"Can't sleep?"

"No." Hilda's bedcovers shifted in the darkness.

"Thinking of Wilhelm?"

"*Ach*, don't make me admit it."

Christina smiled into the dark. She felt warm and snug inside. The hardest part of her plan was accomplished. Hilda had fallen for Wilhelm. "He's a good man."

"Enough."

"Tell me exactly what you're thinking."

"That you're keeping me awake."

"You weren't sleeping anyway."

Hilda sighed. "No."

"Out with it, then."

"*Ach*, I'm thinking that Wilhelm would prefer a woman like you. Someone who laughs a lot and plays with the children and brightens everyone's day."

Christina's smile widened. "I know you spoke of it earlier today, but I still can't believe you think of me that way."

"I can't believe you didn't know it. But I'm not good at telling how I feel. You know that."

"*Ja*."

"The problem is . . ." Hilda made a sharp sound in the back of her throat and sat up. The quilt slid against her linen shift and settled across her feet.

Christina leaned onto one elbow and stared at the moon-lit silhouette of her sister. Hilda looked small and uncertain, which was unusual. Hilda was stout and compact, but she never looked small. She had an imposing presence that made up for her short stature. "You may as well tell me everything," Christina said. "Heaven knows you've kept it in long enough. What have you to lose?"

"My pride, I suppose."

"Which an Amish woman should not have. You taught me that."

"Ah. You've got me. Very well." There was a long silence. Christina was just about to interrupt when Hilda finally spoke. "Amos Schneider. That was his name."

"I don't remember an Amos Schneider."

"No. He moved away and married someone else after I refused him."

"Because of me."

"*Ja*." Hilda pulled her knees up and wrapped her arms around them. "But I left out the last part of the story."

Christina waited in the darkness. She could hear the soft rasp of her sister's breath and the howl of a wolf far away.

"You know the first part—he asked me to marry, but said we couldn't afford to take you in. Times were hard, people were hungry." Hilda sighed. "The crops had failed for the second year in a row."

"I remember that time."

"*Ja*. Well, when I told him I could not marry him because I would not send you to live with our aunt—"

"Aunt Helga?" Christina flinched. "Not her, surely."

"*Ja*. You remember her then. *Ach*, she was a bitter woman. You would have found no happiness there."

"No."

"Anyway. When I said no to Amos's proposal, he told me that he was not so sure he wanted to marry me after all. He said I was too serious and that he would find a woman who was more fun. He said I never laughed. He said I frowned all the day long."

"Hilda, he said that because he was angry at your rejection. He was trying to hurt you."

Hilda did not respond.

"I thank *der Herr* that he would not take me in," Christina said. "If he had, you would have married him and that would have been a terrible mistake. He sounds like a rotten egg."

Hilda snorted. "A rotten egg. *Ja*. That sounds about right."

"I hope you realize you escaped a bad marriage." Christina felt a weight lift from her chest that she had not realized she had been carrying. She had not ruined her sister's life. She had saved it. "He would have kept hurting you. He showed his character when you rejected him. People always show their character when they don't get their way. Imagine the things he would have said, the hurt he would have caused, during a lifetime together. You need a man who is honorable and kind even when he does not get his way."

"And you think Wilhelm is that sort of man?"

"*Ja*. I do."

"What makes you so sure?"

"Haven't you seen him with his boys? He thinks of no one but them. He never thinks of getting his own way, only theirs."

"Ah."

"He would never speak to you as Amos Schneider did. He would never ask you to abandon your sister. I cannot imagine it."

"No. I think you are right. He would not ask me to

abandon you and he would not say those things. But he might *think* them."

Christina considered Hilda's words. Would Wilhelm appreciate Hilda's stern nature? Would he prefer a woman who could laugh and flirt? She did not know. What she did know was that Wilhelm would never hurt Hilda. That mattered more than anything. Christina felt more determined than ever to make the match. Hilda had been on the shelf too long. This might be her last chance for a good man. Christina would never allow her sister to end up with a man like Amos Schneider. They would have to do whatever it took to snare Wilhelm. "I know Wilhelm will make a good husband, and that you already feel affection for him. That affection will likely grow into love, *ja*?"

"*Ja*. I believe it will. For me, at least."

"Then we will just have to do what it takes to make him see you are the one."

"Oh, Christina. How on earth do you propose to do that?"

"You said that men like a woman who smiles and giggles and makes them feel like the center of attention, *ja*?"

"Something like that."

"You'll just have to do that."

"*Ach*, I don't know."

"Do you want him for a husband or not?"

"I do."

"Then do what it takes."

Hilda laughed. "It's too ridiculous. You want me to act like you!"

Christina shrugged and settled back into the pallet. "*Ja*. I did just get a proposal, you know. And it would not have been my first if you had not scared away my other suitors."

"That's true—you have always attracted suitors."

"Then it's settled."

"I suppose so."

"Good. Now get some sleep. Being enchanting is exhausting."

Hilda laughed. "This is absurd."

"*Ja*. It's going to be wonderful good fun."

Hilda did not respond. Christina knew that her sister did not think it would be fun in the least.

Chapter Eighteen

Christina thought she would feel a renewed sense of hope after her conversation with Hilda. She did not. Oh, sure, she felt a thrill of excitement at the prospect of a match for Hilda. Finally, her sister had admitted that she was not made of stone. She needed love and affection just like other people—more than other people, probably. For people with the hardest hearts are the ones who secretly crave the most love.

Christina never made a secret of her need for love. She longed for the right man to come and sweep her off her feet, just as Johan had when he'd appeared atop the wood-pile. Johan. Christina rolled her shoulders to readjust the yoke. She could not stop thinking of him as she trudged through the forest. The wooden buckets swung with each step and sloshed water down the sides of her overskirt. She barely noticed. Worry over Johan Lantz consumed her.

What if he was no better than Amos Schneider? What if he had fooled her just as Amos had fooled Hilda? What if the arrogance of his proposal had revealed his true character? Christina glanced around the empty path. "Come along, Fuzzy." Fuzzy did not follow as willingly as Bruno. The cub was easily distracted. Everything in the woods seemed a wonder to him. While Christina drew water, he had waded into the creek to chase the minnows. He watched the silver flash of their scales with a serious expression, then struck at them with a floppy, furry paw. He did not catch anything, but he did manage to get thoroughly soaked. On the way back, he stumbled over a log as he chased a blue-winged butterfly.

Christina watched the cub wander through the underbrush and whistled for him to follow. He ran to catch up and opened his mouth in what looked very much like a grin, if bears could do such a thing. He zipped past her and bounded through a patch of ferns. A flock of birds exploded into the sky. "You'll scare them to death, Fuzzy. They don't know you're a harmless little thing."

Christina watched Fuzzy nip at the sky as the birds landed on a branch above his reach. "But you won't always be harmless, will you?" She knew that he was a bear and that bears could not stop being bears. Fuzzy would grow up soon and go on his way to live as all bears must. Bears were not complicated. They were straightforward and understandable. Men, on the other hand . . .

Christina stepped over a stone and pressed her hand against the trunk of an oak tree to steady herself. The buckets swung, knocked against her hips, and sloshed cold water. She could feel the dampness soak through her skirts to her thin linen shift beneath. She shivered even though the day felt hot.

Her thoughts left her colder than the water. What *was* Johan's nature? Was he prideful? Was he arrogant? Was he bossy? Did he think only of himself? What if, like Hilda, Christina had been saved from a terrible marriage? She knew these questions would keep circling her mind until she had an answer. But how could she ever know Johan's true nature? How could she ever know who he really was inside his heart? A man's heart lay hidden, deep within.

There was simply no way to know. The only clue was through his actions. She could know a tree by its fruits. But that only made things more confusing! Johan had seemed so fun and carefree. He had seemed kind. They had connected. But then, his words had been self-serving, arrogant, and bossy. And words *were* actions.

Well, there was only one solution. She would have to investigate. "I have to figure that man out, Fuzzy." Fuzzy did not respond. Instead, he sank his claws into the pine tree where the birds had landed. They flapped their wings, shifted on the branch, and stared down at him with beady eyes. "I have to spend more time with Johan," Christina said. "Although I will have to be careful to guard my heart. I cannot let him sweep me off my feet again. Not until I have figured out his true nature." Christina stopped and looked back at the cub. "Fuzzy! Where in heaven's name are you going?"

Fuzzy had shimmied up the pine tree. He climbed higher and higher, until the birds took flight in a whirl of sleek, shiny feathers and the highest branches quivered from his weight. Christina steadied the buckets with her hands and peered upward. "I know just what to do." She raised her voice loudly enough to carry to the top of the pine tree. Fuzzy twisted his head and stared down with lively, black eyes. "Not about you. You'll have to get yourself down on your own. I know what to do about Johan. I'll invite him to the shearing. That will give me a chance to investigate. And Wilhelm will come too, so Hilda can work to win him over." She nodded. "Yes. I think it will go very well indeed."

It was a good plan. Except for the fact that she was not on speaking terms with Johan. She would have to figure out how to get around that.

Johan was surprised to see Hilda stride out of the forest with Bruno at her heels. He lowered his ax, wiped his brow, and waited for Christina to emerge from the tree line. She did not. He stared at the shadows beneath the hemlocks for a long time before he picked up his ax again. He wanted to see those sparkling blue eyes, dash it all, and that cheerful grin. Johan shook his head and brought the ax down hard on a tree trunk. The thud reverberated through the clearing.

Hilda nodded to Johan and headed straight to Wilhelm. Interesting. Even more interesting was the strange expression on her face. She looked . . . different. Happier? No. The smile on her face seemed strained and out of place. So did the soft giggle that carried across the clearing as she spoke to Wilhelm. Mayhap Christina was ill. He felt a stab of concern. It wasn't like her to stay at home. What if she was ill and Hilda had come to fetch help?

Johan frowned and pulled his attention back to his work. He should not be thinking of Christina Dresser. She had made it clear she held no affection for him. If her rejection of his marriage proposal had not been enough, she had made her feelings clear when she snapped at him at the work party. Enough was enough. He was not a man to sit around and pine for a woman who did not want him. He had his dignity.

Johan hacked at the tree again. There was just one problem. He was not a man to give up. He would cut down this tree, then another, and another, until he had cleared a field large enough to yield a good crop of wheat and barley. He would spend hours and hours plowing and planting. He would not stop until he had finished the job. He would not stop until he had overcome an untamed wilderness.

So why had he given up so easily on the woman he loved?

Johan heard footsteps cut across the clearing and looked up. Wilhelm jogged toward him with a furrowed brow. Johan had not noticed that Hilda had left.

"Strange, that was," Wilhelm said when he reached his brother. "Hilda is not herself."

"No? Has she taken ill? The fever and ague mayhap?" Worry for Christina shot through him, and he fought to keep a calm expression.

"No." Wilhelm shook his head.

Johan felt a surge of relief. "What, then?"

"I cannot say." His frown deepened. "She giggled like a young girl and wouldn't stop smiling."

Johan shrugged. "Nothing wrong with that."

"There is when it's Hilda. You know how serious she is."

Johan laughed. "*Ja*."

"She's asked us to come help with the shearing."

"Ah." He would see Christina. No, more than that—he would spend a day with Christina. Did he still want to avoid her? Would he give up that easily?

He would not. He had not sailed across an ocean and hacked a living out of the wilderness to give up on love. His life was in his own hands. He would not fall short of his dreams now.

"Will you go?" Wilhelm studied his brother's face. "You

barely spoke to Christina at the last work party. I cannot imagine that you want to face her again."

"On the contrary, brother."

Wilhelm's eyebrows shot up.

"I will not give up so easily."

A soft smile crept up Wilhelm's tanned face. "You will apologize, then?"

Johan frowned. He had envisioned sweeping her off her feet with sweet words and charming smiles. Apologies were another thing entirely. "Let's not get ahead of ourselves."

Wilhelm shook his head. "You'll be a bachelor all your days, Johan."

Clearly, Wilhelm did not know what he was talking about. Johan knew that he, Johan, had it all figured out. He felt confident he would be married soon. Not as soon as he had originally thought—but soon enough. By the planting, certainly. How had he allowed doubt and rejection to creep into his heart? He needed to push onward and convince Christina that he was the man for her, not cringe away like a whipped puppy. Johan grinned. He felt a renewed sense of hope and purpose. The shearing could not come soon enough.

When they arrived at the Dresser homestead, Bruno looked as if he would burst from excitement. The dog could sense a change in the air. He ran circles around the sheep, barking and nipping at their heels. The sheep stirred, restless and uneasy. They rolled their black eyes and pushed against one another. "There, there, now. You're all right." Christina wound her way through the flock with gentle hands. She petted and cajoled the sheep until they calmed. Johan smiled as he cut across the clearing. She was softhearted and kind. He liked that about her. No, he loved that about her. He loved *her*.

Johan squared his shoulders and straightened his spine. He was on a mission. He would not fail.

Bruno bounded over as Johan neared the sheep, jumped up, muddied Johan's waistcoat with his paws, then dropped back to the ground and darted away. Christina's attention jerked to Johan when she noticed he had arrived. She sucked in a little gasp of air before she regained her composure and turned back to the flock. She pretended to focus on the sheep, but her complexion gave her away. Her cheeks reddened until they looked as bright as fresh picked apples. Johan smiled. She was happy to see him—even if she didn't know it. His smile widened.

The only question was how to win her over.

Wilhelm looked from Johan, to Christina, and back again. "An apology would take care of everything, I think. That's all she wants." He shook his head. "She's ready to fly into your arms."

"Yes, all she needs to do is apologize to me and everything will be all right."

Wilhelm shot his brother a look.

"I'm joking," Johan said.

"Are you?"

Johan shrugged. "I suppose it's not completely a joke if it's true. . . ."

Wilhelm shook his head again. "Dash your pride, Johan. You'll let her slip right out of your hands. Happiness is right there, waiting for you." He motioned toward Christina with an agitated wave.

"What's troubling you, brother?" Johan's lips slid into a half smile. "Worried happiness might pass you by as well?"

Johan could tell Wilhelm was concerned about more than just his brother's love life.

Wilhelm frowned. "You know how good Hilda is with the children, *ja*?"

"*Ja.*"

"I suppose it would be nice if something worked out between us."

"You suppose it might be nice?" Johan gave his brother a knowing look.

"All right. It *would* be nice."

"Just for the boys' sake?"

Wilhelm rubbed the back of his neck. "All right. For my sake too. I like the woman, dash it all. She is grounded and intelligent and knows how to have a good, meaningful conversation. I haven't met a woman like that since . . ." Wilhelm looked down and softened his voice. "Well, since I lost my Anna."

"I like Hilda as well." Johan put up a hand. "For you, I mean." He shuddered. "Personally, she scares me. I've never seen her smile."

Wilhelm laughed. "That's what I like about her. She's thoughtful. She understands life."

"The same with Christina. She just shows it in a different way."

Wilhelm sighed. "Then we both have to find a way to win their hearts."

"Oh, we will, brother. We will."

"I wish I had your confidence." Wilhelm studied Johan for a moment and grinned. "No, scratch that. Your confidence will be your undoing."

"A woman likes a confident man."

"Only if he can balance it with humility."

Johan had plenty to say about that remark, but he could

not. Hilda was walking to greet them and had just passed into earshot. It was just as well. Johan did not want to have to justify himself. He wanted to keep on acting in a way that felt comfortable and safe. If he had to explain himself, then he might begin to doubt himself. And that simply would not do.

Christina did not mean to stare at Johan. And yet she did. He looked calm and confident as he strode out of the woods and flashed a smile at her. His tanned, chiseled features made her knees weak as he stared back at her. She knew she needed to look away. But her gaze held for another moment before she managed to tear her eyes from him. She needed to focus on her work and remember that today was about investigating. *Not* swooning for a man who might be a mistake.

And yet . . . that strong jawline and quick smile. That crinkle in the corner of his eyes as he grinned. The connection she felt when he laughed with her. Christina clenched her hands into fists and forced herself to focus on the sheep. She would not give away her heart so easily, even if it were already lost to him. She would not.

They needed to herd the flock to the river for washing. She would focus on that. Not on Johan Lantz. But she glanced at Johan five times as they wound through the woods. She kept count of each stolen glance. And each time she told herself to stop. And each time, he flashed that dazzling grin of his. And each time, their eyes met and his gaze made her knees weak.

Her plan was not working. How could she determine his character if one glance from him sent her swooning?

Oh, it was intolerable! How could she be so taken by a man who might be bad for her? She patted a ram on the shoulder to steer him in the right direction and glanced at Johan again. He was already watching her. Her heart walloped into her throat and she held his gaze for three heartbeats before she managed to tear her eyes away. Oh, it truly was intolerable.

Christina tried to pry her attention from Johan and concentrate on the task at hand. The sheep bleated and pushed against one another. Their wool felt soft and familiar beneath Christina's palms as she urged them onward. Wilhelm's boys shouted and clapped as they ran around the edges of the flock to round up strays. Bruno's sharp bark echoed through the woods as he circled the sheep and nipped at their heels. The scene felt so familiar—except the green rolling hills of the Rhine River Valley had been replaced by towering hemlocks and endless oaks. The smell of fresh grass and hay had been replaced by the smell of damp moss and pine needles. The Pennsylvania backcountry was as different from her quaint German village as night was from day. And yet, here she was, surrounded by her people, keeping the old ways. She had brought home with her. The thought made her smile. She could accomplish anything she set her mind to do. She had managed to transport a way of life into a vast, unknown wilderness. Some people had warned that the new world was unfit for sheep. And yet, here she was, finding a way.

If she could manage a flock at the far edge of the Colonies, why couldn't she manage her heart?

Fuzzy growled, stumbled away from a belligerent ram, and tumbled against Christina's leg. The movement startled her from her thoughts. "Careful, little one. The sheep will trample you if you fall underfoot." She shook her head and laughed. "You've forgotten how to be a bear, *ja*? Afraid of a sheep." Fuzzy stared up with friendly eyes. He opened his mouth in that carefree, smiling way of his.

"He thinks he's one of us," Johan said.

Christina started and gave a little gasp. "Oh." She had not realized he was behind her. His deep, cheerful voice washed over her in a wave. She swallowed and tried to push away the emotion. "*Ja*. He is adorable."

Johan looked at her for a moment. He hesitated. Then his eyes twinkled as his lip curled up in a playful half smile. Oh, but he was a dashing one. Christina's heart contracted and she swallowed again.

"Not as adorable as you, Christina."

Oh. Oh my! Had he really? Yes, he had. Christina stared up at Johan with wide eyes. The sheep and the forest and the clang of bells and shouts of children disappeared. There were only the two of them. Christina did not know what to say so she said nothing. The thump of her heart spoke loudly enough.

He held her gaze for a long moment before turning his eyes back to the sheep and jogging away to catch a stray ewe. Christina stood and stared until a ram thumped her in the back of the knees. She shook herself to her senses and stepped aside as Bruno chased the straggler back into the flock. "Steady there, old fella." But her thoughts could not stay on the sheep. They returned to the charming young man who strode through the woodlands with an easy smile and easy words, as if he hadn't a care in the world.

He had called her adorable. *Adorable.* Not beautiful or lovely or pretty. Adorable. What did it mean? Dash it all, she could spend hours analyzing if she let herself. A shallow man would call her beautiful, *ja*? A shallow man would be caught up in her appearance. But a man who liked her for who she was would call her adorable. That single word suddenly felt quite significant.

Or did it? She had said the word first. Perhaps he had merely tossed the word back to her. If she had said Fuzzy was delightful, then he would have called her delightful in return. Christina's lips tightened. Perhaps the compliment was actually a bad sign. Flattery could be a dangerous thing. Johan could be the type to whisper sweet nothings without giving his heart away. How many other women had he called adorable? Or beautiful, or lovely, or pretty? He had said that other women had wanted to marry him. Many other women. No. Being called adorable was not a good sign. He was a flatterer. A shallow flatterer who wanted to sweep a woman off her feet. And then what? She would marry him and find happiness until another woman turned his head? Was that his way? Surely not. He was a good Amish man.

And yet, he had said that many women had wanted to marry him. How many women had he drawn close to? Christina shook her head and imagined a list of pros and cons in her mind. She imagined a big checkmark in the cons column. Johan was too quick with his compliments. Even if that sparkle in his eyes seemed so sincere and so dashing. Oh, how she wanted to believe that the compliment was real.

She would not.

Johan grinned as he loped through the woods. He had made an excellent impression on Christina. She had been quite taken by his compliment. He felt warm and confident inside. *Not as adorable as you, Christina.* Yes, he had done well. And the day was still young. He had plenty of time to draw her in until she was weak in the knees and ready to accept his proposal.

Normally, he would be careful around a lovely young woman who had developed feelings for him. He could not help but smile around those women—it was in his nature to be cheerful and friendly—but he would not encourage them with compliments. Christina was the only woman he had ever wanted to encourage. She was the only woman he *had* encouraged. He hoped he had done well enough. Had he come across like a shallow flirt? Surely not. He was Amish—not some brash, worldly man who might toy with a woman's affections.

Dash it all, he had just been complimenting himself on a job well done, and now he was questioning himself. What was it about Christina Dresser that tied his stomach in knots and made him second-guess his every word?

Love. That's what.

He had not asked to fall in love. He had not wanted to fall in love. Johan flexed his jaw and patted the back of an anxious ram. "Steady now." Did he wish he could cast aside his feelings and return to his old way of life, in which no one caused him to second-guess himself? No. He enjoyed his time with Christina too much. He enjoyed the way her smile sent a shiver up his spine. He enjoyed the way her laughter made his stomach flip-flop. He enjoyed the connection he felt when he stared into her clear, blue eyes.

Then why was he so worried about his approach? Johan patted the ram's sturdy back again. "Almost there, old fella." He would win her over. He had to. Perhaps he was not trying hard enough. Perhaps he needed to compliment her more. Johan gave a little, decisive nod. He would double his efforts.

She would be his.

Eli, Abram, and Gertrud were already in the river when the flock arrived. Catrina had stayed behind to prepare a shearing day feast with her grandmother while the rest of her family helped with the work. As weavers, Eli and Catrina would benefit from a good day of shearing. Between the flax harvest and the shearing, the settlement would have enough fiber for the couple to weave into cloth to supply their neighbors for another year. New Canaan families worked together to meet one another's needs, trading goods and exchanging work so the settlement could survive.

Eli and Abram stood knee deep in the river, wrestling with a heavy log. "You've done well," Hilda said and nodded. The men had stacked logs across a narrow tributary to dam the water and create a pool. Eli wedged the last log in place, waded to the shore, and splashed out of the river with a grin. He had taken off his leather shoes and woolen hosen to keep them dry and wore only his knee breeches, linen shirt, and waistcoat. "Come on in." His grin widened. "It's freezing." He ran his fingers through his bright red hair until every strand stood on end.

"Fix that mop of hair," Abram shouted from the pool. "Catrina's not here to tell you that you look like a rooster."

Eli smiled sheepishly and smoothed his hair. Abram chuckled.

"We'll have our work cut out for us if the water's cold," Hilda said.

"Oh, it's not cold," Eli said. "It's freezing. Didn't you hear me?"

Hilda responded with a faint, distracted smile as she surveyed the flock to formulate a plan. "Let's start with the ewes to show them they need not fear for their lambs. Once they feel safe, the entire flock will rest easier."

Wilhelm emerged from the woods with a lamb balanced on his shoulders. He held her legs securely as she rested her soft white chin on the top of his head. "Found a straggler," Wilhelm said as he lowered the lamb to the ground. The little animal hit the ground running and shoved her way into the flock until she found her mother and snuggled against her side.

Hilda's expression changed. She looked as if she had just remembered something. She frowned, cleared her throat, and smiled. "Oh, Wilhelm. Thank you." She lowered her voice so that only Wilhelm could hear, but Johan stood close enough to catch the words. "I was just wondering what we should do. I'm sure you can tell us." She looked up at him and smiled as she batted her eyelashes. Wilhelm looked surprised, and no wonder. Hilda looked very strange indeed.

"Do you have something in your eye?" Wilhelm asked.

"No." Hilda's face fell. She stopped batting her eyelashes.

"Are you all right?"

"*Ja*. Of course." She widened her smile. "I'm waiting for you to tell us what the plan should be."

Wilhelm frowned. "They're your sheep. Don't you know how to wash the wool?"

Hilda's eye twitched. She looked as if she wanted to say something, but she did not. She glanced at Christina, who nodded encouragingly. Hilda took a deep breath and forced a cheerful smile. The expression did not fit her face at all. "Oh, *ja*. But you are so smart, and I just thought . . ." Hilda cleared her throat. She looked miserable behind her smile.

Johan watched and wondered what on earth was wrong with the poor woman.

Christina watched Hilda interact with Wilhelm and exhaled with exasperation. Hilda was not very good at building a man's confidence. Christina had told her sister to make Wilhelm feel smart and competent—men loved that—but to make it seem natural. She had warned Hilda to speak only the truth or it would seem forced. Not to mention that she would be dangerously close to telling a lie. Telling a lie would not do, of course.

Christina knew the trick was to focus on the positive and make sure a man knew he was appreciated. Hilda did not seem to understand that. Instead she was making herself look foolish. Acting as if she didn't know how to wash the wool! The very idea. Christina knew Wilhelm would not be impressed. Indeed, he was not. He looked down at Hilda with a quizzical expression as he rubbed his fingers across his beard. His mouth opened, closed again, and he shook his head.

Hilda gazed up at Wilhelm with adoring eyes. She smiled a fresh, innocent smile. Or at least it was supposed to be a fresh, innocent smile. Christina had practiced with her over breakfast that morning. But Hilda's smile looked more like a grimace. This would not do. This would not do at all. Christina pushed her way through the flock to reach Hilda and Wilhelm. "What my sister means to say is that she would welcome your advice. Of course, she knows how to wash her sheep. We've done it for years. But we've never had the pleasure of doing so with you and Johan." Christina flashed her fresh, innocent smile (the one Hilda was *supposed* to give) and turned to look for

Johan. He stood a few paces away, watching her. Their eyes met, and he returned her smile.

Oh dear. That was not the signal she wanted to give Johan. Now she had done it! Now Johan thought she wanted to smile at him like that. Well, she did, but that was beside the point. She had worked hard all morning to avoid smiling at him like that, and now she had. It could not be helped. She had to show Hilda how it was done. And she couldn't give Wilhelm that smile; it was a smile she reserved for the man she loved. Dash it all, she did still love Johan, like it or not.

That didn't mean she would agree to marry him.

Johan's expression softened as his eyes connected with hers. He looked happy for the first time since the disastrous proposal. She would have to be careful not to encourage him further. Not until she had figured out his true character.

It would not be easy. She wanted to fall into those deep, gray eyes of his. She wanted to run into his arms and melt. Christina raised her chin and turned away. She ought not to want to run into the arms of a man who thought he was *der Herr's* gift to women. Humph. She should not even be tempted.

"Let's get them in the water," Christina said as she turned back to Hilda and Johan. "We've a long day ahead of us." A long day of avoiding Johan's smoldering gaze. Heaven have mercy!

Hilda gave a quick, decisive nod. She whistled to Bruno and pushed into the flock. Eli splashed into the water to take his place beside Abram in the pool while Christina, Hilda, Gertrud, Johan, Wilhelm, and his boys steered the ewes down the riverbank. The sheep shuddered and bleated as they sank into the pool. Eli and Abram led each one through the water quickly, patting their necks and whispering soothing woods. The sheep trotted back onto the riverbank in a long, wet row as water dripped from their fluffy coats.

A ewe bleated and kicked against the water as she splashed into the pool. She slipped from Eli's grasp and spun around in the water. Her eyes flashed with agitation. Christina kicked off her leather shoes and jumped in without taking the time to remove her woolen hosen. The water shot a shiver of cold refreshment up her spine. Her toes squished into the mud. She wiggled them and laughed. Christina loved shearing day. It made her feel alive. She relished a challenge and a change in the daily routine.

The anxious ewe splashed past Christina and tried to escape the way she had come. "Steady now, old girl. You're not clean yet. Nobody wants dirty wool. Let's take a little swim, *ja*?" Christina ran her hand along the ewe's back in a smooth, reassuring motion. "Just a little swim, *ja*?" She scratched behind the animal's ears and hummed a cheerful tune from the *Ausbund*. "There, there now."

Christina heard a big splash behind her, followed by a smaller one. She turned to see Johan wade toward her with Fuzzy paddling behind. "Silly little bear." Christina laughed.

"Let me help," Johan said as he waded through the water. "You'll catch your death in those wet hosen."

"So will you," Christina said as she peered down into the cool, clear water. "You've left yours on as well."

Johan shrugged. "You needed me."

Christina beamed. She could not stop herself. He had come to her aid. He cared. He did not want her to wrestle the sheep alone or catch cold in the water. His hand moved to steady the ewe and brushed against hers. The warmth of his touch rippled through her body, all the way to her toes. She curled them into the mud and grinned.

"That little fellow's got the right idea," Johan said and nodded at Fuzzy. The cub paddled furiously toward the shore, sneezed three times, and clamored out of the water. He collapsed onto the bank and stared at Christina.

"He's looking at me like I'm crazy," Christina said and laughed. Maybe she was crazy. Here she was, laughing with Johan and feeling weak from his touch. She was supposed to be keeping her distance while she observed his character. Well, he *had* come to her side when she'd needed him. That was a positive mark for him. It reminded her of the time he had rushed to her side when the brush caught fire at his homestead. Oh, he did know how to be gallant. Christina felt bright and cheerful inside. She leaned closer to him and their foreheads almost knocked as they bent over the sheep. They both laughed. She loved the sound of his deep, masculine laugh. It always sounded so carefree and genuine.

Then again, he could be helping her just to prove a point. He could be trying to convince her that he was good and trustworthy. Dash it all, she had to stop overanalyzing. For now, she would let herself fall into the joy of the moment. She would grin with him as they splashed through the water and felt the thrill of being young and alive. She would worry about his character later. Goodness knows there would be time enough for that.

Chapter Nineteen

Johan felt a surge of relief when Christina laughed with him. She wanted him near. He knew she did. Their eyes met over the back of the ewe, and he felt that familiar connection between them. Her joy and exuberance shone through her eyes and filled him. He wanted to pick her up, spin her around in the water, and shout that he loved her. He did not.

She could not reject him now. She would have to see the truth. Who else would laugh and play as they herded wet, irritable sheep through cold water? She would have to see they made the perfect team. They both loved life. They fed off one another's happiness.

The morning passed quickly. Johan did not notice that his feet were numb until the last sheep huddled on the riverbank, basking in the yellow sunshine that dappled the shore. He took Christina's elbow to help her out of the pool and up the riverbank. She gave a little gasp at the unexpected touch and turned to look up at him. He smiled and nodded ahead of them. "Let's get you dry, *ja*?"

She nodded with big, blue eyes. Her face glowed with sun and moisture. Water clung to her skirts and prayer *kappe*. A thick blond curl had escaped and hung wet and limp against her cheek. She had never looked more beautiful, more vibrant, more alive. No woman had.

Gertrud and the boys had built a fire on the shore to warm everyone. Johan sank down in front of it with a grateful sigh. He peeled off one wet, woolen hose, then the other, wrung them out, and hung them from a branch. His knee breeches were wet to the waist and they clung to his skin uncomfortably. He barely noticed. He only noticed Christina's bright smile and eager laugh. She kneeled close to the fire, wrung out the wet lock of hair, and tried to push it back under her prayer *kappe*. She only managed to loosen more hair. Soon, she had a tangle of damp, blond curls framing her face. Her woolen hosen were caked with mud and her apron was stained with dirt. Johan wondered if she felt self-conscious.

"I've not had so much fun in months," she said and leaned back into her hands.

No, she did not feel self-conscious. She was confident and full of life. She knew she was beautiful but did not flaunt it. She was not afraid to be real. Dash it all, he wanted her to be his wife. He wanted to work by her side like this through every season. What joy they would have in the years to come. He just needed to win her over.

Johan considered for a moment. He needed to say just the right thing. Too much and he might scare her away. Too little and she might not feel properly appreciated. His heart quickened and his chest contracted. He frowned. Never before had he felt this nervous about what he said to a woman. There was nothing to do but plunge forward and hope for the best. "I've never seen a woman look more beautiful," he said in a voice so low that only she could hear. There, he had done it. He could not take it back. Anyway, he did not want to. It was the truth.

Christina flinched. Her eyes cut to his, and her mouth opened. She closed it before saying anything. Her brow furrowed and she stared at him for a moment. He wondered what on earth she was thinking.

"You flatter me," she said at last. Her expression looked careful and guarded.

"*Ja*," he said and flashed his signature grin.

She sighed and looked away, into the fire. "You flatter me too much."

Now it was Johan's turn to flinch. What had she meant by that? "Flattery is never too much when it is the truth."

"But you do not speak the truth." She picked up a damp curl, held it up, and dropped it again. "I look as sorry as a wet sheep. That is the truth. Your words prove that you speak sweet nothings. There is no sincerity in them."

Sweet nothings? Dash it all, did she really think he was making it all up? Did she think he said things just to flatter her? Did she not realize he was madly in love with her?

She did not.

Oh, it was intolerable. What could he say now without digging a deeper hole for himself? He swallowed and pushed ahead. "A woman of true beauty is beautiful in all circumstances."

"Beautiful words, Johan."

For a moment, he thought that everything was all right. He thought she liked his explanation. But she pushed off the ground, rose to her feet, and wiped her palms on her apron. "You are full of beautiful words, *ja*?" She strode away without looking at him.

What had he done wrong now?

Christina wanted to cry. She wanted to stomp her foot at the unfairness of it all. She did neither. Instead, she forced a smile and nodded to Abram as he chased a stray ram out of the woods. She turned away and pressed her fingertips to her eyelids. She would not let the tears leak out. She would not. How could Johan say such a thing? How could he say she was beautiful?

Someone grabbed Christina's sleeve and she jumped. Was it Johan? She turned and saw it was not. She felt disappointed and relieved to see Hilda standing at her side. "You look a sight," Hilda said.

"It's nothing."

"Nothing?" Hilda put a hand on her hip. Her face tightened. "I know you better than that." She shook her head. "If it makes you feel better, you are not the only one who has failed to impress today."

"Oh, Hilda." Christina gripped her sister's arm. "You're doing fine."

"No." Hilda glanced around and shook her head again. "I am not." She lowered her voice and leaned closer. "You witnessed that ridiculous interaction about how to wash the wool."

"You did fine," Christina repeated.

Hilda raised her eyebrows.

"All right. Maybe it wasn't fine. But you have to start somewhere. You'll get there."

"*Ach*, you didn't witness what happened later."

"Go on."

"I giggled. No, I *tried* to giggle when Fuzzy jumped in the water. It sounded more like a croak."

"Surely not."

"Wilhelm asked if I had something in my throat."

"Oh."

"He offered to bring me a cup of water."

"Oh dear."

The sisters stared at each other for a moment. Christina wanted to offer encouragement, but she did not know where to start. She had her own problems to tackle with Johan. "I'm sorry, Hilda. But I promise you'll manage. Just a bit more practice, *ja*? You'll have him in the palm of your hand." Their eyes moved down the riverbank to where Wilhelm leaned against a tree, one knee bent, the sole of his shoe casually braced against the trunk. He chewed a blade of wild grass as he watched the sheep. His tanned, rugged face looked open and friendly. Christina wondered why everything had to be so complicated. Wouldn't it be easier if everyone just said what they wanted to say and meant it? Perhaps. But would that approach win Hilda a good man?

Hilda sighed and looked back to Christina. "Enough about me. You looked on the verge of tears when I stopped you. What's happened?"

"*Ach*, it's Johan again."

"Of course, it is." Hilda gave an encouraging nod. "What did he say this time?"

"He called me beautiful."

"How thoughtless."

"No. You don't understand." Christina motioned down the front of her body. "Look at me!" She picked up the edge of her muddy apron and shook it. "Just look at me! Any man who calls me beautiful today is just whispering sweet nothings. He's a flatterer, that is all. And this proves it."

"Christina. Really."

"Don't act so sure that you know his intentions, Hilda! You weren't there!" Christina's hands curled into fists. "He gazed into my eyes with that slick, dashing gaze of his and the words flowed from his mouth like honey. He's too smooth with his words, sister."

Hilda frowned. "Mayhap he really thought you looked beautiful. When a man is in love, he sees beauty everywhere." A teasing half smile crept up Hilda's face. "Even in a sopping wet, bedraggled mouse."

Christina laughed. "You frustrate me so! But I can't stay frustrated with you because you make me laugh. And that makes me even more frustrated!"

Hilda looked satisfied. She almost smiled.

"Do you really think I look like a wet, bedraggled mouse?"

"No. Truth be told, I think you look like a drowned rat."

"Hilda!"

"A beautiful drowned rat."

Christina laughed again. She glanced back at the fire. Johan sat with his elbows resting listlessly on each bent knee. His body slouched. He did not look happy. "Do you really think he meant what he said?"

"*Ja*. I do."

Christina pursed her lips. She would have to be sure. "We shall see." A sheep wandered past and butted Hilda aside. Hilda hopped a step and regained her balance. "Easy now," Christina murmured and patted the wet, wooly back. "We'd better get them back for the shearing. But don't forget we've more at stake today than this year's wool. We've got your future to consider. Don't stop trying, Hilda. You will win Wilhelm's heart. I know you will."

Hilda rubbed her eyes with the heel of her hand. She did not look at all confident. Christina's stomach sank. For the first time since she'd met Wilhelm, Christina began to doubt her plan would work.

The morning had passed, and the sun shone directly overhead by the time they herded the sheep back to the Dresser homestead. Catrina and her grandmother appeared with the noonday meal. They ate the hearty brown bread and roast venison quickly. There was much work still to be done. The feast would come at sunset, after the last sheep had been sheared.

Johan watched Christina from a distance throughout lunch. She did not return his gaze. In fact, she made an obvious effort not to look at him. Dash it all, what was wrong with her? Didn't a woman want to be told she was beautiful? She *was* beautiful. He studied the way the noonday sun shone across her nose and cheeks. Each eyelash caught the light. Her face glowed pink from too much heat. She had forgotten to wear her scoop again.

Johan picked up a pebble and tossed it aimlessly. Since when did he notice little details about a woman? Since when had he noticed a woman had forgotten to wear her hat? Since he had fallen in love with Christina Dresser, that's when. Johan tossed another pebble. Time to get back to work. He would drive himself crazy if he kept staring at Christina while she ignored him.

He had never been ignored before.

Johan wondered if he should be upset with her. It did seem rude for her to respond to being called beautiful by stomping away in a huff. He rose from the ground and stretched his back. He could not feel frustrated with her. She was simply too adorable. No, he felt something far more dangerous. He felt challenged. He would not give up, even if the effort tore his heart from his chest. He would find a way to show his love, even if it killed him. And, indeed, at the moment, it felt as if it might.

Especially when Christina turned on her heel to avoid him. Couldn't a fellow shear a sheep next to a lovely woman who had won his affection? Apparently not. Johan picked up a pair of shears and leaned over a restless ewe. Shearing was a difficult skill to master. Blades the length of a man's forearm had to be wielded just so. A good shearer knew the contours of a sheep's body and could cut the wool in careful strokes so the fleece peeled away in one large piece without nicking the animal's skin. A good shearer kept a sheep calm and relaxed as he worked.

Johan was not a good shearer. He knew the basics, but he was no expert. He worked slowly and carefully with his jaw clenched and his hands unsteady. He was worried he might accidentally hurt the sheep—or himself. Thankfully, he did not. But the blades looked frightfully sharp and his fingers had a habit of getting in the way. He sheared two sheep before he stood up, kneaded his back and forearms, and wiped his brow. Dash it all, shearing was backbreaking work. It wasn't easy to hold down a sheep and stoop over it at an unnatural angle while wielding heavy shears that exhausted the muscles in his wrists, hands, and forearms. Plowing and harvesting were tough, but a man got used to it. Shearing used muscles he had forgotten he had. And since sheep were only sheared once a year, those muscles never got used to the job. His arms would be burning by day's end. And for days after.

Johan stole a glance at Christina. Seven fleeces lay piled

by her feet. Seven! Good night. He felt like a weakling. He had managed two to her seven. Hilda was on her ninth fleece. Dash it all, the woman's hands were flying. Wilhelm looked as lost as Johan. He clenched his teeth as he frowned with concentration. He had only sheared two sheep. Well, at least Johan wasn't the only one who had fallen behind.

Abram looked comfortable with a pair of shears. He had sheared five sheep. A decent number, but fewer than the Dresser sisters. Gertrud did not try. She had never sheared before and said it would be foolish to start now. There was not time to learn. She helped Bruno bring the sheep to each shearer while Abram teased her over her muddy feet. She had given up on her shoes after stumbling into the river.

Although the work was hard, Johan heard lively chatter and laughter throughout the clearing. Abram joked with Eli. The children shouted and played as they helped Gertrud mind the sheep. It felt like home. It *was* home. He had not expected to find a little piece of German village life in the wilderness. But here they were, working together on shearing day, just as people had for generations. Afterward, there would be feasting and fellowship, just as there always had been. Sure, they worked in a muddy clearing, surrounded by wild woodlands, rather than a tidy village green. They heard the empty rustle of wind through pine needles, rather than the familiar rattle of wagon wheels over cobblestone. They smelled the damp mustiness of rotten logs and forest floor, rather than the scent of fresh cut hay from the fields. But they were together. They were doing what people had always done, while finding a new way and a new place to do it.

Johan felt a surge of confidence. Everything would

work out. It had to. The Dresser sisters had managed to raise sheep in the backcountry, despite the wolves and uncertain food supply. They had managed to organize a shearing party, as they had in their villages back home. They would manage to keep the settlement alive. They would manage to bring the old ways here and create new ways.

And he would manage to win the right woman. If all other things were possible, surely that was too.

A man stepped in front of Christina and blocked the sun. She stopped squinting against the light but did not look up. Her hands flew across the fleece as the shears whispered and snipped. She knew who stood in front of her without looking. She could sense the confident, masculine presence. If she looked up, Christina knew Johan's dashing smile would meet her gaze. She kept her eyes trained on the sheep.

"You've a way with that," he said at last. Christina did not know how to reply. She clipped the last strands of wool and gave the ram a solid pat on his haunches. The animal scrambled to his feet and dashed away. He looked half the size he had been just moments earlier.

Johan shifted his weight from one foot to the other. Sunlight emerged over his shoulder and pierced her eyes. She squinted, cupped the blade of her hand across her brow, and looked up.

"You've bested me," he said and flashed that dashing smile she had expected to see. Her stomach leapt at the sight. She wished she could calm herself. She could not. His smile lit her up from the top of her head to the bottoms of her feet. When he grinned at her, she felt as if she were the only woman in the world.

Perhaps that was his plan. He seemed quite skillful at making her feel special. Did he flash that smile at every woman? He had admitted—no, bragged—that many women had fallen for him. Was she really special to him? Christina replayed Hilda's story about Amos Schneider in her mind for the hundredth time. He had been charming too. It would not do to blindly trust a handsome, charming man.

"Have I?" she answered. It seemed a safe, neutral response.

"I thought I might offer you my assistance, but I fear it is not needed." He looked hopeful.

Christina considered. "No, it is not."

"Ah, well. If you find a need, I am here." He gave a boyish smile. "My talents are wasted on the shearing. Painfully slow going, it is."

Christina glanced at his pile of fleeces and laughed. "I'm sorry. I don't mean to make fun of you." She laughed again. "But that is a pitiful day's work."

"Indeed it is. Which is why I've come to see what I might do to assist you."

She felt her resolve fade. "Actually, there is a ram who has been unwilling to cooperate. He's the last to go."

Johan glanced around the clearing. "We're finished?"

Christina laughed again. "*Ja*. You didn't notice?"

"No. I've been too busy to notice anything at all." Except his aching back. He noticed that quite well.

"Poor Johan. Worn out after shearing two sheep. You've little practice with shearing, *ja*?"

Johan shrugged. "Not as much practice as you, anyway." He gave an encouraging smile. "You're the best I've seen."

Christina frowned. He was trying to flatter her again.

"That can't be true." She nodded toward Hilda. "Hilda is better than I."

Johan looked as if he knew he had made a mistake. "True." He thought for a moment, then grinned. He had regained his confidence. "But she is not as cheerful at her work. Your smile makes you the best. It lights up the entire clearing."

Ah. A good save. Christina wanted it to be a sincere compliment. It was true she was known for her cheerful smile. Mayhap he *was* telling her how he really felt.

He gazed at her for a long moment with those twinkling gray eyes of his, then nodded and turned away. "I'll round up that ram."

"Thank you." She did not know if he heard her. Her voice had sounded hoarse and dry. She wanted to run after him and shout, *Yes! Yes, I will marry you!* He was handsome and charming and full of life. He made her feel alive. She swallowed the words and looked away. She had been impulsive all her life. She had to be more thoughtful. Hilda had warned her often enough. Marriage was not something to rush into. Even if every bone in her body shouted at her to rush after Johan and melt into his arms.

Johan whistled and sang as he cornered the ram against the cabin. The animal lowered his head and pawed the ground with a hoof. The whites of his eyes showed. Johan did not hesitate at the sight of the curled horns. He lowered his voice to a gentle tone and eased closer. "Steady there, old fella."

Christina watched with a lump in her throat. He sounded so gentle and comforting. Even so, she expected the ram to charge. Johan did not flinch. He just smiled at the animal and kept speaking in a calm, low voice. He flashed that happy grin of his. He was enjoying himself. Christina smiled and leaned forward. She loved how carefree he was. He knew there was a solution to every problem and that there was no sense in getting worked up about it.

That reminded her that she did not see a solution to *her* problem. She had been keeping score all day and the tally felt even. Her opinion flopped back and forth with every interaction. Mayhap it was because her heart longed for him. She could feel the rightness of it all, deep within her. Or mayhap it was because she was prone to foolishness and could be easily persuaded. Even Hilda had fallen for a man of poor character. How much more vulnerable was Christina, with her open heart and emotional nature?

Christina watched as Johan led the ram to her. The animal looked calmer, but still skittish. He rolled his eyes and flung his head about when Christina reached for him. "You're all right, old fella," Johan said in a soothing voice. "Got to get that wool coat off, *ja*?" He held the ram steady as Christina picked up her shears. "You'd be mighty hot come summer, *ja*?"

Christina worked quickly. Johan teased and joked as the shears flashed against the fleece. A few minutes later, the ram trotted away, looking much smaller and humbler without his great wooly coat. "Funny little thing," Christina said as she set down the shears for the last time. She watched the ram lower his head and taunt a rival with his great, curled horns. "I think he's trying to regain his dignity."

Johan chuckled. He looked down at Christina with cheerful eyes. "What would you do without me, girl?"

Christina stiffened. He was teasing, but he was on dangerous ground.

"You ought to stop fighting and admit I'm the man

for you." He nodded toward the ram. "We make a good team, *ja*?"

She stared at him without answering. She was not sure if he was charming or arrogant. It could be so hard to tell with a man like him.

"You ought to trust me to know what's best for you."

Now he had gone too far.

"What's best for me?"

The spark faded from his eyes. "Marrying me."

"And you know what's best for me?" Her eyes narrowed.

"Well, I like to think that I know—"

"That's quite enough, Johan Lantz. I know very well what you think. You think you know everything, don't you? You are all smiles and charm. And yet your arrogance shows despite your best efforts to hide it." She smoothed the front of her skirts, turned, and marched away as fast as propriety would allow. She did not speak to him the rest of the day, even when the others chatted and feasted and wistfully remembered the old ways. She did not break her resolve when Johan watched her with confused eyes and brought her a slice of Catrina's dried apple pie. Christina had heard all she needed to hear from Johan Lantz.

Chapter Twenty

Christina and Hilda both felt out of sorts the next day.

"It's hopeless," Hilda said.

"Nothing's hopeless," Christina said. But she released a long thin sigh as she said the words. Her shoulders sagged. "We ought to be happy. It was a wonderful shearing day." Except that it wasn't.

"*Ja*," Hilda said. "Wonderful." She did not sound as if she thought it had been wonderful either.

Christina and Hilda stood at the big black cauldron in the middle of their clearing. They had risen early that morning to eat a cold breakfast, drag the cauldron into the yard, and build a fire. "Let's try not to think about anything but today's work," Hilda said. They had to extract lanolin from the wool. The waxy, waterproof goop was good for many household needs, from axle grease to hand lotion and medicinal salves.

The sisters picked up handfuls of wool and pushed them into the hot water with a wooden paddle. Fuzzy sniffed the pile of wool on the ground, decided he could not eat it, and scampered away to chase a butterfly. Bruno lay in the sun with his head on his paws, but his ears twitched whenever the sheep bleated. He looked ready to spring into action, despite his half-closed eyelids.

Christina stoked the fire until the flames licked the sides of the cauldron. "Almost boiling."

"*Ja.*"

They spoke little as they stirred the wool and kept the flames high. After a long silence, Hilda cracked her knuckles and said she felt quite foolish.

"Why?"

"Because I could not win Wilhelm's attention, much less his heart."

"Don't be so hard on yourself. There's time yet."

"He just stared at me as if I were some strange creature. The more I tried, the more he gave me that confused look."

"Then you will just have to try harder."

"*Ja.* I suppose so."

"There is too much at stake to give up now." Christina considered the situation as she pushed the wool under the surface of the water. Her eyes watered from the steam and heat. Her arms felt stiff and sore from the shearing. She patted her forehead with the edge of her apron. "I'm at a loss, Hilda. I don't know what to think about Johan."

"He seems like a good man, Christina."

"*Ja,* but that is what you thought about Amos Schneider."

"Oh." Hilda looked as if she had been struck.

"I'm sorry. I shouldn't have said that."

Hilda shook her head. "No. It's true. He fooled me." Her lips tightened into a thin line. "But I was young and naïve then."

"You, young and naïve? I can't imagine it, Hilda."

Hilda laughed softly. "You know I was."

"Mmmm." Christina used her back to force the paddle

through the water. Wet wool was remarkably heavy. "It's still hard to imagine."

"I like to think that I've learned to recognize a man of good character from one of poor character." Hilda gave a sad, wistful smile. "But perhaps not. I did not realize that Amos was the one at fault until you pointed it out the other day."

"You didn't realize?" Christina's mouth fell open. How could serious, no-nonsense Hilda have been fooled? "But no one pulls the wool over your eyes."

"Ah, but he did."

"Surely you realized a good man would not taunt you so."

"Love does strange things to us. I thought it was all me. I thought if I had just been what he wanted . . . if I just could have been good enough for him."

"No, Hilda. Love does not work that way. Love should not hurt. Love should never hurt."

"Oh, it hurt for years and years."

"Don't you see, Hilda? Love should not hurt because of what a man says or does. If it hurts for those reasons, then something is wrong. Love should make one feel, well, *loved*."

"Then perhaps I have never been loved by a man," Hilda said.

"Not by Amos Schneider," Christina said.

"No. Not by Amos Schneider." Hilda looked thoughtful. She wedged a stick of wood into the fire and watched the sparks fly. "I fear that I have encouraged you to make the same mistake."

"With Johan?"

"*Ja.*" Hilda stared into the fire with hardened eyes. "Johan seems a nice young man. He seems like a perfect match for you. But now that I realize how badly I misjudged Amos, I fear I could have misjudged Johan."

Christina shared the same fear. Her heart felt heavy in her chest. What would she do if she could not trust Hilda's opinion? A cry from the edge of the forest cut into Christina's thoughts. Fuzzy exploded through the tree line followed by two laughing boys. The cub looked back, opened his mouth in what looked like an impish grin, and scampered to Christina.

"Franz! Fritz!" Christina waved them over. "There's a cold meat pie on the table, if you've missed breakfast."

Fritz shook his head. "We can't. We've lost Papa. Fuzzy found us. Or rather we found him and followed him here. Papa is looking for us in the woods."

"Wilhelm must be near," Hilda said. "Fuzzy couldn't have wandered far. I hadn't even noticed he'd left before he came back again."

"Right you are," a deep voice boomed from the edge of the clearing.

"Papa!" The two boys ran to their father and threw their arms around his waist. "We found you!"

Wilhelm smiled indulgently. "No. *I* found *you*."

"How did you find us?" Franz asked.

"I followed the sounds of two rowdy boys. It was like following a trail of breadcrumbs."

The boys hugged their father and then raced away to chase Fuzzy.

"Be more careful next time," Wilhelm shouted after them. "The woods are no place for two little boys. What if night had come before I found you?"

"Oh, you don't have to worry, Papa. We will always be loud enough for you to find us."

"What am I going to do with you two?" Wilhelm smiled

and shook his head. The boys did not answer. They were too busy patting Fuzzy and scratching his warm, soft belly. Fuzzy nuzzled against Fritz's knee and nibbled the hem of his breeches.

"I sent them for water ages ago," Wilhelm said.

"It is fortunate you found them," Christina said.

"They would have made their way home eventually," Hilda said. "They only needed to follow the river. It would lead them to Jacob Miller's homestead if they headed in one direction and Eli Webber's if they headed in the other."

Christina caught her sister's eye and shook her head slightly, then glanced at Wilhelm to make sure he had not seen the signal.

"Oh. What I meant was that I don't know what I would have done. Two boys alone in the wilderness? It makes me shudder! They are blessed to have a father who knows how to rescue them." She cleared her throat and cut her eyes to Christina, who nodded encouragingly. Hilda swallowed. She hesitated. "A strong, handsome father." Hilda looked mortified as she said the words.

"Oh. Well." Wilhelm looked equally mortified. He cleared his throat and looked down to study his leather boots.

Hilda frowned. She tried to giggle. Wilhelm's eyes swung back up to her.

"Are you all right?"

"*Ja*. Of course. Quite all right."

Wilhelm rubbed the back of his neck. He looked uncomfortable. "I best be going."

Hilda nodded. She looked as if she might run away if he did not first. Christina stepped between them. "Won't you and the boys stay for breakfast?"

A shriek of joy kept Wilhelm from answering. The three

adults turned to see the boys wrestling atop one of the stacks of soft, white fleeces. Christina gasped. The boys had tracked mud across the clean wool. It would have to be washed again. She looked at Hilda. Hilda would know what to say and how to handle the situation fairly but firmly.

But she did not. Hilda started toward the boys, then stopped. She opened her mouth and closed it again. "Oh, I just don't know what to do," she said and put a hand on Wilhelm's sleeve. "But you can rescue us from this situation, *ja*? You know just what to do, I'm sure."

Wilhelm looked frustrated and confused. He glanced from Hilda to the boys and back to Hilda again. "What's gotten into you, Hilda?"

Hilda giggled. "Oh, I've just realized how much I need a strong man like you to take care of everything." Hilda's shoulders tightened. It looked as if her body fought the words even as she said them. She looked at Christina for support.

Christina smiled and nodded. "Oh, *ja*. Wilhelm is sure to help you, Hilda."

"Um. All right." He stared at Hilda for a long moment, then strode over to the boys. He spoke in a low voice. Christina could not make out his words, but she saw the reaction on the boys' faces. They looked down at the ground and appeared very sorry indeed.

Wilhelm turned back to Christina. "The boys will take the muddy fleeces down to the river and bring them back after they've cleaned them." He stood over the boys and gave his most serious expression. "You know the path home. Don't stray from it. No matter what."

"Of course not, Papa." They looked as innocent as

angels—angels who could not help but leap into every imaginable mischief.

"You'll stay for a late breakfast?" Christina asked. "We have half a meat pie." They had left it on the table, covered with a white linen cloth, to finish at lunch.

Wilhelm shook his head and backed away. "Thank you, no. I must be away." He spun around and jogged into the woods before either sister could protest.

"Well!" Christina said and put her hands on her hips. "I never."

"He could not get away from me fast enough," Hilda said. She sighed and looked down at the cauldron. The oil from the wool had risen to the surface of the boiling water to form yellow, buttery blobs. "Let's pretend that never happened." Hilda began to scoop the lanolin from the surface of the water with the wooden paddle.

"Stop."

"Why? It's ready."

"I'm not talking about the lanolin and you know it. I'm talking about you. Stop acting as if it's hopeless."

"I'm making a mess of things," Hilda said as she pulled the paddle through the water. Steam moistened her prayer *kappe* and made her face shine red with heat.

"I told you, it takes time to get it right. You'll figure out how to win his heart."

Hilda shook her head. She wiped her forehead with her sleeve. "Mayhap I should give up and just be myself." Hilda exhaled and plunged the paddle back into the water. She stared at the water for a while. "Never mind. Being myself never won any man's heart before. Why should it now?"

Christina looked at her sister but did not respond. She did not know what to say.

They did not talk as they poured the lanolin into a clay jar. Hilda looked tight-lipped and distracted. Christina knew she had to solve the problem. She racked her mind for a new plan. When the idea came, it was wonderful. It was foolproof. It would fix everything.

The idea hit her as she remembered how Wilhelm had rushed into the clearing as he searched for his lost boys. What if Hilda were lost in the forest? What if Wilhelm had to rescue her? A damsel in distress, a hero waiting to act— oh, it was almost too perfect. Sparks would fly.

She could not tell Hilda, of course. Hilda had already shown doubts about her ability to win Wilhelm's affection. She would never agree to a harebrained scheme in which she pretended to be lost. More importantly, it would be dishonest if Hilda knew. She could not say she was lost if she was not really lost. That would be a lie. So Hilda could not be a party to the plan. Christina chewed on her bottom lip as she thought things through. She would have to take Hilda deep into the woods and leave her. It was the only way. Hilda would not mind. She was not easily frightened. It would all be worth it in the end.

There was no time to waste. Christina had to think of a plausible reason to lead Hilda into the wilderness. Hilda was too practical to go flouncing about the woods without reason. Oh, it would have to be a good reason. Christina could not lie either, so it would have to have some truth to it. Christina closed her eyes. She imagined the great, wide forest and the winding footpath that disappeared at the edge of the settlement to fade into the roots and trees. She imagined the Blue Mountain that hovered above the forest in the distance and huddled in the morning mist. What could draw Hilda there?

"Are you all right?" Hilda asked.

Christina's eyes flew open.

"Do you have a headache?"

"No. Why would you think that?"

"Because you were squeezing your eyes shut."

Christina did not respond. She was too busy being inspired. Headache made her think of fever, and fever made her think of yarrow.

Yarrow! The answer was yarrow! Christina felt a spark of excitement shoot through her chest. This plan would not fail. It was far better than any other she had ever attempted.

"If it is not a headache, then what is it?" Hilda asked as she fastened the lid atop the jar of lanolin. "Something is distracting you."

"*Ja*. It is." Christina's lips curled in a satisfied smile. She knew just what to say—and it was all honest and true. "Do you remember the fever that sickened Jacob Miller and the Webbers?"

"*Ja*."

"And Greta treated them with yarrow tea?"

"*Ja*."

Christina waved toward the cabin. She knew there was not any yarrow beside the dried herbs that hung from the low wooden rafters. "We don't have any."

Hilda frowned. "No, we don't."

"What if we sicken? Every household should keep a good store of yarrow."

"The season for fevers has passed."

"Not for the fever and ague. That is a summer illness."

Hilda nodded. "*Ja*. You're right. We ought not to be slack in this matter."

"There should be plenty growing along the riverbank. Let's gather some today. I'd feel better if we did." It was true, she *would* feel better if they went. Christina just didn't specify *why* she would feel better.

"I suppose we can spare the afternoon," Hilda said. "Baking day isn't until the morrow. We've finished the last batch of lanolin and the sheep are shorn and happy." Hilda nodded decisively. "*Ja.* Let's go."

Christina gave a little leap and clapped her hands.

Hilda narrowed her eyes. "Is it that exciting, sister mine?"

Christina hoped she had not given herself away. She could never hide her joy—especially when she was in the midst of a successful scheme. "It is a lovely day to be outside. I do love spring, don't you?"

"I like it fine. Better than winter, I suppose. Although there is more work to be done."

"Oh, Hilda." Christina linked her arm in her sister's and tugged her toward the tree line. "Always practical."

Hilda shrugged. "Why would I be any other way?"

Christina laughed. It was going to be a wonderful day.

Chapter Twenty-One

Johan heard the shout before he saw Hilda. She caught sight of him across his clearing and barked at him to hurry. Something was wrong. He flung his ax to the ground and jogged to meet her as she emerged from the tree line. Her brow creased as she motioned behind her, into the vast forest that surrounded the settlement. "I've lost her, Johan."

His stomach dropped to the ground. Oh, *der Herr,* no. "Not Christina."

"Of course, it's Christina. Who else would it be?" Hilda had never looked so severe. She closed her eyes, took a breath, and reopened them. "I'm sorry I snapped. I am not myself." She nodded across the clearing. "Let's fetch your brother. We've no time to waste. The sun will set soon."

He took off across the field before she finished the words. Christina. His Christina. Alone in the wilderness as night fell. He would find her. He had to find her. He thought of the silent predators that stalked the shadows of the deep woods. He would find her.

They were both winded when they reached Wilhelm. He looked at Hilda with quiet, concerned eyes. "What's happened?" he asked as she reached for his sleeve.

"Christina is lost in the woods." Her face looked calm and even, but Johan could sense the fear hiding beneath the surface. Gone were the giggles and uncertainty of the last few days. This was the Hilda they knew, in control and ready to act. "We'll organize a search party, break into groups of two, and divide the woods into grids. Each pair will search their own grid. That way we won't miss anything."

Wilhelm nodded. He looked relieved, although his expression remained serious and concerned. "That's a good plan, Hilda. No one will wander in circles or travel the same path twice. We'll find her." His Adam's apple bobbed as he swallowed. His eyes roved over Hilda's face with a strange intensity. "It is good to see you well again."

"Well again?"

"You have not been yourself of late."

"Oh." Hilda frowned and looked away, toward the woods. She seemed distracted for a moment, then set her face into a firm expression. "We can talk about that later. Right now, we will find my sister."

"*Ja*. Of course."

They made haste to gather a search party. Soon, the woods were filled with people shouting Christina's name and carefully marking where they had searched. Hilda made sure the search remained organized and efficient. She did not lose her head. Wilhelm commented to Johan several times on that fact. "She's been acting so strange lately," he said just before they went their separate directions. "I had begun to wonder if she was the woman I thought she was." Wilhelm watched Hilda as he spoke, even though his words were directed at Johan.

Hilda stood a few paces away, pointing in different directions as the Webbers, Grubers, and Millers nodded. Eli

Webber took off his black beaver felt hat and ran his fingers through his hair in a nervous motion. Catrina clung to his arm and dabbed her eyes with the edge of her apron. Jacob Miller frowned and pulled Greta closer. She glanced up at him with wide brown eyes, then back at the woods. Already, the evening shadows were lengthening and bathing the forest in shades of purple. Darkness would be upon them soon. Every settler feared the dark beyond New Canaan. Few could imagine a worse fate than being forever lost in that vast unknown.

The wilderness reminded Johan of the ocean they had crossed to come to the new world. A man could sail for weeks and weeks and never see another soul. If set adrift, he would die of thirst or exposure before he found land. The settlement of New Canaan lay like a small island within an ocean of trees. Christina could die of thirst or exposure before she found the settlement. How easy it would be to miss it in the enormous forest! No one knew how far the woodlands stretched to the west. They might go on and on forever.

Johan shuddered, picked up his Jaeger rifle, and rested the long muzzle against his shoulder. "I'm leaving, Hilda." She glanced over and nodded, then continued giving directions to the small group of settlers.

"I'm going with Hilda," Wilhelm said. "I won't let her face this alone."

Johan expected that. He was the only man without a partner to search alongside, so he volunteered to bring the two older boys with him. Felix would stay with the Widow Yoder, along with a handful of other children too young for the search. Wilhelm had suggested they leave the older boys as well. "They know the woods well," Johan had argued. "They explore and play when they are supposed to fetch water."

"They were lost just this morning."

Johan shook his head. "I don't think they were lost. They just wanted to run ahead and romp through the woods."

Wilhelm frowned. "I suppose. But keep a close watch on them."

"They are old enough to handle themselves."

"*Ja*. It's hard to remember that sometimes."

Johan nodded and headed into the forest with Fritz and Franz. He prayed to *der Herr* as he crashed through the underbrush and into the lengthening shadows. He would find Christina. His heart beat like a hammer against his eardrums. He would find her.

Christina could not understand what had gone wrong. She had strolled to the riverbank with Hilda and suggested they travel farther into the woods when they could not find any yarrow. She had been in control of the situation.

Until she was not.

Christina had planned to lose Hilda in a safe place, double back to the Lantz homestead, and come racing back with Wilhelm in the lead. Oh, it would have been glorious. Wilhelm would have come tearing through the underbrush, shouting Hilda's name. He would have beamed when he saw her, picked her up, and swung her around in the air. Hilda would have blushed and played the damsel in distress. Wilhelm would have played the heroic gentleman with his swift and dashing rescue. He might even have proposed on the spot. Hilda would have said yes, of course. It would have been perfect.

Instead, Christina huddled against the base of a hemlock,

arms wrapped around her knees for warmth. She had not brought a cloak. The entire event should have been over by dinnertime. She was not supposed to need a cloak. Dash it all, she was not supposed to be lost.

How had it happened? How had she managed to lose Hilda and her sense of direction? She did not know. That was the thing about getting lost; one did not know quite how it happened. If one did, one would not be lost. One would be safely in one's bed, wrapped in a quilt with a hot cup of tea.

A screech owl cried out, and Christina jumped. How could a bird sound so sinister? She heard the soft whisper of wings and another eerie shriek. It sounded like a woman's screams. She had heard that cougars also made high-pitched screams. Abram Ziegler said the cry sounded like a terrified girl. Christina did not want to find out if that was true.

Christina tried to imagine her snug cabin, filled with the familiar smell of woodsmoke and the sound of fabric rustling as Hilda sewed by the fire. She tried to imagine the warm light of a Betty lamp, flickering against the dark. She could not. All she could imagine was the hot, wet breath of a cougar and the sharp, white claws that could pierce the hide of a running horse. Cougars hunted from the trees, stalking their prey on silent paws until they dropped from the branches for a surprise attack. There could be one above her now, still as a statue, waiting. Christina looked up and glanced from tree to tree. She strained to see the yellow glow of narrow cat eyes. She saw only darkness.

That did not mean she was alone.

There were wild things about. She could hear the crunch of leaf litter on the forest floor. She could hear something scratch the tree trunks and swoop above the branches. A howl broke out somewhere in the distance. It pierced the night air like fingernails scraping stone. Christina stiffened. Her heart thudded in her ears and her mouth went dry. Her tongue stuck to the roof of her mouth. The wolf pack might be headed her way. They might have scented her already. She would make a fine meal. She had nothing to protect herself but the sticks that lay on the ground and her bare hands. Oh yes, she would make a fine meal for ravenous wolves.

If only she had brought Bruno. But they had left him at home to guard the flock. They had left Fuzzy at the homestead too, so that he did not slow them down. Christina had distracted him with a bowl of warm sheep's milk while they slipped away. She would have to survive the night on her own. She said a prayer to *der Herr* and shrank against the tree trunk as the wolves howled again.

Christina had never been afraid of the woods before. She had never been afraid of wolves before. She had always been bright and bold and careless. She loved to explore the stark, hidden beauty of the wilderness. But she had never been alone in the wilderness after dark before. Darkness changed everything. Darkness created shadows in her mind. Darkness crept in and cast out all reason. She wanted to go home.

Time passed slowly. The stars wheeled overhead in a curved, sluggish path. The tiny pinpoints of white light felt cold and distant as they rolled across the night sky. Christina wanted to sleep so the night would end sooner. But she wanted to stay awake so she would know if the wolves came. Or would it be better to be surprised? There would be less time for fear that way. A sharp crash into wakefulness, the glare of yellow eyes and wet, stinking breath, then—but no, she would not think that way. She would not allow herself to imagine it.

She tried to sleep. She could not. The tree trunk dug into her spine. The soft animal noises made her feel as if she could hear the night breathing, as if it were a living thing. The slip of tiny feet, the whisper of wind through pine needles, the distant howl of wolves filled the empty wilderness.

But the wilderness was not empty. People said it was, but it was not. It was filled with as much life and hope and energy as her bustling village back home in the Rhine River Valley. Here, there weren't any stout wattle and daub cottages, or church bells, or vast patchworks of barley fields stretching to the horizon. There wasn't the heavy thud of boots on cobblestone, or cartwheels rumbling, or songs on the wind as the milkmaids led the cows into their stalls for the night. But there was life here, and it was everywhere.

Christina stood up abruptly and shook out her skirts. She would not wait for the end to come. She would not succumb to fear. She would find her way home.

Johan plunged through the darkness. He held a Betty lamp high, but the weak flame made him feel small and alone in the overwhelming darkness. Fritz and Franz pretended to feel brave. They puffed out their chests and swaggered. But their small hands clung to Johan's whenever a strange noise echoed through the canopy.

The air felt cold and tight against Johan's lungs. "Christina!" His voice was hoarse from shouting.

Fritz pressed against his uncle's side. "Don't worry,"

Fritz said in a cheerful voice that sounded strained. "We'll find her."

Johan tousled his nephew's hair in a casual, familiar gesture. "*Ja*. Of course, we will." He wished he believed the words. What if she were wandering in the wrong direction? What if she kept walking and walking in the wrong direction until she could walk no longer? She could disappear forever into the unknown.

Johan shivered. He told himself it was the cold. But he knew it was not. It was his heart, crying out for the woman he loved. How foolish he had been! He should have apologized to her days ago. What did it matter that he thought he had been right? He had upset her. He owed her an apology for that simple fact. He had not intended to upset her. He had only wanted to show his devotion. It hurt so much that she did not see he had a pure, loving motive. That was why he had not apologized. The hurt had made him stubborn and prideful. He had thought that if he kept pushing, he could force her to see his love for her—and her love for him.

Johan's jaw flexed. He realized that it had been more than pride—as if that weren't enough! It had also been fear. He had feared she would not return his love. He did not want to admit he was afraid. Men were not supposed to be afraid. Men were supposed to protect and defend and stand strong.

Perhaps admitting he was afraid was the strongest thing he could do.

Dash it all, he did not like where his thoughts were going. All he wanted was for Christina to recognize his love and love him in return. Franz tugged at his sleeve. "What is it?"

"What do you mean?"

"You stopped talking and you've clenched your hands into fists. Are you afraid?"

Yes, he was afraid. He was afraid that if he didn't try hard enough to convince Christina of his love, she would not see it. And so he had panicked during the proposal. He had told her she ought to marry him. He had not asked her. He had said not to worry her pretty little head about it. He had told her other women had dreamed of getting a proposal from him. He had not meant it the way it had sounded. But she had taken it the way it sounded. Of course she had.

"Uncle Johan?" Franz tugged at his sleeve again.

"It's all right," Johan answered and forced a brave smile. "There is nothing to fear."

But there was. Rejection was the most frightening thing he could imagine. Except for Christina wandering alone until she dropped from thirst and exhaustion, lost forever.

This was the worst night of his life.

Johan shouted her name again. He strained to hear a response. Silence. They kept walking. The Betty lamp cast strange, elongated shadows against the forest floor. The trees loomed like the soldiers that had roamed the Rhine River Valley back home. Branches reached out like grasping hands. Johan tried to swallow his fear for Christina. He could not. What must she be feeling right now, all alone? She did not even have the faint light of a lamp or the company of two rowdy children. He shouted her name again.

A faint murmur caught on the wind and carried back to him. He froze and put out a hand to stop the boys. They looked up at him with wide eyes and round mouths. He called her name again and motioned for silence.

There! He *had* heard it.

"She's near," he whispered. His nephews gave solemn nods.

"Christina! I'm here!" He strained to hear her voice. It carried like a thin ribbon on the wind. He could not make out her words. "Stay where you are! I'm coming!"

Johan broke into a run. It was reckless to run in the darkness, but he could not stop himself. Energy surged up his spine and exploded into his chest. His feet flew. His breath came out in hard, sharp bursts. "Christina!" He heard his nephews crash through the brush behind him as they struggled to keep up. "Christina!"

"Johan!" Her voice sounded stronger now. He was closer.

"Don't move! I'll find you!"

"Johan!"

He imagined her flushed face and reckless curls that always fell from her prayer *kappe*. He imagined the fresh, cheerful smell of her starched linen jacket. He imagined the warm comfort of her smile. He imagined her wandering alone in the wilderness. She was near. He had almost found her. His heart beat harder. He could feel it in his fingertips and throat.

"Johan!" Her voice sounded clear now.

He crashed into a low branch and caught a flash of movement. He shoved the branch aside and held the Betty lamp high. A pale face appeared. The rest of her body was lost in shadow. But she was there. He could hear the sharp rasp of her breath. And then she was in his arms, laughing and shouting. He had found her. They had found each other.

Chapter Twenty-Two

Christina melted into Johan's arms. He had come for her. He had found her. She was safe. Nothing had ever felt as comforting and secure as his strong, firm arms. She pressed her face against his chest and listened to the steady pound of his heart. He smelled of wood smoke and leather. She never wanted him to let her go.

But he could not hold her forever. He eased away from her and looked down into her eyes. The weak flame of the Betty lamp flickered across his features. She could see the joy on his face. "I have to signal that I've found you," he said and slipped the shoulder strap of his Jaeger rifle from his shoulder. Christina pressed her hands over her ears as he pointed it skyward and fired a shot. She felt the boom in her chest as a flash of light brightened the forest. A flock of birds burst from the branches. Christina could not see them, but she heard the wild whoosh of their wings and their startled cries.

Christina watched impatiently as Johan reloaded the Jaeger rifle. He propped the butt of the gun against the ground and poured a measure of black powder from his powder horn into the end of the long gun barrel. Then he set a small cloth over the barrel, placed a lead ball on top, and rammed them both down the barrel of the gun. "Won't you hurry?" Christina asked. She wanted him to hold her again.

He grinned as he brought the butt of the gun up and pulled back the lock. "I have to let everyone know you're all right." His eyes shone with emotion. "And then I'm all yours." He poured a few grains of gunpowder into the pin, closed the pin cover, and pointed the gun skyward again. "Cover your ears."

He reloaded and fired a third time before setting down the gun and drawing her close again. "You're not hurt?"

"No," she murmured into his chest.

"We thought you might have been eaten by a bear," Fritz said in a cheerful voice.

"Oh!" Christina pulled away from Johan and laughed. She had almost forgotten the boys. "I should hope not."

"Fritz." Johan shook his head at the boy. "That isn't a nice thing to say."

"But it's true. You were afraid that a bear might get her. Or a wolf. You made us run all night."

Christina swung her attention back to Johan. "Is that true?"

Johan shuffled his feet "Well . . ." He rubbed the back of his neck with his hand. "We didn't run *all* night."

"Just most of it," Franz said.

"I've never seen him so flustered before," Fritz said. "He looked like he might faint."

"Now, wait a minute." Johan shook his head. "That's not exactly—"

"Thank you, boys." Christina beamed at them and clasped her hands under her chin. She looked up at Johan. "Thank you, Johan."

"I did not almost faint," Johan said as she stared up at him. "Just to set the record straight." Christina could make out the curve of his smile and the rich gray of his eyes in the lamplight. She laughed and kept her eyes on his. Her heart felt too full to speak.

He slipped his hand around hers. He had large, rough hands that made her feel safe. "I did think about a lot though. It was a long night."

"*Ja*," Christina said. "A very long night."

"I . . ." Johan rubbed the back of his neck again. "I'm sorry about the things I said when I proposed. I shouldn't have made it sound like you were lucky to have me. And I shouldn't have told you what to do. I should have asked you what you wanted to do."

"It was the worst proposal I have ever heard." Christina sounded serious, but her grin showed him she was not.

"*Ja*. You are not the only one who thinks so."

"You spoke of it to someone else?" Christina's grin widened. "You were worried!"

"*Ja*. I was worried."

Fritz tugged on Johan's sleeve. "Can't you stop talking yet? We don't want to hear about all that mushy stuff." He made a face. Franz mirrored his expression.

Johan laughed. "You don't have to listen."

"We won't," Franz said. The boys found a place to sit and settled in with their backs against the trunk of a tree.

Johan squeezed Christina's hand. "Where was I?"

"You were worried."

"Right. I was worried."

"You should have been. No woman in her right mind would accept a proposal like that." Christina smiled. She could not help but tease him a little. He deserved it.

"*Ach*, it wasn't that bad."

"It was."

"All right. Fine." Johan shrugged. He looked sheepish.

"Why was it so bad?" Christina asked. She wasn't joking anymore.

Johan shifted his weight from one foot to another. "I was afraid." He cleared his throat and looked away.

"Why?"

"Because I wanted you to love me as much as I love you."

"You silly, adorable man."

"Does that mean you love me?"

"Yes." She stared into his eyes. They were barely visible in the dim lamplight. Every noise in the forest stopped. The world hovered in silence. Nothing existed but the two of them. He loved her and she loved him. "I love you."

He had run all night until he found her and apologized. He had shown her he was not arrogant or prideful. He was afraid. He was human, with all of the complex and exasperating emotions that come with being human.

She loved him for it.

Her scheme to lose Hilda in the woods had not worked out as she had planned. It had worked out better than she ever could have imagined. It had been a wonderful plan.

Christina explained everything on the way home. Johan had marked the way and led them through the underbrush until they reached the river and could follow it back to the settlement. It was a long walk, but Christina no longer felt cold. Johan's heavy wool cloak warmed her. So did the strong, firm arm that he kept wrapped around her shoulders. The cloak was far too long, and she tripped over it every so often. He caught her every time.

"So you thought I was arrogant," Johan said after she finished telling her side of things.

She nodded. His arm shifted against her shoulder.

"Well, I can't blame you. Although I thought I sounded perfectly reasonable." She twisted her neck to look at him.

"All right. Not perfectly reasonable. But not terrible. I was just trying to convince you. I didn't want you to say no."

"I would have said yes if you hadn't tried so hard."

They both laughed. "You could have said something, you know," Johan said. "You could have told me why you were so offended."

"Ah. And you could have told me you were afraid of rejection. That would have solved everything."

He lifted a branch out of her way.

"Thank you."

"Does that mean I'm forgiven?"

"Of course you're forgiven. Do you forgive me for believing you were insincere?"

"*Ja*." He paused, then laughed. "Is that why you were so out of sorts the day we worked the flax? Is that why you were angry when I called you beautiful on shearing day?"

"*Ja*. I didn't believe you really thought all those nice things about me. Well, I thought you might. I wasn't sure. I kept trying to figure out why you stopped acting like yourself."

"Fear makes a man do strange things. I was willing to try anything to win you over. I turned on all my charm." He looked down at her. "You didn't like it?"

She laughed. "No. I like the real you. And the real you *is* charming. Just not quite so forcefully charming."

Johan chuckled. "Forcefully charming?"

She shrugged. "*Ja*."

"All right. I promise to be myself from now on. Although I warn you, I am naturally dashing and debonair." He grinned into the darkness.

"I know." She returned the grin. "Didn't I tell you I love you? Don't you know I could only love the most dashing of men?"

The next morning, Christina woke to the sound of metal clanging against metal. Fabric whispered against the stone hearth. The fire crackled and popped. Wood smoke and the scent of roasted meat filled the small cabin. Christina rolled over and buried her face in the quilt.

When she woke again, sunlight slanted through the window from higher in the sky. The cool of morning had disappeared along with Hilda. She had banked the fire and left the cabin. Red coals glowed from the hearth. Birdsong drifted into the still, silent room. Christina threw off the quilt and stretched. She smiled and breathed out a long, happy sigh. Johan had found her and she had found Johan—the real Johan. The mystery was solved. He *was* the man she had fallen in love with. The world was full of Amos Schneiders. But it was also full of men like Johan Lantz. For every bad man, there was a good man, waiting to be found. Life was not over after a rejection. A man who made a woman feel unworthy of his love could never be her perfect match. The thought made Christina feel hopeful and alive. Wilhelm was one of those good men. He was not an Amos Schneider. He could pour his love into Hilda's life, just as Johan had poured his love into Christina. He could be Hilda's perfect match.

Christina just had to figure out how to get them together.

So far, Hilda had been unsuccessful at winning Wilhelm's heart. Thankfully, today was a new day. Anything could happen. Hilda had been trying so hard to gain his attention. They must be close.

Christina heard the low murmur of a male voice outside the cabin door. What had she missed since yesterday? Was Hilda any closer to a proposal? She laced her stays, pulled her skirts and bodice over her linen shift, pinned on her sleeves, and threw on her jacket. She had slept in her hosen, so she slid on her leather shoes as she stumbled across the cabin. Her head was bare. She groaned, doubled back for her prayer *kappe*, smoothed her hair, and tried to look calm.

Sunlight struck her when she flung open the door. The day felt bright and hot and full of promise. Johan leapt up from where he had been sitting on a stump in the yard. "Christina!" Franz and Fritz stopped throwing pebbles and looked up. Christina started to run toward Johan. And then she remembered. She swallowed and scanned the clearing. Hilda stood amongst the sheep, staring at her. Christina caught Johan's eye, shook her head, and slowed her pace. She forced a calm expression. Johan gave a slight nod and stayed where he stood. He seemed to understand her signal. They made a good team. She would bring him in on her plans for Hilda. They would have Hilda settled in no time, if they worked together.

"Ah. She has finally decided to join us." Hilda sounded stern, but she smiled at her sister. "I was just about to take the sheep to pasture. Johan and the boys called to check on your welfare. I was just telling them you are no worse for the wear, just tired."

"I missed breakfast," Christina said and yawned. "The morning is half gone."

"You had a late night," Hilda said. "I imagine you did not sleep in the woods."

"No. But you did not sleep either."

Hilda shrugged. "Ah, well. The sheep are hungry whether or not I've slept. I didn't want to leave you. I waited as long as I could, but I need to take them now."

"I'm fine. Really. I feel wonderful good. It's a beautiful day, *ja*?" Christina's eyes slid to Johan when she said the words and he grinned. "Johan was quite the hero last night, *ja*? What might have happened if he had not found me?"

"We found you too!" Franz said. Fritz leapt up. "We both did."

"How brave you both are," Christina said and beamed at them.

They raised their chins in satisfaction. Fritz put his hands on his hips and stood up tall. "We would have fought the wolves, had there been any."

"I am sure you would have," Christina said.

"We ought not forget Hilda," Johan said. "She organized the search party. She must have been afraid for you, Christina, but she never showed it. She took the lead and directed everyone. It was remarkable."

"*Ach*, it was nothing." Hilda whistled to Bruno. He barked, tore across the clearing, and skidded to a stop beside Hilda.

It was remarkable? Hilda took the lead and directed everyone? *Everyone?* Christina stiffened. She frowned. "Hilda, can I speak to you for a moment?"

"*Ja*?"

Christina gave her sister a look.

"What is the matter with your eyes?" Hilda asked. "They look about to bulge from your head."

Franz and Fritz laughed.

"I'm trying to signal to you," Christina whispered.

"We can hear you," Franz said. Johan laughed. He gazed at her with open affection.

Christina let out a sharp hiss of air. "I was trying to signal that I need to speak to you *in private*." She whispered the last two words.

"We can still hear you!" Franz shouted.

"*Ach*, all right." Hilda glanced at Johan. "Though it is impolite to leave our company out."

"He understands," Christina said. "Don't you, Johan?"

"Of course." He gave a magnanimous bow, then motioned for them to leave.

"See, he understands."

Hilda looked heavenward. "I cannot imagine what this is going to be about," she muttered.

"I heard that," Christina said. "Apparently I am not the only one who cannot manage a whisper."

The boys laughed. Johan chuckled.

Hilda stalked across the clearing. "I haven't time to waste," she said without looking back. Christina glanced at Johan, winked, and hurried after her sister.

"What is it?" Hilda asked as soon as they were out of earshot.

"You directed the search?"

"*Ja*."

"You led everyone?"

"*Ja*. I suppose so."

"*Everyone?*"

"*Ja*, Christina. *Ja*." Hilda glanced at the position of the sun in the sky, then at the sheep.

"How could you?" Christina's voice did not sound appreciative or surprised. It sounded frustrated and disappointed.

Hilda's attention shot back to her sister. She stiffened. "How could I?"

"*Ja.* How could you?" Christina threw up her hands. "We were so close! What will Wilhelm think? A man doesn't want to be bossed about!"

Hilda looked shocked. "Are you suggesting that I should have sat back, giggled, and let Wilhelm take control?"

Christina shrugged. "Well . . . *ja.*"

"Oh, Christina. For heaven's sake."

"Don't 'for heaven's sake' me, Hilda. This is serious."

"No. Your getting lost in the woods was serious."

"This is not the time to lose sight of the goal! We have to reel him in!"

"*Ach*, Christina. He's not a fish." Hilda shook her head. "You could thank me, you know."

Christina pursed her lips. She swallowed. "All right. *Ja.* Thanks are in order. Thank you."

"You're welcome. All that matters is that you are safe at home." Hilda closed her eyes and rubbed her temples. She opened her eyes and turned away. She hesitated and turned back to Christina again. "Do you really think I made a mistake with Wilhelm?"

Christina did not know what to say. She did not want to discourage her sister. But she was worried for her. "I don't know."

A lamb scampered past on long, delicate legs. Bruno barked and trotted after it. "We can finish this conversation later, Christina. I'm taking the sheep to pasture now."

"I'll go with you."

"No. Stay here and rest. I need to be alone to think. I don't know what to make of things anymore."

Christina nodded. She did not know what to think either.

"What was that about?" Johan asked as soon as Hilda disappeared behind the wall of pine trees. They could hear the sheep bells clang in the distance.

"Oh, Johan. I've so much to tell you. Where to start?"

"Come here," he said. "That will be a start."

She leaned into his arms as they closed around her. He rested his chin atop her head. "Everything is all right now. We've found each other."

Christina pushed away from his chest to meet his eyes. "*Ja*. And it's wonderful good. But I can't marry you until Hilda is settled." She told him everything. Christina could never keep a secret. And now, she didn't have to.

"You told Hilda to act foolish in front of Wilhelm?" Johan tried not to laugh, but the corners of his mouth turned upward. He coughed and looked away.

"Not foolish. Feminine." Christina put her hands on her hips. "Really, Johan. Don't you understand how these things work?"

"I understand how they work for you and for me, but not everyone is you and me."

Christina frowned. "Hilda is not the type to catch a man's eye."

"*Ja*. And Wilhelm is not the type to catch a woman's eye."

"You see the predicament."

"*Ja*. I do." Johan laughed. "Those two might never get

up the courage to declare their affection—or even notice it. They are too busy being responsible."

"Precisely. I thought that if Hilda made herself irresistible, Wilhelm would not be able to resist."

"How logical."

"Indeed."

"But it isn't working."

"Of course, it is." Christina looked confused.

"No, it isn't."

Christina frowned. "But it must have. I taught her everything. How to giggle, how to gaze up at a man, just so." She demonstrated, and Johan smiled.

"Ah. I see."

"So, of course, it worked," Christina said.

Johan shook his head.

"I believe Wilhelm used the phrase, 'sounds like a dying billy goat' more than once."

Christina sucked her breath in through her teeth. "No."

"Yes."

"Oh. Oh, no." She covered her face with her hands. "But what else can poor Hilda do? She simply doesn't know how to win a man's heart!"

"I don't know about that. Men don't just want a giggly, pretty face. Oh, some might." He shrugged. "But I can't speak for them. Those men are too shallow to bother with, anyway. Men like Wilhelm want a woman who knows how to handle herself. They want a woman who can carry on an intelligent conversation, or forge a new life in the wilderness, or organize a search party." He winked at her when he gave the last example.

"You mean . . ." Christina did not know exactly what he

meant. Was he speaking for Wilhelm, for men in general, for himself? If he was speaking for himself . . .

Christina began to feel uneasy. "I've been wrong about everything."

"*Ja.*"

Christina's unease grew and her stomach felt unsteady. Johan agreed that she had been wrong about everything. *Everything.* Did he mean . . . ? Could he mean . . . ? She gazed up at him. Her lip trembled. Christina knew that Johan loved her, but did he admire her too? Christina did not just want to be loved. She wanted to be admired. She wanted to be respected. She wanted Johan to look at her and see a woman who could accomplish anything. Did he see her as just a giggly, pretty face? That was how most people saw her. Why should Johan be any different? Was he trying to tell her that he didn't want her to be the way she was?

Was he trying to tell her she should be more like Hilda?

Oh, he was. It was intolerable. But she would not be defeated. She never had been before, and she would not start now.

"Do you mean . . ."

"Mean what?"

Christina cleared her throat and tried to sound dignified. The amused look on Johan's face told her she did not look very dignified at all. She raised her chin a fraction. "That *all* men prefer serious-minded, down-to-earth women? That *all* men admire that type of woman more than other types?"

Johan stared at her for a moment. Christina did not know what to think. He was going to tell her that he wished she were different. But instead, he laughed. Laughed! He wiped his eyes and planted a kiss on the top of Christina's head. "You adorable, wonderful thing."

Christina frowned. "You didn't answer my question."

"Not all men. Not *this* man." His arms tightened around her shoulders. "I love and admire you for who you are. I love everything about you."

"Even my ridiculous harebrained schemes, like getting lost in the woods when I'm trying to lose my sister in the woods?"

"Especially your ridiculous harebrained schemes. They brought us together, didn't they?"

A satisfied smile crept up Christina's face. "Why, yes. They most certainly did." She almost melted into the moment and the security of his arms. But instead, her eyes narrowed with purpose. "One down, one to go."

Chapter Twenty-Three

Johan gazed down at Christina. She was perfect, and she was his. He wondered how soon they could set the wedding date. Why not this week? There was no reason to wait. Except that Christina could not marry him until Hilda was settled. Dash it all, he wished he could marry her now, this very afternoon.

"I'll talk to Hilda," Christina said. "I'll have to tell her what you said." She glanced back up at him. "You're sure you're right?"

"*Ja.*"

She dropped her eyes. Johan could see the tiny tremble in her bottom lip. It was adorable. She was adorable. She must feel sheepish about steering her sister the wrong way. But he loved that about her. She was full of plans and schemes and fun. And, even though she had missed the mark, her plans for Hilda were all made out of love. That made them worth something, even if they failed. He had never met a woman with a bigger heart. Her heart was so big it even had room for an oaf like him, who had almost chosen pride over the perfect match.

"Everything will work out with Hilda and Wilhelm. Don't worry." He took her hand and held it between both of his. Her skin felt warm and soft. "Let's talk about our wedding."

"Oh, no." She shook her head. "I can't possibly. Not until Hilda is settled." She shook her head again. "And now I feel more responsible than ever. I've made such a mess of things."

"Shhhhh." He squeezed her hands. "It's all right. You don't need to get upset about it. We all make mistakes. It will work out."

"No." She shook her head harder. "I have to fix it. I *will* fix it."

Ah. That was the Christina he loved and admired. He respected the way she fought for what she wanted. She would not rest until she saw her sister settled.

"No. You won't."

She gasped and looked offended.

"Not by yourself, I mean. *We* will."

"Oh!" She laughed. "*Ja*. We will together."

Franz shouted at Fritz from behind the cabin. "Be nice," Johan shouted back in an indulgent tone.

They heard a thump and another shout. "All right, Uncle Johan," two voices said in unison.

"I don't want to know," Johan said. Christina laughed; then her face dropped into a serious expression. "We need a plan."

"All right. Let's think."

Christina brightened. "I've got it."

"All right. That was quick."

"If you're right and he wants to see that she is serious and competent—"

"I am and he does."

"—then she just needs to be herself. If Wilhelm doesn't like giggles, then he'll get no more giggles!"

"No more giggles."

"He'll get no-nonsense, hands-on-her-hips, everyone-better-watch-out Hilda."

Johan did not know why his brother would want a woman like that. But, he thought, it seemed like a good match. Wilhelm's first wife had been thoughtful and firm, but kind. Hilda seemed the same. Wilhelm did not want to play practical jokes or whisper under the stars or splash in the river on shearing day. Hilda did not either. It sounded quite dreary to Johan, but to each his own. Johan had what he wanted. He had found a woman who wanted to joke and whisper under the stars and splash in the water on shearing day. "*Ja*," Johan said. "Wilhelm will get exactly what he wants." *And*, he thought as he gazed down at Christina, *so will I.*

"We've no time to lose," Christina said. "We need to put everything we have into this."

Franz shrieked and Fritz shouted. Both boys came flying around the corner of the cabin with Fuzzy nipping at their heels. The boys had lost three hosen between them and both their hats. Their shirts had come untucked from their knee breeches, and Fritz's waistcoat had lost a hook and eye.

Johan and Christina looked at the boys, then at each other. Their eyes twinkled. "Are you thinking what I'm thinking?" Johan asked.

"*Ja*," Christina answered with a sly smile. "I believe I am."

Johan and Christina arranged for the two families to dine together that evening. Christina told Hilda and Wilhelm that she wanted to cook for the Lantzes to thank them for searching for her. Neither Hilda nor Wilhelm questioned that, fortunately. Christina kept herself busy with cooking and housework to put off the inevitable conversation she had to have with Hilda before their guests arrived. She dreaded the conversation and did not know how to bring up the subject. As it turned out, she did not have to.

"I won't do it," Hilda said as she stirred the corn porridge bubbling in the cauldron. The smell of roast rabbit rose from the hearth as fat dripped from the spit and sizzled against the hearthstones.

Christina stopped sweeping the dirt floor and looked up. "Won't do what?"

"Act the fool."

Christina cringed. "Oh, it hasn't been that bad, has it?"

"*Ja*. It has. And I was wrong to do it."

Christina sighed and set the broom against the wall. "And I was wrong to encourage it."

"I'm glad you've come to your senses," Hilda said. She scooped out a spoonful of corn porridge and blew on it.

"Ha! I'm glad *you've* come to *your* senses!"

Hilda laughed. "It was your idea. You're the one who kept pushing it."

"But you're the one who is supposed to keep her wits about her. I think with my heart and not my head, remember?"

Hilda laughed harder. "Christina, what would I do without you?"

"*Ach*, you'd probably be happily married to Wilhelm by now if I hadn't meddled."

"But we would have missed out on so much of the fun." Christina beamed. "Do you mean that?"

"No."

They both laughed. Hilda wiped her eyes and shrugged.

"I can't blame you though. I could have said no to you. I could have believed in myself." She tasted the corn porridge, nodded, and set the pewter spoon on the hearth. "I suppose I'll have to be content living alone. I know you and Johan will marry. I can see it in your eyes."

"You can tell?"

"*Ja*. And I know you're keeping it a secret."

"You do?"

"Christina, I've known you all your life. You are such a sweet girl that you won't marry until I'm settled. Am I right?"

"*Ja*." Christina collapsed onto the rough wooden bench beside the hearth. "You weren't supposed to know."

"You don't owe me anything. It's not your fault that I'm on the shelf. You have to go on and live. I've decided that I don't want Wilhelm if he doesn't feel affection for the real me." She stared into the fire for a moment. "So I'll just have to get used to being alone."

"Oh, Hilda! You still don't see, do you?"

"See what?"

"That Wilhelm does feel affection for the real you."

Hilda's face jerked up to look at Christina. "Oh." She had been crouched over the hearth, and she sat back hard on her bottom. "Oh." She looked surprised. "He likes that I'm slow to smile and quick to frown?"

"Apparently."

"Oh."

"Hard to believe, I know."

Hilda laughed. "Don't push it, Christina."

"I wouldn't dare."

Hilda still looked surprised, but a goofy smile crept onto her face. "How can you be sure?"

"Because Johan told me. And as you pointed out, we are soon to be wed. He tells me everything."

"Mmmm." Hilda looked thoughtful.

"Apparently Wilhelm was impressed by your leadership and courage last night."

"Was he, now?"

"Hilda, I don't know what to make of you right now. You are sitting on the floor, smiling like a lovestruck young girl."

Hilda shook her head, stood up, and straightened her skirts. "I am. And I cannot help myself. My affection for Wilhelm has grown into love, Christina. I never thought I would feel this way again."

There was a knock at the door. Christina's hands flew to Hilda's, and she squeezed them between hers. "I never thought I'd say this, but just be yourself."

Johan wanted to run into the cabin and shout the news of their engagement. He did not. He winked at her from behind Wilhelm's shoulder while Hilda's attention was on the corn porridge and roast rabbit. "Remember what I told you," he whispered to his nephews and nodded. He was not sure that Felix understood the plan, but he knew the two older boys did. They looked like cats that had gotten into the cream. Smiles such as that meant no good.

And that was a good thing.

Wilhelm looked unsure of himself as he entered the dim, one-room cabin. He took off his black beaver felt hat and turned it in his hands. Johan had noticed that his brother had taken extra time to get ready after setting down his ax for the day. He had changed into a clean linen shirt and waistcoat. He had combed his hair and splashed water on his face. He had even wiped down his brown leather boots, which made no sense at all because they would be covered in mud again by the time they reached the Dresser homestead. There was only one explanation, and it confirmed what he already knew. His brother was in love. In love with Hilda Dresser! What a strange, happy world it was. Who would have dreamed that two brothers would fall for two sisters? Who would have dreamed that Wilhelm would find a woman as stuffy and responsible as he was?

Hilda turned from the fireplace with her usual expression. Johan smiled to himself. Oh, they really were perfect for each other. Wilhelm was shy and insecure. Hilda was restrained, but sure of herself. He imagined them growing old together, sitting by the fire, not speaking and not needing to. They understood each other very well. Except for one thing. Wilhelm had no idea that Hilda was in love with him.

Felix stubbed his toe on the table leg and howled. "What have you done with your shoes?" Wilhelm asked. The child rubbed his eyes instead of looking for them. Johan pulled Christina aside and whispered to her as Hilda slipped outside to see to the sheep. Johan knew that Wilhelm would not hear his words over Felix's howls. "Are you sure we can't tell Wilhelm about Hilda? Can't we put the poor fellow out of his misery?"

Christina's eyes widened. "No! Absolutely not."

"It would make this a lot easier."

"Hilda trusts me, Johan. We can't tell Wilhelm what Hilda told me in confidence."

"You told me."

Christina gasped. "We are soon to be one flesh, Johan! It hardly counts." She hesitated. "But perhaps I should not have told you. I will ask forgiveness. *After* we put them together."

"But if you've already told one person . . ."

"Telling Wilhelm—the object of her affection—is very different from telling my betrothed. She would be mortified."

"Ah." Johan shrugged. "I guess we have to do this the hard way." He nodded at his nephews. They nodded back. "Here we go," Johan said.

Christina looked surprised. "You mean they haven't started yet?"

"No." He swept his hand across the room. "This is just a normal day."

Christina chewed her thumbnail. She wondered if Hilda would be in over her head. Felix was still howling. Franz had already lost his hat, and Fritz had spilled the water bucket on the dirt floor. The dirt had turned to mud, and that mud covered half of Fritz's knee breeches. "This isn't part of the plan?"

Johan smiled and shook his head.

"Oh my."

"And you wonder why Wilhelm assumes Hilda won't have him for a husband."

"Oh, she'll have him all right. And by the end of this night, Wilhelm will not be able to resist asking for her hand!"

They could not finish the conversation. The boys began to shout so loudly no one could speak above the noise. Wilhelm looked mortified. He tried to tell them to hush, but they shook their heads and looked confused. "We can't hear you, Papa!" they said and shouted louder. Fritz fell into the mud and rolled. Franz grinned, tripped over his brother, and landed face down in the mud. The fall was not very convincing. It looked far too dramatic.

"Heaven help me." Wilhelm put his hands over his face. "We are guests, boys! Guests!" He turned to Christina with a stark expression. "I am sorry for their behavior. I'll get them under control. Just as soon as I can make myself heard." At that moment, Franz slipped a frog from his pocket. The creature leapt out of his grasp, hopped across the floor and onto the bench beside the table. Franz and Fritz scrambled to catch it, but it jumped from the bench onto the table. The boys shrieked and dove for it. Franz landed in the platter of roast rabbit. The platter flipped over, and the meat skidded across the table to land with a thud in the mud. The frog leapt to avoid the roast rabbit and landed smack in the middle of the corn porridge. The porridge splashed up and splattered the table and the boys' laughing faces. The frog croaked, leapt out of the bowl, and dropped to the floor. Franz and Fritz squealed and took off after the frog. They did not notice when the cabin door swung open and a stout, no-nonsense silhouette filled the threshold. That silhouette had her hands on her hips in a most intimidating manner. She was not smiling.

"What is the meaning of this?" Hilda asked. She did not move from the doorway, and she did not raise her voice. Somehow, her voice carried above the chaos. She had a talent for that. Franz, Fritz, and Felix froze. They stood and stared up at her with big, guilty eyes.

Johan swallowed and surveyed the scene. Mud covered all three boys, the table, and his own waistcoat. Dash it all, how had they gotten mud on *him*? The roast rabbit lay on the floor. The porridge was everywhere. The bench was overturned. Thankfully the frog was nowhere to be seen.

Hilda towered over the scene with a raised eyebrow.

Or at least she seemed to tower over them. She was a short, stout woman, but her stern presence made her seem twice as big. She commanded the room with her eyes. The cabin was so quiet, Johan could hear the rustle of pine needles outside the window.

Fuzzy pushed past Hilda's legs and bounded into the cabin. He scampered straight to the roast rabbit on the floor, skidded to a halt, and pounced on it. Wilhelm looked even more mortified—if that were possible—as he watched the cub devour their dinner. Wilhelm swallowed and ran his hand across his forehead. Beads of sweat formed at his hairline. Johan almost felt sorry for him. Almost. A lifetime of happiness was well worth this momentary discomfort. Ah, yes. Things were going very well. Very well indeed.

"I'm sorry," Wilhelm said. "We'll be going now." Wilhelm shook his head. "I'll just take care of this mess first."

"I won't hear of it," Hilda said. "We've invited you for dinner and we will have dinner." She scanned the ruined food and narrowed her eyes. "Despite present circumstances."

"I'll just get this place cleaned up," Wilhelm said as he bent to pick up the overturned bench.

Hilda opened her mouth and closed it again. She cleared her throat. "I would not dream of telling you how to handle your own children," Hilda said. "But, seeing how this is my home . . ."

Wilhelm nodded encouragingly.

". . . perhaps you would allow me to handle the situation?"

Wilhelm looked relieved. "By all means."

Johan and Christina exchanged glances. Johan tried not to smile. He could tell that Christina was doing the same.

"Boys, you ought not to wreak havoc in someone else's home. I know you meant no harm, so this will soon be forgotten." The boys grinned. Hilda did not. "But not before you clean up your mess." At that moment, the frog hopped out from behind the open door and landed on Hilda's leather shoe. She looked down. "A friend of yours?" she asked while keeping a straight face. The room broke into laughter, and the tension died.

The boys cleaned cheerfully. Hilda taught them to make a game of it. She promised whoever cleaned the most porridge and mud would get to name the frog. They all wanted to win and scrubbed as fast as their fingers could fly. Afterward, Hilda sent them outside to wash the mud from their faces, hands, and clothing. Fuzzy scampered behind them in a comical parade. They came back from the river shivering, but smiling. "We're ready for dinner now," Fritz said.

"Oh?" Hilda gave her signature, no-nonsense look. "And what do you propose we eat? Would you like porridge that a frog has bathed in?"

They shook their heads.

"Then you will have to prepare something. That is only fair, *ja*?"

"But we can't cook!"

Hilda shrugged. "I am sure three resourceful boys can figure something out."

Wilhelm sat on the bench watching his children. He looked surprised and pleased. "Just look at that!" he whispered to Johan several times. "Hilda is a godsend, I tell you! An absolute godsend!"

"For your boys?"

"*Ja*."

"For your boys only?"

Wilhelm shook his head. "She is an amazing woman."

Johan just smiled.

"How can a man keep himself from falling for a woman like that? She can do anything! Have you ever seen a woman so confident? So calm, yet in control?" Wilhelm's eyes spoke even more than his words. They gazed at Hilda dreamily. "And she is quite lovely, *ja*?"

"Is she?" Johan was enjoying himself. His brother had almost admitted that he was in love.

Wilhelm sighed. "More than lovely. She's beautiful."

Johan elbowed his brother. "Then what are you going to do about it?"

"Do about it?"

"Just look at her, Wilhelm. Are you going to let a treasure like that slip through your fingers?" Johan nodded toward the hearth. "She's got your boys cooking, Wilhelm. Cooking!"

Wilhelm just stared at Hilda as though she was the most extraordinary woman he had ever seen.

Johan nudged his brother's shoulder.

Wilhelm shook his head. "There's nothing to do about it."

Johan raised his eyebrows. "Are you sure about that?"

"You don't mean . . ."

Johan shrugged. "Why not?" He leaned closer to his brother. "Unless your only interest in her is as nursemaid for your children."

Wilhelm turned red as a beet. He cleared his throat. "No, brother. I'm afraid I want her to be my wife."

"So she can be nursemaid to your children?" Johan already knew the answer to that question. But he thought it best to push Wilhelm along.

Wilhelm turned a shade redder, if that were possible. "No." He looked sheepish and dropped his eyes to the floor. "I . . . I love her." He shook his head. "Foolish, I know. Why would she take me? A fine woman such as herself. She could have her choice of men."

Johan tried not to look amused. He could not imagine Hilda with any man but Wilhelm. She would scare most of them away. "Mmmmm." Johan shrugged. "So you will let her get away? What if one of those other men sweeps her off her feet before you even try?" Johan motioned toward the hearth. "Ah, dinner is ready. She's taught the boys to make corncakes. Quite an accomplishment, *ja*?"

"Quite right, Johan. I can't let her get away. If she says no, she says no. But, by thunder, I'll try my best!" Wilhelm leapt to his feet. "Hilda!"

Hilda turned her head.

"You are a most impressive woman."

Hilda stared at him from across the room.

"Will you do me the honor of . . . of . . ." Wilhelm cleared his throat. "Will you do me the honor of marrying me?" The words flew from his mouth before he could stop himself.

"Marry you?" Hilda looked shocked.

Wilhelm turned as pale as his linen shirt.

The boys erupted into cheers. "Yes! She'll marry you!" They jumped up and down in front of the hearth. Hilda motioned for quiet.

Wilhelm looked contrite. "I'm sorry." He said the words much more quietly than before. "I didn't mean to shout it out quite like that." He shuffled his weight from one foot to the other and rubbed the back of his neck. "I just got carried away."

Johan glanced at Christina. She had her hands clasped beneath her chin and was holding her breath.

"Carried away?" Hilda asked.

Johan could not read Hilda's expression.

Wilhelm swallowed hard. "*Ja*. I watched you with the boys, and it struck me how thoughtful and resourceful and kind and . . ." He swallowed again. ". . . and lovely you are."

Hilda's careful expression broke. A smile spread across her face. "Lovely?"

Wilhelm returned her smile. Their eyes locked on one another. "*Ja*. Lovely."

"Oh." Their eyes stayed on one another.

"And I guess I've been thinking that—feeling that way for a while. You are a remarkable woman, Hilda Dresser, and I love you. Will you marry me?"

"*Ja*." Hilda nodded. She beamed. Actually *beamed*. Suddenly she looked like a young girl with her whole life ahead of her. Johan had never seen her look that way before. He suspected she had not looked that way for many, many years.

Christina could not contain her joy. It was the perfect ending for all her hopes and plans. Her entire heart strained for Hilda to say yes. And Hilda did say yes. The boys jumped into the air and cheered. They leapt for Hilda and smothered her with hugs. Hilda never stopped smiling. Wilhelm watched his betrothed with warm, happy eyes as his boys crowded her.

Johan waited until the shouts and whoops died down. Then he stepped forward and took Christina's hand. "We have an announcement to make as well."

Hilda and Wilhelm smiled. "It's about time you two figured it out," Hilda said.

"You're one to talk," Christina said to her sister as Johan

pulled her close and rested his chin atop her head. They all laughed.

"Does this mean that Hilda is going to be our mother *and* Christina is going to be our aunt?" Fritz asked.

"*Ja*," Christina and Hilda said in unison.

"Then Fuzzy will be our cousin!" Franz said.

The room broke into laughter again.

"You can have that double wedding, Christina," Hilda said.

"*Ja*." Christina clasped her hands together. She was too happy to speak. No words could capture her joy.

Three days later, the two couples stood in Jacob Miller's clearing, waiting for the worship service to begin so they could say their vows. The weather had dawned clear and mild, so the men had set up the benches outside, where there was more space. Spring spread its glory across the yard in a riot of yellow and purple wildflowers. The fresh, light scent hovered in the still air. Sheep bells clanged in the distance and Bruno barked. Christina's neighbors nodded as they took their seats.

It was a perfect day. There was just one thing Christina needed to do. She needed to tell Hilda and Wilhelm everything. It was the right thing to do. "Hilda," she whispered.

"*Ja*?"

"I have to admit something."

Hilda's eyebrows went up. She did not look surprised.

"I made a plan."

"Oh dear. A plan. You didn't. Not one of your plans." She glanced around as if something might ambush them.

"No. Not today. Before. It's over now."

"Oh. Thank goodness." Hilda frowned. "What did you do?"

"I made a plan to set you up with Wilhelm."

"Ah." Hilda did not look surprised. "And you waited to tell me until we were about to walk down the aisle so the joy of the moment would overtake my frustration."

Christina looked sheepish.

Hilda sighed. "Tell me about this little plan of yours."

Christina looked down. "I got lost in the woods over it."

"Oh, Christina. Why am I not surprised?"

"And I set the boys loose in the cabin to wreak as much havoc as possible."

Johan put his hands on Christina's shoulders and gave his wry half-smile. "That was a conspiracy. We were all involved."

"All of you?"

"Except Wilhelm of course." Christina looked at Hilda with concerned eyes. "I would never betray your trust. And I only told Johan about your feelings for his brother after we were betrothed. He promised to keep it a secret and to help me play matchmaker."

"And the boys?" Hilda did not look amused.

"I encouraged them to be as rowdy as possible the night we came to dinner," Johan said. "The frog was all their idea, by the way. I only told them that it would be a happy surprise for everyone if they made as big a mess as possible."

"The poor dears!" Hilda looked contrite. "I was quite firm with them. And to think they were only following your orders!"

Johan laughed. "Oh, no. They understood. And afterward, I explained the entire scheme. They thought it was worth having to clean up."

"And cook?"

"And cook."

"Well." Hilda shook her head. "I never." Hilda shook her head again. "Why on earth did you do it?"

"So that Wilhelm would be unable to resist you," Christina said. She realized her voice had been a little too loud, and she clamped her hand over her mouth.

Johan smiled. "And it worked. Wilhelm could not stop talking about how remarkable you were."

Wilhelm rubbed the back of his neck and looked down. "Well . . ." He shrugged. "It's true. I could not resist you."

"How long have you been playing matchmaker, Christina?" Hilda put her hands on her hips and gave her sister a hard stare.

"Since the day we met Wilhelm."

"Do you mean to tell me, Christina, that the entire time I thought you were mooning over Wilhelm, you were trying to get *me* to moon over him?"

"*Ja.* Of course."

Christina turned her face to look up into Johan's eyes. "I've been in love with Johan since the moment I found him atop our woodpile." She gazed into his eyes for a warm, delicious moment before she turned her attention back to Hilda. "I'm sorry I kept my plans from you. I didn't think you'd go along with them, and I couldn't let you sabotage your perfect match. And I'm sorry I told Johan you were in love with Wilhelm without getting your permission. Are you upset with me?"

Hilda stared at Christina for a few beats. Christina could feel the tension in her chest. Johan's hands tightened around her shoulders. His grip felt sure and comforting. They waited for Hilda to frown and tell Christina to stop thinking with her heart. But instead, Hilda did a very unexpected thing.

She laughed.

"You're not upset?" Christina grinned. Hilda's laugh felt contagious.

"No. For once, I am glad you thought with your heart and not your head. Where would we be if you had not pushed a match on all of us?"

"Where, indeed," Wilhelm said and took Hilda's hand. "I have to thank you also, Christina. I don't know how your plan worked, but it must have worked in the end, because here we are."

It had worked. Oh, it really had! They didn't blame her. They had *thanked* her. She basked in her success. For once, she had made a plan that worked. Oh sure, she had been lost in the woods overnight, quite by accident, but that had worked out brilliantly. And she had told Hilda to act like someone else, which had been quite foolish.

And yet, here they were.

"Life has a way of working out," Johan said.

"Especially when you know what the heart wants," Hilda said and winked at Christina.

Christina beamed. Bishop Riehl raised his hands for the congregation to be silent and called the two couples to the front. Christina's heart felt so full that she thought it might overflow. Perhaps it had. She knew what her heart wanted, and she knew how to spread what was in her heart to others—even if she had done it in the most ridiculous of ways.

Don't miss any
of Virginia Wise's
Amish New World romances,
available now!

WHERE THE HEART TAKES YOU

Pennsylvania 1737. Greta Scholtz braved a perilous journey—and the loss of her beloved father—to find religious freedom in America. With two orphan children she's taken under her wing, she's trying hard to survive this rugged new world. So she won't let settlement elders pressure her into marrying reserved widower Jacob Miller. She and Jacob simply can't agree on anything— even if the unexpected feeling between them is proving an irresistible force. . . .

After losing his wife and baby, grief-stricken Jacob keeps everyone at arm's length. Duty is the only reason he began helping the headstrong Greta make a life for herself and her charges. Yet he's grown to admire her, especially her strength in the face of obstacles— including him and his wounded ways.
But wrenching misunderstandings and a jealous rival could separate them forever. To find harmony—and perhaps even a future together—Greta and Jacob must take a leap of faith and risk opening their hearts. . . .

WHEN LOVE FINDS YOU

Scandal drove Catrina Witmer from her life as a wealthy *Englischer*'s pampered daughter to reluctant membership in Pennsylvania's thriving new Amish settlement. Surprisingly, Catrina finds contentment and peace in this promising new land, though she won't risk telling anyone about her past. But the unexpected sparks between her and bashful, warm-hearted farmer Eli Webber suddenly have her dreaming of an impossible chance at happiness—as his wife.

Eli never imagined such a spirited woman would look his way. Or that he could ever deserve her, given his own guilty mistakes. But Catrina's vivacity and kindness have him impulsively proposing. Unfortunately, his over-righteous sister, and the consequences of secrets on both sides, threaten to tear their marriage apart for good. Now Catrina and Eli must try forgiving themselves and finding strength in their bond if they are to have a joyous future together. . . .

Connect with Us

Visit us online at
KensingtonBooks.com
to read more from your favorite authors, see books
by series, view reading group guides, and more.

for sneak peeks, chances to win books and prize packs,
and to share your thoughts with other readers.

facebook.com/kensingtonpublishing
twitter.com/kensingtonbooks

Tell us what you think!

To share your thoughts, submit a review,
or sign up for our eNewsletters, please visit:
KensingtonBooks.com/TellUs.